# Jan Mazzoni

# THE
# SNOW FOX
# DIARIES

Previously published as The Snow Fox Diaries
by Jan Mazzoni 2008

Revised 2020

Copyright © Jan Mazzoni 2020

The right of Jan Mazzoni to be identified as the author of
this
work has been asserted by her in accordance with the
Copyright,
Designs and Patents Act 1988


Cover photo by Sue Cresswell
Prints available on request

*Some days, when I look back, I think so what was that all about then? Did it even really happen? It was so unreal it's hard to believe.*

*And then I get out that gorgeous notebook with its handmade recycled cotton paper pages and cover the pink of an Indian sari (he was so pleased with himself for finding it, said how could anyone resist using it?). And I flick through, run my eyes across the black writing with its loops and angry punctuation, entries that started out neat but then became more of a scrawl as my mind began to race ahead.*

*It had been years since I'd written much by hand. Who does these days?*

*But I can still feel the pen in my hand, can remember the excitement, the anxiety, trying to capture what I was thinking or feeling and not having the words. Alone, late at night: the diary writing hour. Too many pages smeared with whisky. Or tears – of sadness, but joy too. Or both.*

*Some nights I still dream of you, my beautiful, wild, snow-white miracle. My obsession.*

*Then I don't want to wake up.*

# WINTER

# ONE

It's as if the world is holding its breath.

There's no sound, just an icy hush. Nothing moves; even a single snowflake drifting down from the leaden sky seems to hang suspended, like a tinsel ornament on one of the Christmas trees that have already been thrown out along with the crumpled wrapping paper, cards with curling corners, the turkey left-overs, littering the streets of towns and villages across the country.

Here, in the frozen white wonderland of dawn on the edge of the moors, there is no litter. Or it's litter of a different kind. After weeks of snow, the birds are dying, dropping frozen from the skies to lie alongside hedges, their wings flapping eerily until they're covered by the next fall of sparkling white powder. Ducks, weakened by the cold, doze on ponds and then wake to find themselves in the grip of a razor-sharp sheet of ice. Even some of the ponies are dying, those stocky little animals bred tough to survive the harshest of winters in one of the most desolate of landscapes. Sheltering in a copse, five yearlings are trapped when the snow drifts that surround them freeze overnight, turn into slippery white walls that leave them no way of escape.

An old sycamore tree, snapped in half by last week's gales, trailing ribbons of ivy, rests propped against the tree next to it, like a drunk who's determined not to fall but can't quite get upright again. Beneath it, the ground could be made of granite. No wonder then that even here the coldest winter for many years has taken its toll. Hibernating hedgehogs, curled into tight prickly balls, haven't so much died as simply stopped living as the blood in their veins becomes clogged with ice crystals. Voles, moles, rabbits, all of them perishing.

The young fox hasn't given up, not yet. Picking her way silently through the stiff white bracken, she stops every now and again, head raised, ears pricked for the slightest movement. She is hungry. Worse, she's starving. Though the extreme cold has resulted in so many casualties, bodies frozen solid and then buried under new snow are hard to locate, almost impossible to eat. She's been forced close to the village, to farms, rifling through bins and bags to find anything edible, foods she wouldn't give a second sniff at other times: pizza crusts, carrot peel, stale cake, occasionally – if she's lucky – some kind of carcass. But at least they helped reduce the hollow feeling inside. It was risky though. Too risky. Once a door had been flung open and out shot a snapping, barking bundle of fury, so fast she'd had to scrabble over the fence and almost not made it. Another time, pawing frantically at a sticky mass of bones and feathers on the road, she'd not noticed an approaching car until she felt the swoosh of air as it passed her, way too close. She'd been lucky not to have ended up like the bird.

The moors are home territory. Here at least she knows her way around, she's safer here. Providing she can find food she has a chance.

Above her, a sudden shriek as a female sparrow hawk drops silently from the branch of a fir tree onto a weakened male of her own kind, the pin sharp claws on her talons sinking deep, the male already half dead, hardly struggling. Bizarre, unnatural happenings. The successful female swoops clumsily over a nearby hedge with her heavy prize, and then down out of sight to start plucking. Two robins sitting close together inside the thorny hedge are disturbed, puff themselves up nervously, blinking, but reluctant to leave their roost they soon settle again.

The fox hesitates, also startled by the scream. Cold, exhausted, she lifts her head and licks at the snow as it settles on her nose. Her eyes begin to close. But then her head swivels. She's heard something, the tiniest whisper in the undergrowth. A long pause, ears erect, as she tries to pinpoint its exact location. Her movement muffled by the snow, she takes a few tentative steps, hesitates, edges closer. Whatever happens she can't afford to lose this chance. Her whiskers twitch. A sharp intake of breath, and she pounces. And misses as the mouse scuttles frantically along behind a curtain of creepers that overhang a large flat rock. The fox lopes around the back of the rock, sniffs, dabs tentatively with her paw. She waits. It's there, she knows it is, she can smell it, smell the fear. Next time she'll get it. The mouse too waits, shivering.

Now, at last, the sun emerges, peering from behind skeletal trees, pale as lemon sorbet though it's strong enough to cast long grey shadows on the white snow. A crow caws from way up in the top of the trees, another answers.

The fox doesn't notice. Her body stiffens, her concentration directed towards just one thing: food. And her next pounce is successful, the mouse trying in vain to press itself into a crevice, a squeak and then silence, its tiny feet pawing the air even as the fox's sharp canine teeth crush its head, fragile bones splintering, warm juices flowing. The fox chews briefly and then swallows, too hungry to eat slowly, to savour the sweet flesh.

She realises that there are humans close by a nanosecond too late. Even as she lifts her head a shot rings out, then another. The pain is red hot, excruciating. She tries to run, stumbles as a back-leg buckles, falls face downwards into the snow, the white mush sticking to her fur, clogging her nose, thickening her already white eyelashes. As the pain spreads her whole body tightens, curling against it, then arching as though trying to throw off this thing that has wrapped itself around her, ensnaring her like a coil of barbed wire. For a moment she's still, then a spasm lifts her up, spins her around before tipping her over onto her side, chest heaving, her breath escaping in ragged white clouds, getting slower, shallower. One front leg jerks aimlessly.

But then the adrenalin kicks in; somehow she stumbles to her feet, and is off and running.

"You got it! Shit, Dave, you hit the bugger. D'ya hear it scream?"

"Yeah, but what the hell is it?"

"C'mon, it's my turn, gimme the gun."

"Couldn't be a fox, not that colour."

"Dave, shut it and bloody give me the…"

"Here. Christ, what if it's a dog? Tell me it wasn't, was it?"

A jeering laugh.

"That's illegal, shooting people's pets."

"Hey, bet it's one of those big cats you hear about."

"Shit, Dave. Shut up, will you? C'mon, it's heading for the river."

"The Beast of Exmoor?"

"See, won't we, as soon as I've finished the bugger off!"

The two lads are no longer concerned about not being heard. They crash through the woods, branches cracking underfoot, boots thudding, tripping and swearing. A flock of starlings swirls up into the sky, black dots against pale blue, circles once and then settles again. A buzzard balanced motionless on a tree stump swivels its head, blinks, but is too stunned to move.

And then, as though someone has shut a door, the calm returns. But something is different. There's a new sound now, the sound of a single drop of water falling from the tip of an ivy leaf onto the ground below. Another fat droplet hangs precariously, and then falls. And another. The thaw is beginning.

On the ground, shiny red beads of blood strung across the snow will fade and disappear well before nightfall.

# TWO

It often starts with a death.

For a new beginning you need something to either die, or change, or simply end. Come to a full stop.

Before her life veered off at a tangent and she had to blink hard, re-adjust her views on a whole lot of things, and learn to live without avocados, Katie hadn't even known about The Rule of Nature. Which is a shame as it would probably have made her feel a whole lot better, about everything.

That same morning Katie wakes at 7.50am, almost the exact time that the gun goes off, though it wasn't that that woke her, obviously, as she's over two hundred miles away in her cosy mews house in west London. Their mews house, that is; she shares it with Ben, her husband of nearly fourteen years, the man she once loved so passionately that it took her breath away just to think of him, she went around hyperventilating gently. Sometimes she found herself pressing the palm of her hand to her chest, as though to steady her racing heart.

She'd been dreaming though she's no idea what about. It had been a good dream though. She feels as though she's been dragged away from a party before she was ready to leave, or from a particularly gripping film, and for a brief moment she resents being back in the real world. Ben is downstairs and though she can't quite recall hearing it, she has the feeling he's dropped something, a glass probably. The slate floor tiles were her idea. He'd have preferred wood, and jute rugs in multi-coloured stripes, which – if she'd realised how clumsy he was becoming – might have been a better option. Though he tells her not to get up on his behalf, to have a lie in, that he can make his own breakfast, she realises he's kidding himself. Besides, she doesn't want to lie in. Why would she? She's not done anything especially exhausting, in fact, the opposite. She's not that old. She's not ill, for Christ's sake.

The door moves silently inwards, Ben's face appears, smiling. There are fine crinkles at the corner of his eyes.

"You're awake? Good. I've brought you some juice."

"You shouldn't have."

She means it. Why can't he understand that she doesn't want him to run around her, to try to make things right when he can't? It isn't his fault her life has come to a halt. That everything she's done over the past five years has been for nothing, not only the ridiculous hours she chose to work, but being enthusiastic about a job that others may think of as mundane or even suspect – how many jokes are there about estate agents? – but that she actually enjoyed, all for nothing.

What she wants is simple: she wants to have a reason to get up every morning, like Ben has. That's what she wants.

"There's going to be a crash. They're saying on the radio. A seriously big one."

She has no idea what he's talking about.

"Economic. You know, all this stuff about the subprime market in the US?"

Still no idea. She shrugs.

He's already got his heavy grey duffle on over his suit; he looks like a teddy bear, well-padded and pink faced. From his pocket, the jingling of car keys.

"Anyway, I'm off. It's icy out there, going to have to take it extra steady." He bends to kiss her, then as she continues sipping the juice he presses his lips against the top of her head.

"One good thing. They're forecasting a thaw. About time too."

Katie nods. Since when did they talk about finances, and the weather? Had they really got nothing more interesting to discuss? When she'd had a career – way back before Christmas, in another era – they seemed never to have time to talk, money matters and social arrangements being exchanged in sound-bites as they passed going in opposite directions, over the phone, on note pads. Occasionally one or other of them would say how crazy it was that they never got the chance to sit and chat anymore. Maybe, Katie is thinking, it wasn't such a bad thing. Maybe it was the secret to them still being together, unlike the many couples they knew who were divorced, separated, or (even more tragic) hating each other but staying together for the sake of the children, or the derelict farmhouse in Provence they both refused to give up. You two are so lucky, friends said. No kids, no money worries. No wonder you have such a good marriage.

"Ben, before you go…"

He's at the door, turns, stands there silently, watches as she pushes aside the duvet, pats the space beside her, combs her fingers through her hair before settling back on the duck egg blue sheets. She feels a shiver of excitement. Or is it just that the room is cool?

"You used to say it was the only way to start the day. Remember?"

She waits. Outside a car horn sounds half a dozen times then stops abruptly.

He sighs, walks across and sits heavily on the bed beside her, the fabric of his coat rough against the top of her leg. Reaching, he runs the back of a finger along the side of her face, down towards her lips, but she takes his hand and directs it down towards her breast. Though she can see by the twitch at the corner of his mouth that he's tempted, his hand stays where she's placed it, heavy and warm and motionless.

"Katie, I've got to go or I'll be late."

"So be late."

"Love, I've got a meeting, it's important."

"And we aren't?"

She curls her body towards him, stretches up and winds her hand around his neck, pulling him gently towards her, and he bends willingly until their lips are touching and she can taste marmalade, their kiss gentle at first, then as she eases her tongue inside his mouth, becoming more urgent. How long since we've kissed like this? she thinks.

Ben pulls away.

"C'mon Katie."

"You don't want to. Me. You don't want me."

"Tonight, OK?"

He's trying to soften his rejection He can't see that what upsets her most is that one day when she wasn't paying attention he turned from someone who never said no, and who was wild and funny in bed in a way she'd never expected, into a middle-aged dullard. She savours the word: dullard. It's so right.

"We haven't eaten out for weeks," he's saying now. "Tell you what, there's that new gastro pub opened at Putney, overlooking the river. You book. We'll get a taxi, drink champagne, come back and screw the night away."

Defeated, Katie swings her legs over the side of the bed, heads for the bathroom.

"Fine," she mutters, clicking on the shower, checking herself in the mirror as she does every morning. "If a slab of burnt steak is what it takes."

He follows her, loiters in the doorway. A weak ray of sunlight crosses the room and she spots a single white hair, the start of one of those streaks you see in hair colourant commercials: woman with streak looking tired and unloved, woman with no grey having her earlobe nibbled by toy boy lover. Without hesitation Katie separates it and tugs hard.

"Katie, I have to go." Ben turns, clumps down the stairs then remembers something.

"Sorry love, forgot to say," he calls up "I broke a glass."

She turns abruptly away from the mirror and steps under the hot stinging spray.

Katie is cycling solo across China, raising funds for some charity or other. She started in Beijing, headed south, followed along The Great Wall passing ancient temples and pagodas, street traders selling hot noodles on plates made of plaited leaves, deep green pools and gorges. Her legs are pumping away slowly, smoothly, and she feels she could go on forever.

A voice over the loudspeaker.

"Intermediate pilates is about to begin. Anyone wishing to attend, make your way to Studio Two, and hurry."

No-one seems to hear. Certainly no-one disentangles themselves from whatever machine they've slotted and strapped themselves into. But then the place is almost empty. Katie is used to being there evenings and weekends, with all the other workaholics, people with lives, all determined to find a window in their schedule to work out, so they don't feel guilty about that extra tequila margherita.

Now of course, Katie can come whenever she wants. She glances around. Only one other bike in her row is in use; further along a girl with orange hair chews gum as she cycles furiously, her eyes on the handlebar machine that tells you everything: the speed you're travelling, how far you've gone, your heart rate, pulse, blood pressure.

"And probably how much you drink, how often you have sex, who with," Katie joked, the first time she visited the gym, trying to talk Ben into joining her. "Then there's a pool, a sauna, a selection of therapies and classes. You get your very own personal trainer too who works out your targets..."

"Can't I just stay flabby and happy?" Ben had said.

"You're not flabby." He isn't. He's a big man: big hands, big feet, with heavy shoulders and legs that could be made of smooth, pale wood. A solid man. The kind you can rely on.

"But you will be if you don't take care of yourself. Anyway, there's a café too."

"Don't tell me. Organic mineral water, carrot matchsticks, low fat pumpkin seeds?"

She'd suspected this was how he'd react.

"Possibly. OK, probably. But coffee too, with caffeine. And soup and sandwiches."

She'd tailed off. He'd not even been willing to give it a try. At first she'd been disappointed, but then it had become just another thing she did without him. And after a bit she'd settled into a routine and been glad he hadn't tagged along and stopped her concentrating. Working out on the machines, lifting weights, going up and down the pool, feeling her body getting firmer and more supple, fitter than it had been twenty years ago – it gave her an unexpected buzz. Ben didn't know what he was missing.

Now she slows, eyes drawn to one of the TV screens strung across the room. Even though there's no sound, Katie can tell at once what's happening, she's seen the same news story time and again. A bomb has gone off on a crowded city street in Iraq, Pakistan, somewhere in the Middle East. There's dust, bricks, a car flipped on its side. People stand around looking stunned. A man in a white robe is hunched down over what looks like a pile of rags. Tenderly he lifts it, stands, holds the lifeless body of a little girl towards the camera before turning and making his way through the rubble. No tears, no accusations or anger. Only a dignified acceptance that this is the way life is.

Katie can hardly bear to watch. What the hell is wrong with people? How can anyone do these things?

She slides out of the seat, picks up her towel. She hasn't been for weeks, not since becoming – how she detested the word – unemployed. Inexplicably, frustratingly, now she has so much time to kill working out has lost its appeal. Worse, it bores her.

That morning had been no different from any other. She'd been sitting one end of the kitchen table, not yet dressed, fingers linked around a mug of tea, Ben opposite her munching toast, saying the same things he'd said the day before, and the day before that.

"Katie, we're living in one of the biggest and busiest cities in the world. You can't tell me there isn't a job out there with your name on it."

"At my age?"

"Come on, you're a young woman."

"I'm nearly forty, Ben. Over the hill as far as most employers are concerned. Skidding down the other side."

"Rubbish. Besides, there are anti-ageism laws now."

"So someone might take me on as a token oldie? Gosh."

He sighed. "It's not like you to give up, Katie. Look how many times you've started again."

"When it was my choice, yes. When I found something that interested me more than what I was doing."

Ben glanced at his watch.

"Remember when you used to lecture me on the power of positive thinking? Some life skills course you did. Drove me crazy."

"I was young. Naïve."

He'd carried on talking, his tone warm and confident in the way she imagined him talking to his clients, convincing them with his manner as much as his words that here was a man they could trust with their building projects, with their money. With their dreams even. It was barely two years ago that he'd taken the plunge and set up as an independent quantity surveyor and already he was being offered more work than he could cope with. Which meant that despite the loss of her income they didn't need to make many sacrifices. None really. Katie knew she should be pleased, even grateful. She wasn't. She was jealous.

When eventually he'd picked up his laptop and hurried off, she'd sat there flicking through a local paper. She'd hardly left the house lately, certainly not during the day, had blamed it on the weather. But look, why stay home when there were so many exciting things happening right there on her doorstep? Well, a short walk away. An exhibition of seventeenth century tulip watercolours. Gothic nightmares interpreted through black and white photography. A demonstration of Brazilian capoeira, whatever that was.

But in the end it was easiest to go to the gym

Now she pushes through the heavy glass door and the cold air hits her, though there are signs that the thaw has started. The gutters are running, water trickling noisily down the drains. The pavement is no longer a sheet of ice. Walking along quiet back streets Katie straightens her shoulders, breathes deeply. The air smells of car fumes, of wine from a bottle smashed on the pavement, glass shards in a red puddle, and then – as she gets closer to a small park – she gets a whiff of fir. It reminds her of the Christmas trees she used to have at home as a child. She and Ben never bother. Instead they've got into the habit of buying an expensive wreath from the florist on the corner. Hanging it on the front door is their token effort. You only really enjoy Christmas if you're a child, Ben used to say, or if you spend it with children. He'd stopped saying that some years ago.

Cutting across a small scrubby park Katie notices an old woman shuffling towards her, a carrier bag in each hand. As she pauses by a bench a pigeon drops down, then another. Then there's a flurry of birds: more pigeons, small brown birds, blackbirds, seagulls, all of them desperate for the food the woman is scattering around, bread, cooked pasta, fruit peel. The birds aren't fussy. Poor things, it's a wonder anything has survived this bitter winter. Without dotty old eccentrics like this most probably wouldn't.

The woman is holding out her arms now, and a few sparrows flutter up and settle nervously on the rim of her open hands to peck at the last of the scraps. She notices Katie.

"Who you staring at?"

"I was just thinking…"

"Well don't. I ain't doing nothing wrong. Go on, sod off."

Katie bristles. But then she can imagine the comments people make: pigeons are disgusting dirty things, seagulls are dangerous, they all carry disease, there are way too many of them anyway. And what about the rats she's attracting with her scraps? Rats freak people out even more than birds.

She tries again.

"But it's great, that you…"

"Didn't you hear me? I said sod off!"

Katie shrugs, moves on. Hurt that's she's been so misunderstood.

Now the sky is turning pink at the edges; soon it will even out to a light grey, then darken, though in the city it never goes black. Already lights are on in the windows of a row of Victorian houses now converted to offices. If Katie looked she'd see people sitting hunched motionless in front of computers, talking on the phone, chatting together as they make important decisions, or it could be just about what they plan to do that evening. But she keeps her gaze straight ahead

A smell of coffee. The café is small, basic, but there's music playing – bossa nova? – and it looks cosy. She takes a seat near the steamed-up window, though she could have sat anywhere; apart from two black teenage boys sharing a can of coke but not talking, both busy texting other people, the place is empty. Like the gym. Like the streets. She used to complain about being jostled by the crowds, so why does she find this emptier, quieter world somehow depressing?

The coffee is tasteless, but it's hot.

A man comes in. His grey hair looks unwashed, is curling over the collar of a camel coat that's seen better days. In a strong, clear voice he orders the all-day breakfast. The man behind the bar nods, and Katie decides this is a regular customer – an out-of-work actor possibly – who comes in every afternoon for breakfast. As he crosses to a table by a radiator, drops heavily onto a chair and unrolls his newspaper, she notices he's wearing slippers.

Ben doesn't wear slippers. He won't wear cardigans either, nor tee shirts. He still actually likes wearing a suit, which must make him unique amongst men. With a tie more often than not, though nowadays he'll knot it loosely. It was one of the things Katie had especially liked about him, his cautious attitude to fashion; it reminded her of her father. With a shock she realises she no longer notices what he's wearing. Or if he has a cold, or is excited about a new project. Familiarity does that, of course. What's that famous quote? Familiarity breeds contempt – and children. She couldn't remember who said it, an American writer?

With a twinge of guilt she realises it's getting late, nearly five, and Ben will be home soon. The music changes to Simply Red. The boys leave. A young woman with a bare midriff arrives to pick up sandwiches ordered on the phone, and Katie has to wait for what seems like forever to pay for her drink.

Thing is, Ben has got used to her being there when he gets home. She should ring but she didn't bring her mobile, and isn't sure that public phones exist anymore. Though he doesn't say much she knows he worries about her these days, feels helpless. He feels anger too – she can see – but whether at her for not coping better, or at Bryan, her bastard sneaky selfish shit of an ex-boss, she's not sure. But before she can head home there's something she has to do.

She's promised herself that she'll put the past behind her, move on – but not today.

Surrounded by antique shops, boutiques and florists, The Hot Property Shop is the only one on that stretch of road that isn't lit up, the wooden Venetians down, slats closed, door padlocked. The Flame Red paintwork they'd had done only last summer is beginning to bubble. Bryan had got a friend of a friend to do it rather than a professional decorator, said why pay more than they had to? She should have known then that something was wrong. And when he'd thrown a fit about the phone bill, accusing them all of rambling on when they were professionals, for God's sake, should keep calls short and to the point. His face had flushed. That wasn't like Bryan, nothing like the quietly spoken man she'd met years ago and decidedly instantly she'd like to work with. And there'd been the day someone brought up the subject of the office Christmas party, they had to have one, the staff were owed that much. A big mistake, that.

She'd missed clue after clue. Stupid of her. Unbelievably stupid.

Inside, nothing would have changed. She could see it, smell it: the leather chairs, the polish she'd insisted the cleaner used on the oak desks (wood, like our faces, needs to be nourished if it's to look good in old age.) The computers would be silent, the glossy magazines out of date. In the kitchen the carton of milk left by the kettle would have turned sour. It had all happened so quickly. One moment they were one of the top estate agents in the area, with an excellent summer behind them, some good sales going through despite the time of year. Bryan had even talked to her about becoming a partner, said she deserved it, and she'd agreed – to both. Next, they were out on the street. No chance to even collect the personal things she'd left in her desk: the hair mousse, the energy bars, the latest Jodie Picoult novel and she still didn't know what happened after the shooting at the school.

Bankrupt. That was what the man with the briefcase had said. He hadn't opened it, and she decided he probably carried it for protection. He'd met her eyes almost defiantly. Mr Shreeve would explain. But Bryan wasn't in the office, hadn't been all day. He couldn't be reached by phone. Katie had driven straight round to his house, rang the bell then hammered on the door, not stopping until her knuckles were too bruised to go on.

Now she stands on the other side of the road, her back against the wall to keep out of the way of the crowds that have at last appeared, everyone hurrying home, dodging between cars and buses that are crawling along the wet, black road. She'd tried to avoid going anywhere in the rush hour, preferring to stay on and get things straight, was always happy to do evening viewings. It had started, this habit of working all hours, a few years ago when Ben went independent. It had felt like he was never there, or when he was, his mind wasn't. So she might as well not be either.

"Katie, hey, is it really you?"

The girl clutching her arm is hardly visible with all the scarves and the pull-on hat, but Katie recognises the voice.

"Hannah?"

She's surprised at the jolt of pleasure she feels. Hannah was a trainee she and Bryan had taken on back in the Spring, both of them won over by her bubbly personality. Clients would adore her. Katie felt especially bad about her when the business folded. She'd felt bad about everyone, being let down the way they were and just before Christmas too, but it wasn't her fault. Except that she'd known Bryan for years, was almost a partner; if anyone should have spotted what was happening it was her.

She must stop it, going over this again and again.

"So how's things?"

"Good. Very good. Busy. I'm working for Dunmore and Taylor, d'you know them?"

Katie shakes her head. The heavy drone of a slow-moving jet overhead makes speech pointless.

"And what about you, Katie?"

A woman with a pram waits impatiently as Katie tries to move aside, her way blocked by a man carrying a large cardboard box who seems to be looking for a taxi.

"This is hopeless." Hannah is almost shouting. "Tell you what – let's go to the wine bar round the corner?"

Katie is about to make an excuse, but she doubts Hannah will be put off. Wasn't that why they took her on?

"Come on, just one glass?" Hannah links her arm through Katie's. "I've missed you."


Inside the wine bar the atmosphere is bright, welcoming, familiar. It isn't yet crowded. They take their glasses to a chrome table alongside a giant fern that looks so green it could be artificial, though may not be, it was something they often debated. Katie used to come here regularly, sometimes with Hannah or other work colleagues, more often with Bryan, using it as an extension to the office. They'd order a bottle of chilled white and sit at a corner table. And Katie would think how lucky she was, having a job she thrived on, and a generous salary, and a boss who she liked and respected and trusted.

"OK, so what I'm doing now."

Hannah is off. All Katie has to do is listen. She envies Hannah's ability to just discard her disappointment, scrunch it up and drop it in a waste bin and move on. She's never been like that.

She takes things too personally, always has. She was an only child, brought up to believe that the world revolved around her. If Bryan was cheating, taking money out of the business to use for his gambling habit, manipulating the accounts, then she was the one he'd let down more than anyone. After himself and his family, that is. Though maybe he'd believed his own lies. Maybe he'd genuinely thought that everything would come right – that his next gamble would pay off, he'd win the jackpot, whatever – and be able to extricate himself from the nightmare and get on with his real life again; with watching his children grow up, going skiing in the winter, Greece in the summer, with making the business that had got off to such a flying start go from success to success.

He'd been stopped at the airport, a ticket to Mexico City in his pocket. One ticket, one way. Even his wife had no idea what was going on.

"And you, Katie, what are you up to these days?" Hannah sips from her full glass. Katie's is nearly empty.

"Not a lot."

"Not working?"

"Giving myself a break."

"Good. You deserve it. You worked twice as hard as the rest of us, all those horrendous early morning viewings, and weekends." An apologetic smile. "You were so willing we couldn't help but take advantage of you."

Katie shakes her head.

"Come on, don't exaggerate. We were a team, we all did our bit."

"Except for that shit Bryan. Sorry, Katie, I know you two were close but…"

"You're right. He was a shit."

"Ever hear what happened to him?"

"No. Something gruesome, hopefully."

No point in admitting how many times she'd driven round to his house, sat hunched in the cold car waiting, though she'd no idea what for. She saw herself talking things over with his wife, sharing the hurt. The curtains remained drawn, there were no lights, not even the security lights came on when one evening she braved the path, determined to find some little chink through which she could see inside. The electricity had probably been cut off.

"Hey, I've just remembered. There's a new estate agent opening, over towards Hammersmith. You can imagine the panic at my place. Worth you getting in touch?" Katie shakes her head.

"Been there, done it for longer than I should have. No, I'm waiting for something new to turn up. Something different."

"Like?"

Katie empties her glass, shrugs.

"Won't know till it does, will I?" she says, getting to her feet. "Another glass?"

"I really shouldn't." Which means yes. The bar is busier now. Quiet conversations intertwine, voices lift and fade, there are little eruptions of laughter, people unwinding before they get the crowded tube back to their wives and husbands and their partners. Katie feels she's come home as she edges her way through them to the bar, says hello to a couple of familiar faces though she can't remember their names, if she ever knew them.

She buys a bottle of wine rather than single glasses, orders some pita bread and hummus.

It's only when Katie gets home that she remembers she never did ring Ben. The TV is on, but as usual Ben isn't watching it. He has it on for background noise, for company. Instead he emerges from the kitchen, a can of lager in his hand, stands watching as she slips off her coat, then her mud splashed boots. There's a smell of burnt toast.

"You didn't take the car or your mobile," he says. "I decided you'd either gone to jump off a bridge, or meet a lover, or even, just possibly, to see a man about a job?"

His face gives nothing away, not worry or relief. Ben has learnt to keep his emotions to himself. He's wary of saying the wrong thing too, as he's done so often over recent weeks. Katie knows she's being a bitch, hates herself for it, yet can't seem to stop.

"Sorry, I should have rung. After the gym I went for a walk and bumped into someone I used to work with, Hannah, remember? You met her a couple of times. Anyway, we went for a drink."

"You went to the gym? Was it good?"

"OK. Not really. I wasn't in the mood."

Katie checks the kettle for water, turns it on. She takes a mug from the dishwasher, drops in a tea bag. Out of the blue she feels her eyes begin to fill with tears. Again. She's always tearful these days and hates herself for it. What a wimp. She turns away from Ben but not quickly enough.

"Kate, love."

His arm across her shoulder is like a rug, cosy and protective, but she shrugs him away.

"It's nothing. Too much wine."

"Katie, come here."

This time she lets him turn her towards him and they both ignore the rush of steam from the kettle, the sharp click as it switches off. From the TV comes a gasp then cheers as someone scores a goal. Katie presses her face against his shoulder.

"Ben, what's wrong with me?" she mumbles. "Other people lose their jobs, they lose a lot more, and they pull themselves together and get on with life. Why can't I? Everything feels so pointless. Like because no-one needs me I've got no right to exist anymore."

"I need you."

She wants to reply I know, and I'm grateful, it's very flattering but it's not enough, can't you understand? Instead she pulls back, manages a smile.

"Your confidence has taken a knock. You'll bounce back, Katie. I know it."

And now she can see that there's something he's waiting to tell her.

"Meanwhile, you know you keep saying you want to try something different?"

A flutter of panic.

"I've had an idea for a project. It would mean a complete change of scenery, a chance to…"

"Ben, stop right there. I hate projects. They're things set by teachers or, I don't know, marriage guidance counsellors…"

"Trust me. You'll enjoy this one."

"And I don't want a change of scenery. I like it here."

"I don't mean permanently."

"Not even for the weekend."

"Come on, Katie. Please?" He's disappointed. "You haven't heard what I've got to say yet."

"OK. You're right. I'm sorry."

"Then just listen, will you?"

Again he catches her shoulders, making her face him.

"This idea of mine. I was talking to someone at work today and it came to me. I think it's what you need, what we both need. You may disagree, I'm not going to bully you into anything. But please, love, don't set your mind against it before you even know what it is."

He's right. Katie takes a deep breath.

"So go on then. Tell me."

**SPRING**

# THREE

*Is it because you're white, I wonder?*

*I've always been drawn to white things: white lilac, mozzarella cheese, frost rimmed leaves, snow. The eerie white light of the moon. My cousin Andrew used to say it was a cold colour, cold and puritanical. He said in Imperial Rome it was the colour of death, mourners wearing it at funerals, corpses being wrapped in white shrouds.*

*I remember that summer I insisted on wearing only white – white shorts, a cotton halter top, white wedge heeled shoes, even a floppy white hat I found in a skip though I told my mother someone at school had given it to me – he said it told the world I was a cold person, frigid, a PT, and that boys would run a mile rather than have anything to do with me. I didn't care. I was nine years old, maybe ten. I wasn't even sure what a PT was.*

*Andrew was always goading me, trying to elicit some kind of response: a blush, a tantrum, best of all, tears. Throughout those long holidays we spent together on Exmoor he'd follow me around like a puppy who can't stay still for a minute, is always up to something naughty, pushes you until you want to smack him hard but then suddenly flops at your feet, rolling onto his back and demanding to be tickled. And forgiven of course. I always forgave Andrew. Eventually. He was my older cousin, two and a quarter years older, sarcastic, witty and worldly wise, who was going to go to university, was destined to Do Well. He wore an old corduroy jacket with jeans and made it look trendy. He hated football, any sports come to that, and though I realised this made him some kind of nerd, I couldn't help but admire him for having the courage to say so. There was a time when he collected slugs, took them everywhere with him in little boxes, said they were his friends. He made me hold one and though I thought I'd throw up I managed not to flinch, and he was impressed, said most girls would freak out.*

*Once my mother found me sitting out under a tree in the garden in the rain. It was almost dark, there were sinister rustlings coming from the bushes, and I wanted to be inside with everyone else, but I was sulking. When I eventually told her what Andrew had done – whatever it was, I've forgotten now – she'd hugged me, dabbed at my tear stained face, and told me that he only teased me because he liked me so much.*

*"Well I don't like him," I'd replied, secretly pleased. If my mother said it, it must be true. "I hate him. I hope he catches some horrible disease from those disgusting slugs, and his teeth fall out and his fingers fall off, and his innards turn to jelly."*

*"OK," my mother said. "So are you coming in now, while there's still some ice cream left?"*

*He'd been delighted, of course, when I told him about the house on Exmoor, how Ben and I were taking it on for a year or so, and how of course he and Tess and the girls*

*had an open invitation to come any time they
liked, as often as they liked. I'd meant it
then, knowing how I'd miss them. Him
especially. They've only been down once,
but it doesn't matter, not anymore. Nothing
matters now I have you.*

They finally move into the house on April 17th. Or rather,
they move in the necessities that will make life down in
Devon as comfortable and convenient as their lives in
London. Kitchen things: assorted pans, a whisk, a wok, a
food processor a grateful client had given Katie three years
ago, still in its box. For the bedroom, duck feather pillows
and duvets, Ben's eye mask for keeping out the light. Plus a
radio, a CD player, a handful of CDs. No television.
There's already one, an ugly black box balanced on a
spindly table in the corner of the lounge which Ben has
promised to tinker with, see if he can get working, even
though Katie says it would do her good to go without for a
while.

They've not been to look at the house again after that
first time a few months ago, and nothing has been touched,
it's still exactly as it was then. Which is as it was when the
old lady was rushed off to hospital where she died a few
days later, leaving a half cup of tea balanced on the edge of
the frayed floral armchair, an unwashed frying pan now
rimmed with mould, an apron with a recipe for lasagne on
it looped over the door handle. There are dead flies
everywhere. Probably mouse droppings too, if they looked
closely. Despite the bright spring sunshine it's dim indoors,
the air cool and stale. Ben flicks a switch on the wall.
Nothing.

"Must be fused," he mutters. "Rachael did warn about
the state of the place. Said she hasn't had a chance to get
down since the old girl died."

"It's like stepping back fifty years," Katie says, the heels of her strappy red sandals clipping on the lino as she trails a hand across the square wooden table that almost fills the room. There's a scratched stainless-steel sink in a corner, a curtain hiding shelves beneath, and alongside it a very small, very old electric cooker.

"How can anyone live like this?"

She's talking to herself. She tries to open one of the two smeary, un-curtained windows but they've been painted shut. Inside the wall cupboard she finds tins of rice, tuna, tomato soup. There are also – she counts – thirteen packets of chocolate cream biscuits. And a bottle of brandy, opened but still virtually full. Medicinal, then. Sad that Rachael's aunt didn't get to enjoy it.

"It's not the fuse." Ben bursts back into the kitchen and Katie thinks how large he seems, larger than ever in this small, cramped room. Large and so full of life she can almost hear the blood whooshing around his veins. He brushes at cobwebs on his sleeves. "Bet the electricity's been cut off. Bloody nuisance."

He spies the brandy.

"Ah ha, so what've you got there then?" He holds the bottle. "Martel. Excellent. Don't suppose you've found glasses too?"

Katie looks in the obvious places, can only find teacups with roses, and matching saucers. She rinses two under the tap, shakes them. Ben measures a generous slug of brandy into each. They clink cups.

"To Rachael's aunt," he says.

"To good times."

"To hard work, you mean."

Katie shakes her head. "No way. A few coats of paint, new curtains, dried flowers. A little bit of imagination. I'll soon have the place tarted up."

"You're looking forward to it, aren't you?" There's a combination of surprise and told-you-so in Ben's voice.

"Possibly." She softens. "OK, yes, I admit it."

He wants her to thank him for getting her away from London, for encouraging her to take on something that will give her back her confidence. Or at least to acknowledge that his idea had been a good one.

"This brandy isn't at all bad," Katie says instead. "Even out of a teacup. Wonder what she drank it from. The bottle?"

"Judging by the amount that's gone, I'd say an egg cup."

Taking advantage of the lull – a silence interrupted only by a sudden loud trill of a bird from outside the open front door – Ben drinks his in one go. Katie sips hers, feeling the firewater trickle down her throat, way too strong for her usually but today is special.

And to memories, she adds, though only to herself. One of the reasons she'd agreed to come to Exmoor was that it gave her the chance to revisit the past. But they're her memories, her past, not Ben's, so she doesn't say it aloud.

"So," she says, going through into the lounge, noting the faded wallpaper, the plywood mock fireplace she suspects – hopes – covers a real one, the beaded oriental style lampshade inside which there's no light bulb. "Where to start?"

It's in worse condition than she remembers from their one brief visit, but then that's the whole point of the exercise. It's a farm worker's house, or more precisely, two that have been combined, a characterless building in a hedged garden surrounded by fields, and up beyond them, the moors. A house that hasn't heard laughter, or been filled with the smell of fresh baked bread, or flowers for years. A neglected house. A house in which a lonely old woman nibbled chocolate cream biscuits and waited to die.

Katie's job is to use the interior design skills she acquired at college all those years ago (but that she let go to waste as she concentrated on her career) to turn it back into a home. Or, more important – as Rachael made clear when she agreed to them taking it on rent free for a year – to increase its value so that when eventually she decides to convert her legacy into cash, she'll get more than she would if she sold it straight away. Stunning Exmoor location, character cottage in excellent order, ideal holiday home. In other words, she'd said, a pot of gold. Rachael is secretary to the director of the company for which Ben has just completed a sports club for employees. She has ambitions. She'll probably use the money to buy herself a place on the board, Ben says.

Upstairs there's a landing with a grandfather clock that isn't working but that takes up most of the already restricted space. Three rooms lead off the landing: a large and a small bedroom, both crammed with heavy dark furniture, and a toilet with a cistern on the wall and one of those chains you have to pull. She'll make a feature of that of course. The bathroom, she remembers now, is downstairs, converted from a scullery probably, the suite picked up at a sale and some hideous colour. Brown? Avocado probably. God knows what she's going to do about that.

In the main bedroom the sheets are still on the bed, pulled right back as the old woman must have left them the morning of the day she had the stroke. A mixture of pity and disgust catches Katie's throat. On the chest of drawers there are two framed photos: a black and white one of a wedding, and one of a young girl in school uniform. Rachael? Presumably the aunt didn't have any children, which is why Rachael has inherited the estate. Even back then Rachael looked smug.

Katie crosses the room, tugs at the top window which slides down noisily. And there it is, that smell she knows so well from her childhood, desiccated coconut, and below her, threaded through the hedge, a ribbon of yellow gorse. She'd forgotten all about the wonderful mouth-watering smell of gorse, the prickly bushes that attack you if you get too close, though often she'd hidden herself away in a dusty dell surrounded by them and seen them as allies, a protective shield against the rest of the world. She'd tasted the petals too: they were like slivers of cucumber.

Beyond the hedges lies a patchwork of green and the tawny gold of bracken, clumps of trees dotted about, some in leaf, others still bare. Further away there are softly rounded hills, and above them – out of sight, but she knows they're there, she can sense them – a vast sky covering the wild empty spaces that are the moors. There's not a building in sight.

"It's a bit isolated here," he says. "There are a couple of houses along the road, and a farm I think. That's it. Will you be OK?"

"Of course," she says, surprised to find she means it. "I fancy a bit of solitude."

"Even though you won't have your computer? Rachael did say the broadband connection was virtually non-existent up here."

"I'll manage."

"And don't forget you can't count on your mobile working, not all the time. Sometimes it will, other times you'll have to go up the hill or climb onto the roof to get a signal"

Katie laughs.

"There's a landline, isn't there?"

"But what if…?"

"Ben, enough. Stop worrying."

Ben's arms circle her from behind. He kisses her neck, yawns, then turns and collapses onto the bed.

"Got the electricity sorted anyway," he says. "They promised it would be back on in an hour. Meanwhile, just time for a nap." He catches her hand and tugs her towards him.

"You won't get me anywhere near that bed until it's got clean linen on it. And a new mattress. Could we get one delivered, d'you think?"

Stupid question. A four-hour drive down the motorway and she thinks she's in Outer Mongolia. There are plenty of towns in the area, all the usual stores no doubt, their intrepid delivery drivers used to coping with narrow roads that snake between towering hedges.

"Write down everything that needs replacing," Ben says, getting reluctantly to his feet. "We'll organise it soon as we're back home."

Your home, she thinks. This is going to be her home, for a while at least. The plan is for her to spend as much time here as she needs in order to do a miracle make-over of the place. And of herself too is what Ben has at the back of his mind. He thinks it will do her good getting right away for a while. Taking a gap year, as he put it.

"I'll make a list of the jobs that need doing too."

Katie likes making lists, it helps her feel in control. She's missed making lists.

It's the next day that it happens, though not until late.

But when Katie wakes she already has reason to think of it as a special day: last night she and Ben made love. They make love regularly, of course. It's scheduled into their routine, like going to the recycling centre with the usually unread newspapers, or to Tesco's on a Sunday. It's an affirmation that they're a couple. But this time was different. They'd climbed the narrow staircase early, both of them shattered, unused to physical labour and the heavy Devon air, and Katie had gone straight to sleep. When she became aware that Ben was gently tugging at her nightdress, rolling it upwards into a wad of fabric, her legs feeling unexpectedly naked, she couldn't for a moment think where she was. The room was black, not a chink of light anywhere. She'd shifted onto her back, about to tease him, but immediately he'd lifted himself on top of her, his body hot and heavy, nuzzling down between her legs. She said his name but he'd muttered shush. He'd been ready, more than ready, and so – she found with surprise – was she. As he entered her, moving slowly and rhythmically, then faster, the bed groaned and squeaked and she wondered if it had ever been used this way before. Probably not.

Desire, that was it. Their coupling was usually a matter of habit; this time it was about desire.

In the morning she wakes before he does, lies there studying the unfamiliar ceiling, a beige stain in the corner that must mean there's a loose tile on the roof. A line of gold between the curtains suggests it's already late. She stretches her arms. She feels good. She'll run a bath, then see what she can find for breakfast. The fridge isn't working and they didn't bring much food with them anyway, but so what, it's fun roughing it when you don't have to.

When eventually she returns with toast and coffee on a tin tray decorated with kittens, Ben is still asleep. Even when she nudges him he's slow to open his eyes.

"Mm. Burnt toast," he mutters. "I thought that was MY speciality."

"Best I could do," she says, sliding open the curtains. "There's no toaster. Another thing for my list."

The day – this seemingly ordinary day that will turn out to be anything but – passes quickly. Katie is determined to do as much as she can before they head back to London in the evening. Ben bumbles around trying to help, gets in the way, escapes to the kitchen and opens a packet of chocolate cream biscuits. He sniffs them then takes one.

"Ben, really." Katie pulls a face. "They're way past their sell by."

She's sifting through the slithering pile of carrier bags now littering the table.

"Have we got any more black ones?"

"Doubt it. There's no more room in the car anyway."

"There'll have to be. I've got to clear that wardrobe," Katie says. She should have done it first. All those clothes packed tightly together, that horrible musty smell. The sooner they're dropped off at Oxfam the better.

Ben takes another biscuit.

"Leave yourself something to do next time," he says.

"Maybe you could find a shop that sells them?"

"What?"

"Black bags."

Ben gives in. Probably pleased to have an excuse to get out of the house, she thinks. But though the drive to the nearest village isn't far – ten minutes away, according to Rachael – he's gone for ages. Katie feels almost relieved when she hears the car door slam. Bringing in country air he pushes into the room, elbows out, arms full of boxes and bags.

"Come and see." There's pride in his voice. "Free-range eggs. They're still warm, and look..." He holds up a feather. "You forget they come from chickens, don't you?"

He unrolls the top of a brown paper sack.

"Organic potatoes. And I couldn't resist this honey. Smell it. Amazing, huh? Got it at a farm up the road, all of it. A real old -fashioned farm, decaying barns, cow shit everywhere..."

"I'd noticed," Katie says, glancing at his shoes. That explained the smell. "Don't suppose they sold black bags too?"

"No. Had to go to the village shop for them. Got some coffee, too. Only had instant I'm afraid."

It would obviously take more than her nagging to spoil his mood.

They eat before they leave – fried egg on toast and a cup of wine, though Ben tips most of his into her cup. He's the one who will drive them back (she hates motorway driving) and he won't take risks, not when he needs to be mobile for his work. Especially now there's only his salary coming in, Katie thinks. That's what he means.

It's getting dark as they pile things into the car, a calm evening, even the birds finally quietening. Katie's enjoyed their trills and burbles more than she'd have expected; she actually turned the radio off to listen to them. Ben promises to track down a CD of bird song so next time they'll be able to identify their visitors.

"That's us though," Katie says. "The visitors I mean. They live here."

"True, but so do we now."

As he struggles to lock the front door, Katie manages to squeeze one more cardboard box between the mountain of bags in the car boot. She slams it shut. Almost immediately a loud crack makes her jump, followed by another, then a third.

"Did you hear that?" Katie turns and looks towards the back garden and the fields beyond, though there's nothing to see.

"Fireworks? Out here?" People are always chucking bangers in the city: kids, late night revellers. But what's the point when there's no-one around to be startled, or woken from a deep sleep?

Ben puts the key in his pocket, crunches across the gravel.

"Sounds more like shooting."

"D'you think so?"

Katie gets into the car beside him, reaches for her seat belt.

"So someone's actually out there in our back-garden shooting things? God, I don't like that. Besides, isn't it illegal to even own a gun these days?"

Ben starts the engine. He edges forward in a wide circle out onto the road. Though only a couple of cars have gone past all day, he checks carefully in both directions before pulling out.

"Probably miles away. Sound carries, don't forget."

Katie is terrified of guns. Once, when she was at primary school, a man was shot just the other side of the railings. He was a father who'd been banned from seeing his daughters. They were in Katie's class, twins, timid girls with badly cut hair everyone said their mother did with nail scissors. They were never apart. When the courts decided their father was a danger to them – the rumour was that he was a violent alcoholic, which didn't mean much to Katie until her own father explained, then she felt bad about teasing them – he came to the school with a shotgun and shouted that he was there to take his girls. No fucking do-gooders had the right to keep them from him, he shouted. It was fucking cruel. It was killing him. The teachers hustled everyone away from the windows, and one of them shouted that the police were on their way. There was a long silence, then in the distance the sound of a police siren getting closer. Then, a gunshot. Someone started screaming and wouldn't stop. He'd put the gun into his mouth and pulled the trigger. Katie couldn't forget the blood that was still running along the gutter as they were all hurried through the gate past the covered shape on the ground, and sent home for the rest of the day. She'd had nightmares for months.

"What are they shooting at anyway?" she says now.

"Rabbits probably. They were talking about them at the garage. A plague of rabbits, that's what the guy said. Like locusts, despite the cold winter. They've never seen so many."

"So what harm do rabbits do?"

"Don't ask me."

They both go quiet. The road is narrow, the light fading fast. Ben is leaning forward slightly, gripping the wheel firmly as he concentrates, headlights scanning the uneven road and the hedges that seem to be going on forever. Katie resolves to forget about rabbits, thinks instead about all the things she has to do when she gets back to London. Her shopping lists are safe in her bag. She'll start first thing tomorrow.

And then it happens.

Something – an animal of some kind – emerges from the hedge to their left, starts to cross the road, becomes aware of the fast-approaching car and spins around back towards the hedge. As Ben hits the brakes the animal pauses and looks straight at them, its eyes reflecting the car lights. Then it slips easily through a space and is gone.

"Did you see that, Ben?"

"See it? I nearly flattened the bloody stupid creature."

"But what was it?"

"A dog?"

"Possibly. I don't think so. What would a dog be doing out here? There hasn't been a house for miles."

"Then what?"

Though in the grey of dusk it's impossible to be sure, Katie had the impression the fur was white. And from its shape, and from the swish of its tail, and the graceful way it moved it looked to her very much like a fox. But it couldn't have been. Foxes aren't white, or only – she seems to recall from some documentary – if they're Arctic foxes and it's winter. This isn't the Arctic and it's April.

"A spectre? An apparition?"

Katie glances at Ben, knowing how cynical he is about such things. Yet there was something about the animal – about the way it stopped and looked directly at her – not at them both, but at her – that's stunned her.

"Yes. Right." He chuckles. "So why don't you try to get some sleep?"

"Good idea."

She won't, of course. She remembers the first classical concert she went to, persuaded and challenged and eventually bullied by Ben into going along even though she'd always much preferred what she called happy music. As the lights dimmed, the conductor had marched briskly from one side and everyone applauded, then gradually calmed. Facing his orchestra he'd lifted both hands high, there was the longest pause, all eyes on those slim white fingers, no-one daring to cough, even to draw breath. Then he dropped them.

The first few notes of the cello had reached right inside Katie, stopping her breath for a moment, and she'd caught hold of Ben's hand. The Prelude to Bach's Suite No. 1 in G Major she now knew it to be. All she'd known then was that something big had happened – that a door had opened, that she'd tuned in to a new frequency, and that this was only the start.

And she'd smiled to herself, just as she did now, sitting in the car with her eyes closed and her thoughts back there on the side of the road.

# FOUR

Less than two weeks later and they're back again.

"God, what a nightmare journey! I'm shattered."

Ben moves around the kitchen as if it's a room he's long been familiar with, opening cupboards, pulling out drawers. He's always like that, has an ability to be instantly at home. Katie still feels she's in someone else's house and places the bags she is carrying carefully on the table, especially the plastic carrier that's warm to touch, concerned that some of its contents might escape and mark the wood.

"Can't believe our luck, finding a fish and chip van," Ben is saying as he takes out the neat white parcels, unwraps the paper and slides the contents onto plates.

"I'm amazed they still exist."

Katie is trying to remember when she last had fish and chips, the real thing, not grilled Dover sole topped with pink peppercorn butter, or monkfish kebabs, or thin slithers of potatoes oven roasted in rosemary flavoured olive oil. Probably when she was last in Devon. Now she picks at the crispy orange batter which is the bit she likes best, pops a piece in her mouth, tries one of the jumbo-sized chips. Heaven. She won't think about the calories.

"I don't suppose we've got any vinegar?" He means the brown kind of course, not balsamic. Katie shakes her head, offers him salt as compensation, which he sprinkles generously.

They settle on the sofa, plates balanced on their laps, and eat in silence. Katie too is exhausted, and she was only navigating. It took nearly five hours from London, with tractors lurking on corners waiting to nip out in front of them, and lorries sticking together as though linked, like railway carriages. Ben had suggested waiting until evening to drive down, when the roads would be quieter. He'd been right.

And then the mist. It had come down in minutes, billowing silently across in front of them like smoke from a bonfire, swallowing up everything: clumps of bushes dotted along the roadside, the endless sky, the occasional van parked on a patch of scrub, its occupants gazing out of the window drinking tea from a thermos. Grey humps materialised in front of them: sheep hunkered down with their lambs pressed to their sides and no intention of moving.

They'd crawled the last few miles across the top of the moor until the road dropped down and curled between the hills towards the village, and then just as suddenly they were back in the real world where things had colour, and shape, and there was a sky overhead again.

Looking back Katie realised they'd neither of them spoken whilst they were in the mist, though Ben had hummed tunelessly, as he did in traffic jams. Afterwards, the first thing that had come into her mind had been the white fox.

"Wonder if it'll still be there, where we saw it," she said, thinking aloud.

"What?"

"The fox. Or whatever it was. Remember?"

"What fox?"

Ben was concentrating on squeezing between two vans parked opposite each other on the village high street, both drivers hanging out of their windows, nattering as though leaning over a garden fence, oblivious to other traffic. Not that there was much. And not that anyone else seemed bothered anyway. That was what she was going to enjoy about being down here: living more slowly, like people used to.

It was whilst they were waiting to get through that they'd noticed the fish and chip van parked up ahead.

As they drove past the hedge where they'd spotted the fox she'd checked, just in case, though she knew it wouldn't be there. And it wasn't. Further on though they saw a couple of rabbits actually on the road. They appeared to be dead, though as Ben swerved slightly to avoid one Katie had a feeling that it moved. What is it about the other side of the road that's so appealing to animals? she thought.

Both their plates are scraped clean. The cans from which they've been sipping lager are on the floor at their feet, also empty. An electric fire buzzes – the only heater they've found so far, and doing a good job despite the smell of burning dust. Outside the window a handful of stars glitter in a navy sky. It's late, and Katie is far too full to want to do anything. This is a new sensation for her. Usually she eats slowly, pushing food around on the plate, counting calories. Now she feels satiated in a way she'd forgotten. It's not an unpleasant feeling. No wonder they're called comfort foods.

Ben too is almost asleep. His head nods, then he jerks it upright. He smiles sheepishly.

"Go to bed," she says. "I'll just do the dishes then I'll be up."

He stands and stretches, his shirt pulling free from the top of his jeans, yawning noisily.

"Leave them," he says, holding out his hand. "We'll do them together in the morning."

Used to tidying before she goes to bed, Katie hesitates, but only briefly. But though she thinks she'll sleep, she doesn't. Instead she lies there listening to Ben's steady breathing.

He's only staying for the weekend, then on Sunday evening she'll drop him at the railway station in Taunton, and she'll stay on. On her own. She'll drive back to this house with its light switches in the wrong places, with its unfamiliar sounds and even more disturbing silence. She's staying on to get to know it better so that when she begins work on it she'll be able to capture its character, make the best use of natural light, conceal its defects. What she'd describe as doing research.

"If I'm going to do this I want to do it properly," she'd said.

"You always do do things properly."

"I've already collected a wad of colour charts, and some wallpaper samples. I see it as a wallpapery kind of house, don't you?"

Ben, who was watching the news on TV, had grunted.

"So who's your money on for the next mayor of London then?" he called. "Got to be Boris, hasn't it?"

She went and stood in the doorway.

"Ben?"

He caught the note in her voice, turned.

"What's the real reason behind all this? I mean, what will you get out of it?"

"Katie, love, the reason behind all this – as you put it – is to make you happy. Or try to. Nothing more."

He'd said it so seriously that she couldn't help but smile.

Knowing he'd never bother to cook for himself, she'd stocked the freezer with ready meals. She'd bought salad and fruit too though she suspected they'd end up in the bin. She'd left clean shirts and underwear, fresh towels in the bathroom, she'd even hoovered everywhere.

Strange thing was, though they'd had separate working lives for most of the years they'd been together, they'd rarely slept apart. She hasn't thought about it before, but now she realises it's important, a sort of touching base. Even during the bad times they'd shared the same bed, back to back, a carefully maintained space between them, but she'd still been aware of the way the bed dipped and the warmth of his body. Most nights anyway. There had been a week or so when he'd used the futon in the spare room, not wanting to be near her, refusing to even talk, though she'd known his reasons. He'd thought she'd lied. Wrongly.

One more night together before he's gone. She's awake again, noticing as Ben's breathing changes, his foot suddenly kicks out, he moans. It doesn't sound like a good dream. Katie strokes his arm and he quietens. It's going to be odd, not just sleeping alone but waking alone. Not to hear the buzz of his electric toothbrush in the bathroom, the fridge door clunking shut, a spoon stirring against china. She's missing him, and he hasn't even gone yet.

And then she remembers – as clearly as if it was yesterday – the time he'd gone to Paris, the first and only time he'd agreed to go abroad to one of his conferences, a three day affair with specialists from across the EU meeting in a new building that looked from the brochure more like a factory than a convention centre, but that overlooked the Seine, which was a compensation. He was to give a talk on buckling. It had been his specialist subject at university: why buildings buckle. When they'd first met she'd been spellbound by his stories of bridges twisting like snakes in strong winds, tossing cars and their occupants into the river below; of vast domes collapsing under the lightest flurries of snow; of a block of flats folding flat as a pack of cards; of ancient towers suddenly crumbling, like an exhausted old man dropping dead in the street.

"Have you been to the Santa Maria del Fiore in Florence?" he'd asked her.

"Yes," she'd said. "At least, I think so."

She'd been to Florence with a school party and her memories had more to do with giggling with black eyed youths and drinking grappa than cathedrals.

"That incredibly beautiful dome was built without a scaffold over five hundred years ago. And it's still there. Imagine. OK, it's been strengthened, but it's still there."

His eyes had glittered, and she'd thought then that this man may not be handsome in the usual way, may wear the most awful shirts and bite his fingernails, but his voice made up for it. She'd thought, I could listen to him for hours, no matter what he's talking about.

"We should be building things for tomorrow, the next century even. People don't think. They don't care. They want everything to be cheap and instant. And safe of course, yet look how many still fall down."

She'd sat there with her elbows on the table and her chin on her hands, mesmerised.

Katie would have loved to go with him to Paris, but it was during the week, she had work commitments. It was to be the first time they'd been apart and they were both being sensible. Katie planned to see friends, a film, to give herself a pedicure, sort her wardrobe. She'd be fine. But once he'd left the house – once it had sunk in that she wouldn't see him again for three whole days and nights – she was shocked at how different it felt. Like there'd been a power cut, and everything had stopped – the fridge, the radio, the heating system – and instead of that quiet almost imperceptible hum that's the life of a house there was only silence. She'd wandered about hugging his favourite blue and grey striped sweater, pressing her face into it, comforted by the many smells that together could only have been Ben: his skin, his Body Shop deodorant, the faint smell of cement dust that he picked up just by visiting building sites, that no amount of hot washes could entirely remove.

It was when she bent to retrieve a wet towel from the bedroom floor that she saw the folder, inside it his notes. Pages of them, carefully numbered and stapled. The ones he'd spent evenings poring over. Though he could talk with confidence in social situations, he was nervous in front of big audiences, needed his notes on hand even if he didn't refer to them. They were his prompt, his back up. His courage.

Katie glanced at her watch. His plane would have taken off a while ago, had probably landed. She could ring and tell him she'd got them, but what use would that be?

She knew at once what she'd do. It was obvious.

The channel tunnel had finally opened, and the papers had been full of it for months. Now you could get a train direct from London to Paris. You didn't need to book, it didn't cost a fortune, and in less than three hours you'd be dodging traffic outsider the Gare du Nord.

Katie could just imagine his face when he saw her there, folder in hand.

She rang for a minicab, barely had time to scrabble together a few bits and pieces she might need before there was a ring at the door. She was on her way and still didn't know if what she was doing was a brilliant idea, or irresponsible and stupid. There were other ways to get packages delivered urgently, probably quicker and certainly cheaper. She was taking his notes to him herself because it was a crazy, romantic thing to do.

As the train neared its destination, slowing now, outside the window the grey suburbs slipping by, drab and characterless and yet still somehow French, she felt a twinge of doubt. Ben might be relieved to get his notes, but how would he feel about her being there, intruding on his world, the one he shared with men – it seemed it was mostly men anyway – whose strange passion was discussing Binishells and bridle node connections and the like. Would he resent her, like her father used to sulk when her mother insisted on accompanying him to the pub on a Sunday lunch time?

It was raining in Paris, street lights reflecting yellow off the wet pavements. Everyone seemed to have umbrellas and sensible shoes, everyone except Katie. It hadn't been raining in London. Again she caught a taxi, only too aware that in this unfamiliar city she had no choice but to trust the driver as he swung down cobbled alleyways then back to weave his way aggressively through the early evening traffic that was already clogging the boulevards and rues. If Ben seemed at all put out she wouldn't be offended; she'd simply hand him the folder and head back to the station. She'd be home in time to watch News Night.

She stood at the reception desk waiting for the skinny young woman with strangely bronzed skin and blue fingernails to track Ben down, to inform him that someone was waiting. Katie had declined to give her name. Suddenly she felt ridiculous standing there in her old cords and a sweater, her sandaled feet soaking, wet hair glued to her neck. Ben would want to disown her.

When he emerged through a distant door he was chatting to some colleagues, but the moment he spotted her he broke away from them, hurried across the tiled floor.

"You forgot something," she said. holding the folder out to him.

"I know. I've been freaking out."

A quick embarrassed grin.

"I thought you would."

"So you came all this way to give them to me."

"I've been wanting an excuse to try the tunnel."

"You are amazing," he said quietly. He was staring at her in a way she'd forgotten.

"And very soggy," she said, running her fingers through her hair. "God, I'm sorry Ben, I must look a mess."

"You look beautiful. Like a mermaid."

She felt like they were strangers, meeting for the first time, awkward together. Men in dark suits, women smelling of expensive perfume edged around them as they blocked the reception desk.

"I'm frozen too."

"Come with me. My room's tiny, but it's nice. You'll approve."

He'd been right. Everything was cream and pale turquoise, the carpet thick under her bare feet, big lamps casting a subtle light. She'd crossed to the window and put her face close to the glass, could just make out the river, cars with their lights on edging along beside the fast-flowing water, the traffic still heavy though she couldn't hear it.

"Do you mind my being here?" she asked. "I know I'm intruding."

"I love you being here."

"Honestly?"

"Honestly."

"But your colleagues will be waiting for you. That's the whole point of…"

"Let them wait. You get those wet clothes off, the shower's through here."

It felt strange to be there, in Paris with Ben. Wonderful. Even as she closed her eyes and let the warm water trickle down over her head and body she sensed the shower door opening. Ben's arms encircled her from behind, his lips on the back of her neck, one hand curved around her breast, the other moving down across her stomach, down further. She wanted to turn to him but he wouldn't let her, held her tight as his fingers slowly worked their magic, strong stubby fingers, a jolt of exquisite pain as a nail caught the tender skin, Katie reaching forward to press the palms of her hands against the tiles, her breathing unsteady, her body stretched and shivering and yearning for him.

Afterwards he'd wrapped her in the biggest white towel she'd ever seen and carried her to the bed.

Later still they'd sent down for cheese sandwiches, and a bottle of wine.

Apart from the lecture he had to give, and a couple of meetings he felt obliged to attend (he couldn't think of a good enough excuse to get out of them) Ben spent the next three days with Katie. Most of the time they stayed in the cream and pale turquoise room. They didn't talk much. Before they checked out they went to a nearby cafe and sat at one of the round chrome tables set out on the pavement, sheltering from the never-ending rain under a vast plum coloured awning, eating ravenously. They were the only ones sitting outside. People hurrying past glanced at them, the waiter impatient to get back into the smoky warmth, muttering under his breath as they ordered yet more food.

"It's such a shame you missed most of the conference," Katie said. "You were looking forward to it. Are you very disappointed?"

"What d'you think?" Ben was studying the bill. He returned it to the silver platter, started counting out notes. "Shattered, but not disappointed."

Katie sipped at the final dregs of now cold coffee.

"You know what was especially good about being here?"

Ben raised an eyebrow.

"As well as that. It was getting right away from the real world."

It was true. Ben hadn't once mentioned work even though he was in the middle of a dream build, as he put it, a conversion of a canal-side factory to luxury flats. For just about every waking moment of the past few months he'd either been on the site or on the phone. Or he'd been talking about it. He nearly hadn't come to the conference; she'd insisted.

And Katie, too, she'd hardly thought about the department store where she worked in the offices, maybe soon in an office of her own. She'd applied for promotion, had had a second interview, was on the short list. Head of publicity, it said on the door. Imagine if she got it.

She'd never before taken time off. And she'd lied, said there'd been a death, her grandmother, which was not only a cliché but a cruel one seeing as her grandmother was alive and thriving under the Spanish sun. Worse, since putting down the phone she'd hardly thought about work.

At a time when she should have been there, proving she was indispensable.

"Katie, these few days have been…" As Ben struggled for the word the waiter snatched up the platter, the door into the restaurant snapping shut behind him.

They both laughed.

"I know. Couldn't agree more."

Ben glanced at his watch.

"OK, we'd better go or we'll miss the flight."

Katie followed him out onto the street, caught his hand and he wrapped his fingers round hers and tucked both their hands into his pocket.

Of course, she hadn't left her pills behind on purpose.

Ben has only been gone three days, yet Katie's amazed at how quickly the house is beginning to feel like hers. Not even Rachael's aunt's. Hers. Of course, she knows all the trade tricks for turning – as she used to say to potential clients – a house into a quick and easy sale.

Fresh flowers – she'd found some floppy pink and blue blossoms in the garden, had no idea what they were, weeds probably, added fresh green leaves and grasses for contrast, crammed them into jugs and put them everywhere. You wouldn't get wild flowers like this in London, not at any price.

She'd brought down with her some dusky blue throws she'd picked up at a charity event. Made by a women's co-operative in India, she recalled, all of them victims of some kind: battered by their mother in law, raped by brutal husbands. She'd had to buy something. Now she draped one over the sofa, folded the other across the bottom of the bed. On a kitchen shelf she'd neatly lined up her favourite herb teas alongside muesli, a jar of marmalade, assorted crispbreads in a see-through storage box. At first the fruit bowl had added a splash of colour, but now there's only an apple and two speckled bananas left.

Katie walks around the house touching walls. She sits in different chairs. She's taken down all of the pictures and ornaments – plastic framed prints of Constable and Renoir, figures of little girls in straw hats, and playful puppies – and packed them into boxes. Hopefully Rachael would like them, reminders of an aunt who obviously cared about her, even though the feeling didn't seem to be reciprocated. If not, Oxfam again. She wants to start with a clean slate, an empty shell.

Much of the time she gazes out at the overgrown garden that seems to be edging ever closer to the house, a sea of greenery lapping at the walls, tapping at the windows. She imagines waking one morning to find the house resting on the sea bed, fish swimming past the windows, finds the thought unnerving. She prefers to look out on the gravelled yard in front, her car parked on one side, a solid stone shed in the far corner with a small window and padlocked door. At least that's a job she can put off for now, emptying the shed; she hasn't yet found the key.

Katie has to admit that she's ever so slightly nervous of the outside world. Indoors, surrounded by brick walls, she feels safe, but out there is an alien environment full of things to fear, though she's not sure what they are. Nights of course are the worst. City nights are diluted by street lights, security lights, the lights from thousands of windows. Here the night is deep and dense. Like tar, or treacle. She realises she's a true urbanite; her idea of countryside is Hampstead Heath.

This evening has been especially harrowing. She'd been trying to get the television to work. It co-operated when Ben twiddled the knobs. But now the picture is grainy, dissected by moving lines, and she wonders if the aerial has fallen, or even if there is one. The scream is so sudden, loud and child-like that she freezes. A pause during which Katie is sure she can hear something moving along below the window, a frantic scuffling sound, and then more screams. She takes a deep breath. If acts of barbarism are taking place out there in the flowerbeds – if some innocent creature is about to be eaten, or two testosterone-fuelled males are tearing each other apart – it's none of her business. It's nature. She must learn to ignore it.

Then, silence.

Katie pours herself a drop of wine, takes a large sip, decides she needs to speak to someone, to hear a human voice. Not Ben's. He'll only start worrying. She'll try Andrew on his mobile. No point in ringing on his landline; she'd long ago noticed his voice sounded different when Tess and the children were nearby. He'd never tease her, or swear. She'd picture him holding the phone close, his back turned to the room. He answers almost at once.

"Hi, it's me. Can you talk?"

"Katie? To you, any time. If you can hear me over the racket."

From the sound of it he's in a pub, probably the one behind the college where he teaches, where she'd sometimes meet him for a drink after work. She wasn't sure if he told Tess about their meetings. There was no reason not to, of course, except that Tess liked routine, and her carefully organised day included dinner at seven, at which the whole family would eat together. And which Andrew seemed to go out of his way to either be late for, or miss altogether. Tess insisted he did it to irritate her. Katie suspected it had more to do with a need to rebel against timetables.

A chuckle, then she hears him saying he'll be back shortly, imagines him moving away from the bar, pushing through the heavy doors and out into the dark street. She can hear traffic.

"So, you have my full attention."

"It's nothing special. Well, just a question really."

"Ask away."

"When we used to come to Exmoor did you ever feel... I don't know. Frightened?"

"Of?"

"The emptiness. The wildness of it all. The dark. Things that go bump in the night."

"No way, I thrived on it. We both did."

"Me too?" She can't remember. It was all so long ago.

"You used to cry when it was time to go home. Surely you haven't forgotten that? Every year without fail. You'd end up red eyed and snotty nosed, and they'd try to cheer you up with ice cream, which was great 'cause I got some too."

That she remembers. But that was because the holiday was over and soon she'd be back having macaroni cheese for tea on Mondays, fishcakes on Tuesdays, Shepherd's Pie on Wednesdays, with them. And watching TV, with them. She never minded being an only child except at the end of the holidays, when – after spending every hour of every day for four or more weeks with Andrew and his family, and her grandparents, and sometimes other people, friends, once someone's baby – she had to go back to living with just her parents. She adored them, but they were another generation, old. She longed to share her thoughts, worries, silly dreams with someone her own age. Andrew was an only child too – his older brother had died in a horrific road accident, Andrew hardly remembered him – but he had mates as he called them, an inexhaustible supply. Even so, she knew he liked it when people took them for brother and sister.

"You're not serious, are you Katie? It's here in the city you take your life in your hands each time you step outside."

He thinks she's ridiculous.

"I know. I suppose it's all so new to me. And when you're alone you're more aware of things, you hear things you'd miss other times..."

"And imagine things."

"I'm not imagining the slugs that are somehow getting into the kitchen. Great fat orange things. I nearly trod on one the other day, and I had bare feet. Yuk."

He laughs.

"Lucky you, your very own gastropod collection."

"Lucky me."

He sighs.

"You'll be fine, Katie. Give it time, we won't be able to prise you away from the place."

Someone calls his name. A girl. She's often wondered about his students, those moist-eyed young women with their sheets of shiny hair, their confidence. She once asked him if he'd ever had an affair, or a one-night stand, or even a fumble in a cupboard, but he'd laughed and changed the subject.

"Katie, I'm being reminded it's my round. Look, I'll ring you tomorrow."

"Don't worry. I know it's your busiest time of year."

"I've always got time for my favourite cousin," he says. About to say goodbye and let him off the hook, she pauses.

"Andrew, remind me why I'm here. I mean, is this a good idea or am I just running away from things?"

"It's a bloody brilliant idea. Good old Ben. You and I both know it can work magic, that place. Just hang on in there."

"OK. I will, I promise. Now go and buy those poor people a drink."

"Katie?"

"What?"

"I miss you. Next time you're in town we must meet up, have a meal. Just us. We haven't done that for ages."

"Fine. Your treat of course?"

"Of course."

Katie puts down the phone. After a bit she makes a decision. She goes to the back door and opens it wide, leans against the door frame, peers into the darkness, which isn't as black as she'd imagined. In the silvery light of a half-moon she can make out the hedge, the path as it curves away from where she stands to merge with the purple shadows pooled under shrubs and bushes. A whisper-soft touch on her bare arm makes her jump, but it's only a moth attracted by the light in the hallway behind her.

When, from down to her left, she hears a rustling, Katie holds her breath. She waits, her heart thumping. After seconds that seem like hours she decides that whatever it was, it's gone. Or possibly it too is frozen, waiting. From way off comes the hooting of an owl, a sound so familiar it makes her smile. Safe indoors again she feels ridiculously pleased with herself.

You see, there's nothing to be afraid of, nothing at all.

*Was that you searching for food, coming close to habitation when every instinct must have been telling you to stay away, that no matter how much you hurt with hunger it was too dangerous, the risks too great? You shouldn't have needed to of course, not in early summer when the moors are usually teeming with prey, when all a fox need do is sit there and wait for dinner to bob past. But not this year. This year was different.*

# FIVE

The complete solitude was a novelty at first, but it wore off. One week of seeing nobody, and Katie had felt a buzz of excitement about going shopping. She even looked forward to driving past the farm Ben had mentioned, debated stopping and introducing herself. After all, they're her nearest neighbours. But the long low building looks dark and unwelcoming, As she slows the car she can hear the bleating of sheep, sees at once that the front yard is crammed with animals packed so tightly they can hardly move. A lorry – D.W. Frith's Licensed Abattoir displayed on its side but in a discreet print size, she notes, so they don't want the world to know – has a ramp down and ready for loading. But there's no-one in sight. When a dog starts a frenzied barking at the back of the building, Katie accelerates away.

And even further on she meets few cars on the drive to the village where the streets too seem eerily quiet, a few vehicles tucked tidily alongside the shops, a bike, an invalid carriage stacked high with shopping bags. She looks for a double yellow line, can't see one, parks behind a mud-splattered truck that has what looks like a set of drums in the back. Strange, she thinks. But not as strange as being able to park so easily. Ben would be suspicious; he'd go and find a car park – if there is one – just to be safe. He'd pay for a couple of hours too, even though they'd probably only need an hour.

Katie walks down one side of the street noting the shops, crosses and walks back the other side. A butchers, a bakers, a vets with a notice in the window proudly announcing it will now be open three hours a week. A post office that's tucked in the corner of a newsagents shop that also sells local produce, eggs, ready-to-plant seedlings, and that hires out videos and arranges dry cleaning. No hardware store, so no chance of getting half the things on her list.

Still, the mini market looks promising. There's piped music, and people wandering the aisles with trolleys, children tagging behind, and Katie feels as though the real world has been switched back on again. She finds bread, milk, butter, frozen peas. At the checkout the girl – Patrice, her badge says – looks at Katie out of the corner of her eye.

"Livin' round here, are you?"

"Yes. Over towards the moor. For a while anyway."

"Like it?"

Katie nods.

"It's a beautiful place. And so peaceful. I'm going to love it, I'm sure."

The girl doesn't speak again, satisfied. Fiddling with her purse, Katie remembers her list.

"I couldn't find any avocados. You do sell them, don't you?" The girl shakes her head. "Tamari sauce? Tofu?"

The girl shrugs.

"Right. No problem." Katie slips her change into her purse.

"Is there anywhere round here I can buy masking tape, sandpaper, that kind of thing?"

"Not that I know of."

There must be, Katie thinks. Everyone's always doing things to their homes, it's the British preoccupation. She's being deliberately unhelpful, probably hates outsiders.

A man also leaving the shop pushes the door from behind her, holds it open as she struggles through with her two carriers. He's chuckling.

"Tofu. Tamari. You are kidding, aren't you?"

He has a soft twang to his voice. American. Even more of an outsider than her, then.

"Now if you want venison, poached, OK, but who's gonna know, I can help."

"Thanks, but I don't eat much meat." Especially not deer, she adds silently.

"Lobster? I know someone who catches them off the North Devon coast. Monsters, so fresh they dissolve in your mouth."

He's walking alongside Katie as she heads back to the car. If he hadn't spoken she'd have taken him for a local farmer, scruffy, scrawny, his checked shirt half tucked into his trousers, half out. All it needed was the straw clamped in the corner of his mouth. Though if he'd been a farmer his long grey hair wouldn't have been tied back in a ponytail.

"I never know where to start with a lobster," she says, dropping the bags into the boot of her car.

"Of course. Fish fingers, that's what you Brits prefer, right?"

She decides to ignore that comment.

"But I'd give up on the tofu if I were you," he's saying. "Not round here. You could try Barnstaple. Not the most picturesque of towns, but good for shopping. You'll get your DIY store too. And a couple of cool wine bars. You look like the kind of girl who likes wine bars."

Is he chatting her up? Unlikely. Besides, he's considerably older than her. Twenty years, even more.

"I used to, in my past life. Not interested since I moved down here."

"Which was how long ago?"

Katie pauses as though calculating.

"Just over a week."

"Give it a month and I warn you, you'll be desperate for a wine bar. Or a 24-hour supermarket, Or a proper traffic jam where people actually get out of their cars to thump each other."

Katie likes him already.

"You live locally too, do you?"

"Yup. Got a barn about three miles out of the village."

"Lucky you. I've always wanted to live in a converted barn."

"Who said anything about it being converted?"

"Oh. Right."

"It's half way there. Well, a third. Luxurious it isn't, but it suits me."

Katie tells him a bit about the house she's taken on, about how Ben is going to spend as much time as he can with her but that mostly she'll be alone, which is going to be a new experience for her. Especially as she has no near neighbours, and knows no-one.

"OK. Guy Gregory." He holds out his hand.

"Katie Tremain," she says, noting his skin is soft, silky. Not used to manual labour then.

"There. Now you know someone."

She opens the car door, is about to slide into the seat when Guy shakes his head.

"Hate to tell you, but you can't get tyres round here either."

He walks to the front, kicks at the wheel.

"And I didn't see a spare in the trunk."

"Oh no."

Even as she gets back out of the car Katie remembers that she used the spare months ago after another puncture – why is she always getting punctures these days? – and the damaged tyre is still somewhere at the back of the garage. She just hadn't had time, had even lied to Ben, knowing he'd disapprove of her driving around down here without a spare.

"You're right. I don't have a spare."

"Tell you what, if you can wait five minutes I'll give you a lift. If you can stand the smell in the truck, that is. Last thing I had in it was... no, never mind. So? What d'you say?"

"I'd be very grateful."

"OK. I'll be real quick."

He jogs across the road and Katie notices how easily he moves, so light on his feet, like a young animal. She retrieves her bags, locks the car, waits patiently on the pavement. A couple of boys whizz past on racing bikes and she wonders idly why they're not at school.

Guy returns clutching a paper bag, jumps into the truck and waits while she piles her bags onto the floor then pulls herself in, the seat lurching sideways as she sits. He passes her the bag, starts the engine and pulls away without looking behind him.

"Take one. Whichever you fancy except the cream one. That's mine. You can pass it to me, if you would."

Doughnuts. She'd noticed the bakery, now she comes to think of it, had dismissed it instantly as a place full of temptations.

"I don't eat..."

"Hey, no-one turns down Mary Morgan's doughnuts. They're out of this world. Trust me, I'm American, I know about doughnuts. In New York we have a shop selling forty-eight varieties."

Bet he doesn't know how many calories they contain, Katie thinks, nor how much saturated fat, nor white sugar. Probably doesn't care either. She passes him one, can't resist licking her fingers, then thinks what the hell and takes one for herself.

"Good, huh?"

"Wickedly good."

"I'd marry her, even though she's no Kate Bush. If she wasn't already hitched."

Somehow Katie can't imagine Kate Bush being his type.

"And so what was the last thing you had in the back?" Katie says.

"A deer. It got hit by a coach. I went and collected it for some friends who run a pub restaurant. No point in wasting it, not when so many visitors to Exmoor are prepared to pay mega bucks for their venison fillet mignon. They want to see the deer, gush about how beautiful they are, then they want to eat them. We humans, huh?"

Katie wishes she hadn't asked.

"And the drums?"

"They're for this young guy I know. He works on a farm, spends his days spreading slurry and mending fences, and is completely wasted. I thought he'd like to get rid of some of his frustration on... wait, hold on."

Katie winces as the truck bumps over a rabbit, then immediately hits another one. Surely Guy could have avoided them? He's not going that fast and there's nothing else around. True, they were just sitting there, right in the middle of the road, as though hypnotised.

"Poor things." She turns to look out of the side window.

"Rabbits? Not to farmers. They detest them. Recent years there've been way too many. They may look cute, but believe me, they can do serious damage."

He glances at Katie then changes his tone.

"Still, it's a hell of a way to die, myxie. You know, from the time they're infected to the time they snuff it can take thirteen days? You see them everywhere, blind and blistered up, starving."

"Myxie?"

"Myxomatosis. Ask me, I think they head for the roads as a way of committing suicide. I do them a favour. At least it's quick."

"But you're not saying it's been spread deliberately?"

Katie can hear the outrage in her own voice.

"Sure it is. Some farmer over beyond Copperdown Woods started this outbreak. He's boasting about it to anyone who'll listen. Trouble is it spreads like wildfire and soon it's having effects no-one reckoned on."

"Such as?"

"They say back in the fifties the virus killed over ninety nine percent of rabbits. Next few years the buzzards were almost wiped out. Shame, I like buzzards. You ever watched them when they're way up above you and they catch a thermal? It's like they're surfers riding a wave, adjusting their weight ever so slightly, wings motionless."

"Don't they think about the knock-on effect then, these people?"

"Seems not. Stoats nearly coped it too, until the clever buggers discovered squirrels. Then the squirrels were nearly wiped out."

"But it's all so... so cruel."

Guy gives a sound that could be a snort, but that she decides is a chuckle.

"Local folk don't do sentimentality, at least, not about anything with fur or feathers. The sooner you learn that, the sooner you'll be accepted."

Does she care about being accepted? Will she be around for long enough anyway?

"So where is it we turn off for your place? We must be almost there."

He drops her by the gate, the engine still running to show he has no expectation of being invited in? He insists she takes the remaining doughnut.

"It'll make you happy," he says.

But as soon as she's in the kitchen Katie crosses to the bin and drops the bag into it. She stashes things in cupboards, the fridge, arranges fruit in the empty bowl, and as always it gives her a good feeling, the satisfaction of knowing starvation has been staved off a little longer. But despite this, and the late afternoon sunshine patterning the floor, still there's a little black cloud hovering overhead. Why? Because of the rabbits and the deer? This is rural life. At least it's honest, she reminds herself. City people eat meat, wear leather and furs. They just let someone else do the dirty work.

Katie switches on the kettle, makes a mug of tea, then she guiltily retrieves the doughnut and heads outside to the wooden bench she's discovered tucked in a far corner of the garden under what looks like a tangle of honeysuckle, though it isn't yet in blossom so she can't be sure.

Later, she rings Ben. No answer.

She leaves a message. He's coming down the day after tomorrow, so maybe he could get the spare tyre repaired and bring it with him? She misses him, she adds. As she speaks she's standing at the bedroom window looking down on the garden. She's already come to love these last few moments of the day when the sun hangs suspended like a huge drop of water, quivering, edging lower, lower, and then suddenly dropping behind the hills leaving slowly widening ripples of pink spreading across the evening sky.

She tries Ben again. Still no answer. She hates it when she can't reach him. When he's extra busy he switches off his mobile, and she knows he's up against some really tight deadlines right now, but still she feels abandoned. She leaves a shorter message asking him to please just ring her.

It's television time. She has plenty to do during the day, but not the evenings. Collapsing in front of the box is becoming a habit, a bad one. She bought some wine in the mini market; there wasn't much choice, none of her favourite Pinot Grigio, nothing else particularly tempting, so she settled for a cheap red from Bulgaria. In a box. After half a glass it's almost drinkable.

Katie's watching a documentary – another heated debate on climate change – when something outside catches her attention. She hasn't put the light on, nor drawn the curtains, and can see that it's almost dark now. It's much chillier too; she shivers.

There it is again.

If she didn't know better she'd think it was human voices, but it's unlikely anyone is walking along the road; no-one goes past even during daylight. Besides, this sounds nearer. Outside the front door.

She tiptoes along the hallway, opens the door a crack. No-one. But about to close it she hears laughter, and at the same time notices a flickering light through the window of the shed. A candle? But who? And how did they get in when the door was padlocked? And what the hell should she do next?

In the city she'd call the police, or a neighbour, preferably male and muscular. But this isn't the city, and the nearest police station is probably miles away, she's no idea where in fact. She thinks briefly of Guy who'd given her his phone number, but there's no way she could call him. Ben can't help her. No-one can. She's on her own. She turns back into the hallway and picks up the first heavy object she touches – a copper jug that's at the top of a box of things to be got rid of – and a small torch Ben said she should keep by the door in case of emergencies. He'd had in mind a fuse blowing.

As she crosses the courtyard she steps lightly on the gravel, but even so she senses things go suddenly quiet. Then the candle is extinguished.

Counting to three, Katie switches on the torch and reaches for the door.

A scuffling sound, someone swears. The smell that hits her is instantly recognisable; there was a time years ago when no dinner party they attended was complete without someone lighting up a scruffy, loosely wrapped joint and passing it round.

"What the fuckin'…?"

The voice is young, male, high pitched. Katie directs the torch downwards and sees the panic in his face. On the ground beside him is a girl who is frantically pulling a tee shirt over her head.

"That's my line I think," she says, trying to sound stern, to cover her relief. It's a couple of kids having a sneaky smoke.

"Sorry, miss, we thought the house was empty." As he speaks he's mashing the joint into the ground under a grubby trainer.

"The old lady died, didn't she?"

"She did. But I'm living here now. Me and my husband."

Proud of herself for her quick thinking. For not letting on she's alone.

"We didn't know. Honest."

They're both on their feet now, anxious to go. As they file past her she can see they're even younger than she thought.

"Wait," she says. "How did you get here?"

"Cycled out." The boy nods in the direction of the gate, and swinging the torch beam across the yard Katie can see a tumble of metal by the hedge. No wonder she didn't hear them. And there was no car parked outside to warn them the house was inhabited, no lights on.

"And the shed. It was locked. How did you get in?"

"Got the key, ain't I?" He hesitates. "My mum used to help the old lady, did a bit of cleaning for her, brought her out soup and apple crumble and stuff. Mum said she was a miserable old cow, but even miserable old cows have to eat."

The girl giggles and shoves the boy, who ignores her.

"Mum's got a drawer full of keys."

"That's one less for her drawer then. I'll keep it. And you two better cycle off home."

Obediently they turn away, the girl catching the boy's hand.

He hesitates.

"You won't tell anyone, I mean, about the spliff?"

"Not unless you come back and try to use my shed again."

"We won't, miss."

She can't recall when anyone last called her miss. Made her think of The Prime of Miss Jean Brodie, which she loved and had seen more times than she could count.

Once back indoors Katie walks around the house checking windows, turning keys, securing bolts. And now she feels vulnerable, tucked down a lane, well away from habitation, with non-one to turn to, no-one even knowing she's there. What if they'd been real addicts, too wasted to even know what they were doing?

But they weren't. They were kids who you'd expect to be home hunched over computer games, or watching Harry Potter videos, or at worst loitering outside McDonald's chucking chips at each other and plotting how to skip school without being missed.

She dials Ben's number one more time. When he still doesn't answer she leaves a short message saying – in case he's interested – she's just disturbed some intruders.

She's not so much shocked as surprised. How often has she seen hooded kids huddled in litter-strewn doorways sharing a joint, often in full view of a CCTV camera. She's even watched a teenage boy doing deals with children as they emerged from a local primary school. She rang the headmaster about it, but he said it was the Christmas carol concert that evening and he was frantic, half his staff off with flu, none of the chairs in place yet. Ben thought he'd probably been threatened.

That's city life. But she still thinks of the countryside as being somehow untainted, wholesome. Like in the Hovis commercials. Though she supposes children everywhere have to take risks, break laws, it's part of growing up, it's how they learn. Tough on parents of course. Thank God she's not one.

Things might have been very different, of course.

Katie had only been back from Paris a few days when she had confirmation of her promotion. She sat there, swivelling in her specially purchased ergonomic desk chair, trying not to smile. It wasn't the prestige, nor the money though that would be useful, everyone can use more money. It was being trusted to do the job by people who knew the business far better than she did. They were depending on her not to let them down, nor the shareholders, the staff, the customers. And she wouldn't.

The first morning there was a bunch of white roses on her desk.

YOU CAN DO IT, was written in familiar handwriting on the card. YOU CAN DO ANYTHING YOU SET YOUR MIND TO. THAT'S JUST ONE OF THE THINGS I LOVE ABOUT YOU. BEN

He hadn't added kisses. He didn't do slushy, except on very rare occasions. One of the things Katie loved about him.

She reached for the phone. From her fifth-floor window she had a view of the river, watched as a police launch dodged between pleasure boats packed with intrigued tourists, like a footballer showing off his moves.

"Jane, can you come in for a minute please?"

"Sure."

"But first, could you organise a coffee?"

"Of course."

"And one for yourself too,"

First rule of business: bond with those who are going to be most useful to you.

"Oh and Jane, any chance of finding a vase?"

"For the roses? I already have."

Definitely someone to bond with.

"You're really getting a kick out of this job, aren't you?" Ben said over fettucine with artichokes, the fourth night running they'd eaten at their local Italian trattoria.

"You know me. It's like having a brand-new toy to play with."

She snapped the end off a breadstick.

"One day I'll get bored. But it'll take at least a year or two. Can't wait to see how this new project we've planned is going to work out, it's something they've never tried..."

Ben twirled his fork in the pasta.

"You do realise that if we keep eating out like this I'm going to have to start doing more overtime," he said.

"So how often have you threatened to have a go at cooking?" Katie trickled dressing over her rocket salad, looked at Ben, waited.

He grinned.

"OK. You're on," he said. "Tomorrow evening. I'll pick up some ingredients on the way home. Prepare to be impressed."

It was only when she realised her periods were late that the thought occurred to Katie. She couldn't be pregnant, could she? Despite taking the pill, her periods had been all over the place lately. She noticed she was more irritable too, couldn't wait to retire to the sofa at the end of the day. She'd put it down to all the things that were happening in her life. If it hadn't been for Paris she wouldn't even have thought of it. Three days. Would those three days without the pill be long enough?

"Shit," she said aloud to the mirror. "Shit, shit, shit."

She didn't look any different.

Why me, when I'm surrounded by women who want nothing more than to have babies, who consult calendars and thermometers and horoscopes, and drive their husbands crazy demanding intercourse at carefully chosen times, daily if not more often? Who'll go through any amount of pain and humiliation – not caring how many strangers in white coats do embarrassingly intimate things to their bodies – and pay vast sums of money for the chance, the slightest chance, that they might conceive? Whose sole purpose in being alive is to breed?

If she didn't look any different, maybe she was mistaken.

Tess, for example. She and Andrew had only been married a year when she started panicking. Though she rarely talked to Katie about personal things – wary, no doubt, of the affinity Katie had with Andrew, and for good reason – there had been one evening when she couldn't hold back. Whilst Katie slotted the dinner plates into the dishwasher, Tess had sipped her wine and talked. And talked. About how desperate she was to have a baby to hold, fondle, kiss. About how she'd already chosen a wicker crib that was straight out of a fairy tale, a cot light that as well as making patterns on the ceiling played noises from nature, birds and tinkling streams. The envy she felt when she saw a pregnant woman was indescribably awful. Once she'd almost snatched a baby from a pram and made a run for it.

"You don't think I'm going insane, do you?" she'd said.

"I think you're very normal," Katie had said. "Just a bit impatient." For a moment Tess was revolted by her soft, soppy neediness.

"I hope you're going to have some lemon meringue pie," she went on. "I made it from scratch. It's Andrew's favourite, I know."

But then, if Tess and the millions like her were normal, what did that make Katie?

She put off going along to Boots to get a testing kit.

She put off thinking about it. She put off mentioning it to Ben, knowing from the few brief chats they'd had that he would be delighted if she really was pregnant. And she wouldn't, not right now. Maybe never. OK, it was selfish but she'd fought hard for this job and she wasn't ready to give it up. Besides, they'd only recently bought their mews house; for the past months it had been filled with dustsheets, the smell of paint, the incessant thumping of punk rock from the builders' radio. Now, at last, it was finished. No way was it suitable for a baby with its open plan staircase and tiled floors and glass table. The guestroom – which would have to be the nursery – was grey and purple. Even the one indoor plant they'd bought (chosen because it was low maintenance) was a giant and very spiteful cactus.

The only option would be to have a termination. Without telling Ben, of course. Without telling anyone. But even as she thought it she knew she couldn't do it. Or maybe she could?

And then, one evening.

For some days now he'd noticed she was distracted, eating even less than usual, sleeping fitfully; said she mustn't overdo things, that would be silly. She'd said of course it would, and she wasn't. He mentioned it again. She told him to stop worrying, muttered something about him going on and on and how it was the last thing she needed right now. The third time the words had tumbled out before she could stop them.

"OK. Here's the thing." She'd taken a deep breath. "I think I might be pregnant." It was the first time she'd said it aloud. For a long moment Ben had simply stared at her.

"You're kidding," he said then. "Honestly? But how…?"

"Paris. I didn't bring my pills with me, I didn't bring anything, remember? Except your notes." He'd run his fingers through his hair, turned away and then back to her, grinned.

"Wow. That's some souvenir!"

In two big steps he'd crossed to her, wrapped her in his arms, pressed his face into her neck. Rocked her from side to side. She pulled away.

"Ben, wait. Two things. Firstly, I'm not sure. I'll do a test tomorrow, but my periods have been erratic lately to say the least."

He held her at arm's length, his eyes holding tightly to hers.

"Sure. Obviously. Fingers crossed. And the other thing?"

How could she say it?

"I don't know… I mean, I don't think I'm ready to have a baby right now."

His smile had wavered, but he managed to hold onto it.

"I know, the timing is all wrong. But don't worry, love, we'll manage. I'll make it alright, I promise."

Katie had felt sick. She didn't want to be going through any of this. She didn't want to have to be saying this.

"You don't understand. I don't think I can do it. I'd resent it, and be miserable and bad tempered, and the baby would suffer, and you'd grow to hate me."

Now his hands had dropped away from her.

"So you want to get rid of it, is that what you're saying? Have an abortion?"

"A termination. That's the word they…"

"I don't believe this."

He'd moved away across the room. As though he couldn't stand being near her.

"I mean, before you kill off our baby – our baby, Katie, don't forget, ours – can we at least talk about it?"

"Ben, please. Let's wait and see. It might be a false alarm."

"And if it isn't?"

The question hung there between them, echoing in the silence. Katie dropped down onto the sofa, put her face in her hands.

He'd stormed out of the room, thumped up the stairs, down again and then out of the house, slamming the front door. Ben who never thumped or slammed around.

When, next evening, she told him – trying so hard to hide her relief – that the test result was negative, he'd given her a long look, then gone on reading briefly before getting up and leaving the room. It was only much later that she realised that what she'd taken to be disappointment was something else altogether.

It was doubt, suspicion, mistrust. A nasty little worm that would burrow deep into his subconscious, curl up and wait.


Though it feels like ages ago that Katie left the last message for Ben, it's no time, fifteen, twenty minutes. Hearing the ring tone, and then his voice makes everything right. She's sorry if she sounded angry that he wasn't there. She knows he's not ignoring her. It's been one of those days. Ben says of course, he understands, she never needs to apologise to him. He'll get some new locks, replacing them all would probably be a sensible idea. Of course he'll organise the car tyre too. He misses her, he says, lowering his voice. It feels strange in the house without her being there. When she insists it's the same for her he says no, it isn't. The house on Exmoor is her territory, he's hardly spent any time there. But their London home is – well, theirs. Her things are still scattered around, her clothes fill the wardrobe, a novel she was reading lies open beside the bed. There are smells that remind him of her: her face creams, her favourite Costa Rican coffee. He keeps expecting her to emerge from the bathroom with a towel wrapped around her head, or burst through the front door with a Chinese takeaway that'll be cold if they don't eat it instantly, that often is already cold if he's honest.

"Beginning to regret dumping me down here then, are you?"

She hopes her voice shows that she's smiling.

"What gives you that idea?"

She can hear it in his.

So he really is missing her then.

# SIX

*A misplaced maternal instinct. Is that
what this is all about? Ben thinks so. He
wouldn't dare say, of course. But sometimes
I see him watching me when I'm getting
your food – opening a tin of cat mush or,
even worse, defrosting those bright yellow
baby chicks so cute they look like they're
straight off the top of an Easter cake. He
watches me knowing I don't want to be
fiddling with such things, that I'm
squeamish, that my stomach turns easily (as
easily as a rotisserie in the window of a
Greek restaurant, he once joked), but that
I'll do it for you. He equates my
determination to cope with that of a mother
spooning pap into her drooling baby, wiping
away sick, disposing of stinking nappies. He
thinks that having you living here with me is
putting me in touch with my caring side.*

*Typical cliched man-think.*

*You're not a baby substitute, far from it.
You're a wild, beautiful creature from a
parallel world who happens to be in trouble,
and who I want to help. If I can, which I
sometimes doubt. I feel privileged that our
lives have not just crossed but become
intertwined. I also know that one day I'm
going to have to set you free. I want it. Wild,
beautiful creatures have to be free or they
die. Or they're as good as dead anyway.*

Ben arrives a day early bringing all the things he promised,
plus a box full of goodies: avocados, mangoes, couscous,
halloumi cheese, toasted sesame oil. Piled on the wooden

table like a Dutch still life, they make Katie want to take up photography again. Ben finds it amusing, her being so excited. It's alright for him. He can get whatever he fancies from the late night delicatessen a five minute walk away, the stock displayed on glass shelves like ornaments, everything overpriced but irresistible. It's run by an affable Jamaican called Jethro who understands about the tastes of city people.

"I hope you've been eating properly?" Katie says.

"Depends what you mean by properly."

He looks as though he's put on a few pounds – even in that generous grey checked shirt he'd wear every day if it was up to him – though he can carry it. She likes him best in casual clothes, they make her want to be wrapped and safe in the curve of his arms.

"Tell you what, that microwave's bloody brilliant."

"So there's nothing left in the freezer?"

"Not much. A salmon someone at the office gave me. He'd caught it himself, said fish brings him out in a rash and his wife is vegetarian."

Ben perches on the edge of the table, picks up the folder Katie is using to keep together the growing number of fabric swatches, paint charts, her notes. He holds up a square of linen.

"I love this... what is it? Azure? Turquoise? Can see it as curtains, long ones that bunch up on the floor."

"Periwinkle. Did he keep it chilled? If not it won't be edible."

"I doubt it. And there are some Belgian chocolates that old guy up the road left for you. You helped him with some forms?"

"I'd forgotten. That's kind of him."

Not that they're going to be edible either, she thinks.

"So are you going to sit there watching me, or get started?" she says, half teasing, half serious. There are so many things she needs him to do, and he hasn't got long, yet she hates to nag.

"First I'm going to make myself a coffee, seeing as you haven't offered."

It's true what he said on the phone: the house does feel like it's hers and that he's a visitor. But he's not.

"Make me one too, will you?" she says to make the point.

Katie is tackling the woodwork. Some of it is so badly scuffed it will have to be repainted, but she hopes to get away with just cleaning the rest. As she crawls along the hallway floor sponging down the skirting boards, she can hear Ben out on the front doorstep, muttering as he works. Though he's in the building trade he isn't good with his hands. Usually, if something needs doing he'll know someone who can do it.

Sun shining through the small panes of the end window, its rays full of dust, reminds Katie of her resolution to get outdoors more. It's a waste, living here in the midst of all this wilderness and hiding away in a musty old house like a little city mouse. The air is amazing too. Early mornings it actually tastes like iced fizzy water.

"Finished." Ben stands behind her looking pleased with himself. "Every outside door now has a new lock. Here, put these keys somewhere safe."

Katie sits back on her heels, rolls her aching shoulders.

"Fancy a walk later?"

"Where to?"

"Nowhere. Around."

"Sure."

There's no enthusiasm in his voice. He doesn't like doing things without a purpose. Neither does she, usually. Driven, isn't that the word the shrinks use for people like them?

"Never know what we might find out there," she adds.

"Such as?"

"How do I know? That's the point."

Katie accepts she'll have to go exploring alone. But in the end it rains, lightly at first, and then settling in for the day, the rooms now so gloomy that they need to put on the lights, and she gives up and goes back to cleaning the woodwork.

It's early evening, and Ben is in the attic. Having removed the plywood fireplace in the living room he'd found a real one behind it, the tiles needing cleaning, but not damaged. Now he's searching for the missing grate. Ben likes attics. He's been up there so long Katie imagines he's fallen asleep.

"You OK up there?" she calls. She has no intention of climbing the ladder he's balanced precariously against the trapdoor opening.

"Mmm."

It's the sound he makes when he's putting together a particularly complicated quotation. It means I hear you but have no intention of stopping.

"Ben?"

"What?"

"Food's ready."

"OK. OK. I'm coming."

She's not convinced. She leaves the lasagne in the oven, turning the heat low, sits one end of the wooden table and picks at the pistachios he'd brought with him, getting through them too fast, annoyed with herself when she'd resolved to make them last. She'd forgotten how irritating Ben could be at meal times, complaining about how he's starving one moment, then letting everything burn because he's been distracted. She goes back upstairs.

"Ben? What're you doing up there?"

A pause. Then his head appears silhouetted against the attic light.

"Coming down right now."

She's in the middle of dishing up when he comes into the kitchen carrying what looks like a long piece of wood wrapped in a sack. He puts it down tenderly.

"You won't believe what I've found, love."

With a plate in one hand and a serving spoon in the other, Katie watches as Ben unfolds the wrapping. Revealed is a long leather case and she thinks for a moment it's some kind of musical instrument, but as he clicks the catch and lifts the top she shudders. Nestling in a groove of green baize, is a double-barrelled shotgun.

"It's old and needs a clean, but it's in excellent condition. And look at the handle, and the beautiful lines. Feel how smooth the wood is. It's walnut I think."

Katie doesn't want to touch it. She doesn't want it in her kitchen. Ben reaches for a small box wedged neatly into its own groove, takes out a red cartridge, balancing it on his palm as though it's a rare butterfly.

"And the cartridges, they're cardboard. Amazing, huh? Bet they don't make those anymore."

Katie glances at Ben. His face is flushed.

"Ben, let's eat."

"Of course. Sorry, love."

But even as she pours wine he's still standing, buckling a leather belt around his hips.

"How neat is this? It holds... let's see... twenty-four cartridges all ready to be loaded. Probably used on rabbits."

Katie sits.

"They don't waste bullets on rabbits round here," she says, piling most of the salad on her plate. He doesn't seem to want to join her anyway. She was so looking forward to having him there, to sharing meals.

"They give them myxomatosis. Cheaper, easier. Probably more efficient too."

Ben finally sits.

"This looks delicious." He reaches for his fork. "By the way, rifles take bullets. This is a shotgun, it takes cartridges filled with lead shot."

Katie wants to hit him. He knows what she means.

"Besides, I don't think it's spread deliberately, love. I know you think these people are cruel, but…"

"A farmer who lives near Copperdown Woods started it. Everyone knows, so presumably everyone approves."

"Who told you that?"

"Guy. The American who rescued me when I had the flat tyre."

"And he knows what he's talking about, I suppose?"

Katie shrugs.

"Sounded like he did."

Ben glances at her over his almost empty plate.

"Katie, love, you mustn't let these things get to you."

"I don't intend to," she says, giving him a quick smile. "More lasagne?"

When the dishes are washed and Katie goes to see what's on TV, Ben says he'll join her in a minute. Half an hour later he's still in the kitchen. Through the open door she can see him standing at the table with the gun, examining it, passing it from one hand to the other, getting the feel of it. Then he holds it against his shoulder and points it across the kitchen, and as he pulls the trigger she hears a click.

Eventually he comes and drops down heavily onto the sofa.

"Didn't notice anywhere selling firearms in the village, did you? There must be a farm merchant somewhere nearby where I can get a cleaning kit."

He puts an arm around Katie's shoulders and automatically she leans in against him.

"Could be dangerous to use it without cleaning it first."

She glances up.

"What d'you mean, use it? Why? When have you ever handled a shotgun?"

Ben's eyes stay on the flickering screen.

"Come on, it's not rocket science, Katie."

"And excuse me for mentioning it, but aren't you meant to have a license? Who is it that's always going on about people picking and choosing which law they'll obey and which they'll ignore?"

"Give me a chance, I only found it an hour ago. I'll get a license."

"They won't give you one. Not unless you can prove you have a good reason for needing a gun."

He yawns, ruffles her hair.

"Katie love, it's been a long day. Let's not argue."

He's already gone by the time she wakes next morning. She's surprised she didn't hear the car start. She pulls a sweater over her nightdress, heads down to the kitchen where she pours a glass of fruit juice, takes it out into the garden. She's disappointed that Ben's not with her here in the damp, green jungle she's growing to love. Disappointed too that he's off on some new project. She admires the childlike quality that allows him to get so swept away that he completely forgets everything else, yet she could do with his help. And he did promise.

And then, probably the biggest disappointment is that he's forgotten how she feels about guns.

When she hears the car on the gravel she hurries inside and goes straight to the bathroom, drags the plastic curtain with its pink and blue shell design around her, turns on the shower.

"Christ."

The first shot makes her jump, even though Ben had warned her he's about to have a go. But it's his exclamation and the sound of the gun clattering onto the paving stones that has her running out. He's bent double clutching his right shoulder.

"I expected it to have a kick, but Christ almighty…"

"Ben, what have you done?"

What if he's broken his shoulder? She tries to turn him towards her, but he doesn't want to be touched. His face is scrunched with pain. But gradually he straightens up. He examines his hand for blood. Finding none he moves his shoulder carefully, then massages it. Katie glances towards the line of targets he's set up along the top of the furthest hedge: a couple of bottles, some empty cans.

"Did you hit anything."

"A bird? No chance of anything else. The barrel kicked upwards when I pulled the trigger."

Now he's smiling, a small tight smile, and she knows he's alright.

"You better not have. I like the birds."

She means it. Him and his bloody gun. All morning she'd had to work around him as he took over the kitchen table, spreading the gun out on newspaper, fiddling with foul smelling oil and rods and wadding, pleased beyond belief when it came out brown and crusted.

"Look at all that rust? This stuff is brilliant."

She wished he'd clean the windows instead.

"If it's really that old, maybe a collector would be interested in it?"

"Possibly." He'd held the barrel up to his eye like a telescope. "That's better."

"Ben?"

"Sorry, love. What did you say?"

Next he'd rubbed the outside of the barrel until it gleamed, worked oil into the small ring that was the hammer. The trigger, he explained. And this, he'd indicated, is the safety catch. Very important. He'd smiled.

It brought to mind a poem Katie had learnt at primary school, a very old one, probably written over a hundred years ago. It had been a favourite that always made her laugh. As he rummaged around looking for things to use as targets she went and found paper and a pen. She wasn't sure she had it right, but it must be close. She printed it on the back of an envelope.

I saw a jolly hunter with a jolly gun
walking in the country in the jolly sun.
In the jolly meadow sat a jolly hare
saw the jolly hunter took jolly care.
Hunter jolly eager at sight of jolly prey
forgot the gun was pointing wrong jolly way.
Jolly hunter head over heels gone
jolly old safety catch not jolly on.
Bang went the gun hunter jolly dead
jolly hare got clean away
jolly good I said.

Now – as he blasts away in the garden – she looks at it again, secured to the fridge door by a pink pig magnet she'd found in the back of a drawer. It still makes her smile. He won't be able to miss it but he won't say anything of course. He's good at ignoring things he doesn't want to have to face.

But she's wrong. They're in bed with the light switched off.

She'd thought he might already be asleep.

"Katie, about the gun."

She says nothing, waits.

"I know how you feel about guns…"

"Do you?"

"Of course I do. I know why. You told me, remember?"

"So why bring a gun into the house?"

"I didn't bring it in, Katie. It was already here. Guns are part of the way of life down here. Everyone has one. They need them."

"And us, why do we need one?"

"We don't need it. And I'll get rid of it. But humour me, will you? It's a beautiful bit of craftsmanship, I really enjoyed getting it spruced up."

"And shooting with it?"

A pause.

"Yes, that too. I bought a couple more boxes of cartridges. If I could just hit a tin can I'd be satisfied."

Is she being unreasonable? People join shooting clubs, go on clay pigeon shoots.

"If that's what you want. Just keep it away from me."

"I'll keep it in the attic for now. Ought to get some kind of security case, I suppose."

"But you will get rid of it."

"I'll get rid of it. Soon. I promise you."

The silence is as dense as the black that surrounds them.

"Katie, I've no intention of killing anything. I couldn't. You do know that?"

She doesn't speak because she'll say the wrong thing. Instead, she turns away from him, pulls the duvet up around her ears. After a bit he kisses her shoulder and whispers good night.

Katie sleeps badly. She wakes early. She debates various ways of getting back to sleep, knows from experience that they never work. Besides, she's had an idea. She eases herself out of bed, picks up her jeans and tee-shirt. Ben grunts but doesn't wake. Downstairs she pulls on her clothes, uses her fingers to untangle the knots in her hair, noting again how all those expensive layers are growing out, she's looking like the wild woman of the woods and doesn't much care. She doesn't bother with makeup either.

She steps outside. Along the road there's a stile, beside it a signpost that's so entangled in a prickly hedge it's impossible to read, but that almost certainly says Public Footpath. It's a starting point. But the path is so overgrown that within minutes she gives up and leaves it, clambering instead up the rocky side of the bank, her feet slipping on shale, breathing a sigh of relief when she finally reaches level ground. Now, at last, she can look up.

Like the climb, the view is breath taking.

Far below she can see a small white house, the only one, recognises it at once. By now Ben will have found her note. He'll probably go back to bed.

Overhead, a screaming flock of birds wheel around like boys with arms outstretched playing at being fighter pilots. Swallows? Swifts? She's not sure. A mass of low white flowers along the bank has a familiar smell; she presses a leaf between her fingers. Garlic, of course. Didn't she once have a recipe for wild garlic soup?

She can't remember when she last went out without carrying something: her bag, her mobile. The feeling of freedom reminds her of back when she and Andrew used to tramp the moors, Andrew always ahead, eyes down, kicking at tufts of grass and looking for slugs. Later, during the final summers they shared on Exmoor, they'd sit by a stream or on a breezy outcrop sharing a cigarette. Hanging out, being cool.

Now the air has a new smell, and as she nears a sun dappled copse she can see the fuzz of bluebells. She debates picking a bunch, has a feeling it's against the law, goes ahead anyway. She thinks briefly of people heading for work in the city, driving along fume-clogged roads, hot and impatient even before the day begins. And here she is, picking bluebells.

Having said that, she really ought to be getting back. But how?

She climbs a little higher and finds herself on the edge of open moorland with its coarse carpet of bracken, on the horizon grazing ponies silhouetted against the sky. But she needs to go the other way, down into the valley. And now the house is nowhere to be seen.

Best to just work her way downwards.

She's forgotten though that going up is easier than going down. Here the ground is uneven, with slabs of rock interspersed with bramble covered bushes and unexpected holes. Katie is hot; she has a blister on her big toe, which isn't surprising considering she's wearing sandals. The flowers are flagging too, sap oozing from their broken stems along with a new and decidedly unpleasant smell. Or maybe it's not them. When she hears movement in the undergrowth Katie pauses, relieved and delighted when a very small rabbit takes a few hops towards her. Then she steps back. She can see at once the sores on its head, like barnacles clinging to a rock. Its eyes are unseeing slits. Even from where she stands she can see its ribs showing through the tatty fur, its breathing laboured.

She should kill it of course, but she couldn't possibly. Instead she hurries on down. And now she can see them everywhere: scraggy bundles of fur, hunched, motionless, waiting to die, or on their sides and already dead.

"Oh God," she mutters. "This is a nightmare."

At least she now knows what's causing the putrid smell.

There's a loud crack – a jet exercising over the moors, gone from sight before she hears it – and as she looks up, startled, Katie's foot slips and she almost falls, looks down to see she's trodden on a mass of gunge with bits of fur, its head still intact apart from the holes where the eyes once were. Its skin seems to be shivering; it's full of maggots.

Pressing her hand to her mouth she swallows the bile, doesn't want to vomit but knows it's close.

As the bluebells tumble to the ground she spins round and starts running, heading downwards, no longer worried about falling, desperate to get away. It's only when she reaches another clump of trees that she stops, collapses onto a log, struggling to catch her breath. A flock of small birds rises from the ground and she thinks for a moment they're butterflies; there's a clatter of wings as two wood pigeons move to a higher, more secluded branch. She takes a deep breath; the smell of death has gone. Gradually her heart settles.

Minutes pass.

And then, a twig snaps. There's a blur of white, a sound that makes her think of a dog whimpering. Half afraid, half intrigued, Katie stays perfectly still, her eyes straining to see through the tangled branches. Another white shape flings itself at the first, the two of them blending to become a ball that rolls across the ground, over and over, then separates into two again, one chasing the other. As they pass a gap in the bushes Katie can see that it's two puppies playing tag. Except, what are puppies doing up here in the middle of nowhere?

She debates moving closer, but even as she does one of them bursts out of the undergrowth into the clearing and scampers towards her, then stops. It seems unsure what to make of her, stares, but doesn't run away. Katie stares back. And as she takes in its dazzling white fur, its short ears and rounded face, she hears a short low muffled bark and sees another shape, larger than the first two, padding along behind the bushes. Its call has an instant effect. Both of the youngsters scamper to greet the new arrival, jumping up at her face, tails swishing, pushing each other aside in their anxiety to be noticed by their mother. Not a dog, Katie now realises, but a fox. A fox, white as snow.

For a long moment it's as if the world has stopped.

This isn't happening, it can't be. It's against all the rules of nature. Yet even as she begins to wonder about her own state of mind, she remembers the fleeting glimpse of the white animal in the hedge when they were driving back to London. That wasn't so far away from here, only a few miles. It could be the same one. It must be.

Now Katie is aware that the mother is watching her through the brambles, watching, debating. Not panicking, but not sure either. The sharp call of a crow seems to jolt her; she turns and is gone, the two cubs at her heels.

Katie sits there, afraid that if she moves she'll wake and find it was all a dream.

Eventually, somehow, she finds her way back to the house. The door is open and she can hear Ben hammering away at something. There's the dull thud of a brick falling followed by a landslide of small stones. Ben swears. Katie stands in the doorway.

"Ben, you won't believe this."

He's kneeling on the floor by a built-in cupboard they'd thought about taking out. His face and hair are thick with dust. He rubs his eyes before turning to her,

"Hi, I thought you'd left me. So what won't I believe?"

And now she hesitates: what if he really doesn't believe her? Or makes light of it, or spoils it? Would she ever be able to forgive him?

She inhales. Exhales. Inhales again.

# SEVEN

Ben is leaving, going back earlier than planned to start work on a new contract, an office block in north London. It's to be the European base for a Chinese company that makes educational plastic toys. Clever Clogs Toys for Little Clever Clogs. Ben pulled a face. He's seen samples. He thinks they should be banned on the grounds that they're ugly, badly designed, over-priced, and that they teach children nothing that they can't learn in more interesting ways. Of course, he's a traditionalist. If he was a father he'd know these are just the kind of learning aids today's toddlers love. Hence the company's financial success. And the new office block too of course, which he admits excites him. The directors have refreshingly open minds and have taken on an architect Ben has never worked with before, a bit of a maverick known for coming up with some wild ideas, but someone has to do it, push the boundaries. The directors are enthusiastic, Ben even more so.

Or he was, until the worsening financial situation in the US started to make waves closer to home.

"The banks are getting jittery," he says, checking the fridge for a last minute snack, bringing out a chunk of cheese which he immediately nibbles..

"Hm. You weren't saving this for anything, were you?"

Two bites and it's gone.

"Nothing like insecurity to make those wimps in the city slam down the hatches. Bad time to be starting any building project really, but hey, what can we do?"

He's looking around, searching for something.

"We didn't eat all those apples, did we?"

Katie hands him two which he stuffs into pockets.

"Right. I'm off. And you're sure you don't mind me going?"

"How many more times?"

"And you definitely don't want to come back with me? I thought the plan was a few weeks here, a few weeks there."

"Plans can be changed. I'm busy. I'm happy. Stop worrying."

"Katie love…"

She knows what he's going to say, heads him off.

"But when you come back, don't you dare forget my things."

She's written out lists of the items she needs. Some more clothes, some Body Shop soaps and shampoo, six metres of the linen Ben liked which she plans to make into curtains, if she can get Rachael's aunt's Singer sewing machine to work. And a camera. She's found one in a cupboard, an old compact camera that seems to have a few shots left on it, and that will do for now. But she needs something better, one of the new easy to use digitals.

"I won't. Meanwhile, I want you to promise me…"

"Not again."

"You could get lost out there. Or break an ankle."

"I'll take my mobile."

"And who d'you think is going to rush to your rescue?"

"The Search and Rescue team use helicopters. I've always wanted a ride in a helicopter."

Nothing is going to make him smile.

"Katie, the moors are dangerous. People die out there."

"Not in the summer."

He sighs. She wraps her arms around his neck, brushes his lips lightly with hers. Cool lips, unyielding.

"Now go. And drive carefully."

She doesn't need to say it. He always does.

Katie watches as he pulls onto the road. A quick twiddle of his fingers through the open window, and he's gone.

*Ben knew, right from the start. We hadn't been close like we used to be, not for some time, both aware of it, both accepting it as inevitable. It's a fact: all marriages go stale sooner or later. And yet still he knew me well enough, realised that there was nothing he could have said or done to stop me. I had to find you again; it was as simple as that.*

*And I did. Eventually.*

*Not the first day; that was a disaster. Nor the second. The third time I went up to the moors I found the right spot, and I had the feeling you were nearby, but you didn't show yourself. Quite right too. You knew that human beings were the enemy, even a dotty middle aged woman in clumpy walking shoes, flowered shorts and a straw hat. I emptied the little foil package of chicken chunks (I'd scraped off as much of the satay sauce as I could) onto a nearby rock, hoping you'd find them. And like them. But it wasn't about feeding you, not really. It was about winning your confidence.*

*I should have recorded it all at the time, though of course I hadn't yet started the diary. And it doesn't matter anyway because I can remember every little detail. The dew that clung to the grass like tiny glass beads. The nest I found wedged in a fork in a tree, made it seemed of pale grey lichen and lined with feathers. That stream – I had no idea it was there – and the duck that was suddenly gliding along beside me, in her slip stream half a dozen little brown powder puffs, their feet paddling furiously.*

And the woods, your woods, a cool, green cave. I was amazed how quickly the cubs got used to me. And thrilled. Probably a bit smug too, like I'd done something clever. No idea why. Like all young creatures their curiosity overcame any natural fear, and they were soon daring each other to get close enough to sniff my feet. I didn't try to touch them, though I did once wiggle my toes and got a nip which served me right. You were much more cautious. I'd sit on the dusty ground with my legs drawn up, my arms wrapped around them, motionless. Much of the time you'd sit there too, a distance away from me, and together we'd watch your little ones fighting, pouncing on mock prey items, not knowing what to do when they caught real ones. Like that frog. I loved it when they found something new, the way they'd take a stiff-legged jump backwards, ears flattened, noses twitching, but then couldn't resist having another look, sometimes getting bold enough to take a swipe. Or when one chased its own tail, like a cat. More than once I nearly laughed out loud and ruined everything.

Sometimes you and I would exchange a look. You'd sigh. Kids, you seemed to be thinking.

I still found your eyes strangely unnerving. They made me think of pearls.

Of course I longed to tell everyone about you, to show off, as though discovering you was down to my extensive knowledge of the countryside and its wildlife, not to my getting lost. But something made me hold back.

Andrew rang to sound me out about the house. If there would be room for the girls as well as him and Tess if they came down for a weekend, how far we were from the sea, what other fun things there were to do. I said it would be wonderful to have them to stay, all of them, which I meant. Then I realised it would mean missing my visits to you and I was less keen. Never for a moment did I think that you needed to see me. Not needed. But you were coming to expect it, I think? Especially the cubs.

A big mistake, that. Stupid. I should have known better.

Guy turned up one day. Said he was passing, came bearing doughnuts so I had to invite him in and make mugs of coffee to wash them down. I don't believe he was just passing. He's not the neighbourly kind. And he was so restless, couldn't sit, paced about (which probably explains how he manages to stay thin despite his sugar addiction). (Or is he – despite his comments – sweet on MM as well as her doughnuts? I've watched her through the leaded glass window, tugging blonde curls out from under that silly frilly cap she wears to look the part.) He seemed troubled. And again I was tempted to offer you up as a gift, to say here's something to take your mind off things, a fox family that I can guarantee is unlike anything you've ever seen before. I didn't though.

So you remained my little secret. And for a few weeks, I walked on air.

And then there was the day when nothing much happened, nothing special - and yet everything changed.

There had been no warning.

Looking back later Katie could remember how ridiculously pleased she'd been when she spotted the poster. There was to be a Spring Bank Holiday Fayre. Guy said Katie and Ben must go. He said they'd learn more about life on Exmoor from one day at this real traditional rural event than years staying hidden away in that house of theirs.

He thought of them as townies. He didn't hide it. Typical townies, with their designer country wear, their faddish tastes in food and fear of the dark. He was right, but still Katie felt faintly irritated. He was from much further away than them, from the other side of the Atlantic. His childhood holidays were probably spent splashing about in turquoise lakes, tormenting chipmunks, eating popcorn round camp fires and scaring the smaller kids with tales of man-eating bears. Not on Exmoor, like hers. He'd probably never even heard of Exmoor. So now he's lived here for a while and he knows some locals, and where to buy stuff. So what?

"Sounds like he really got to you," Ben had said as they turned into the field between the oil drums, following the big red arrows. "I trust they've got trucks standing by to pull us out of this," he added as he spun the steering wheel to the left and they bumped and squelched across the water-logged field that seemed to be where visitors were meant to park.

"Not really. He's right – everyone should support these events. It's just… I don't know. His manner. I get the feeling he's got issues."

"Who hasn't?"

Ben turned off the engine.

"OK, let's go and fraternise."

Though the rain has only just stopped, the air was warm and buzzing with insects. They threaded their way through an assortment of muddy cars towards a bigger field where clusters of people were milling in anticipation. Most were wearing Wellington boots and already Katie regretted the wedge heels.

Afterwards, she'd remember the day as a series of images.

The greasy smell of hot meat. Skewered like a kebab, a whole pig turned slowly over a bed of coals, its face serene, an apple clenched firmly in its mouth.

A little girl in shocking pink wellies, lost, her face streaked with black tears.

The rifle range. Ben not saying anything, but watching those who came close to the bullseye, noting how they wedged the stock of the gun into their shoulder, the gentle way they squeezed the trigger. The affectionate way they handled the gun, as though it was the family's pet dog.

Birds of prey in an open tent, three of them on perches, motionless, watching, waiting. Katie said she didn't want to see their display later, she felt both sorry for them and a bit repelled. Thought the guy in the denim shirt looked like a ringmaster.

Guy ambling up and introducing himself, exchanging a few words with Ben, winking at Katie before wandering off. They'd never be close friends, those two. They were different species.

Morris dancers. Line dancers. The ugliest dog competition. The cutest baby. Candy floss, the old-fashioned kind on a stick.

Everything stopping as a line of leather-clad motor cyclists wove a path through the crowds. Ben, always fascinated by old bikes, could name most of them: Bonneville, Norton, BSA, a Harley Davidson, a Triumph Tiger Cub. When the riders dismounted there was applause.

And the sculpture Katie bought from a young man lounging behind a table, reluctant to look up from the comic he was reading. Carved from a single piece of wood no bigger than a grapefruit, it was of a calf suckling its mother. Was it his work? she asked. He nodded. She said it was beautiful. Another nod. She paid next to nothing for it.

It had felt like a perfect day out. If they'd left right then it would have been just that, a perfect day.

Katie had been humming the song as she stood waiting for Ben, the crowds thinning now, stalls being dismantled. He'd disappeared into the beer tent to dispose of their plastic cups.

At first she didn't notice the three men grouped nearby drinking lager from cans. Then something about the tone of their voices caught her attention.

"I've had enough, I'll tell you that."

"You're not the only one having problems. You know Fred Markham? Went over to free range chickens a few years ago? He's lost a dozen in the last couple of weeks."

"Trouble is, they're getting desperate, what with having cubs to feed too. It's the one down side to killing off the rabbits."

"There's no down side to killing rabbits. Bloody pains in the arses, they are."

"OK, but think about it. When did you last have trouble with foxes? I've hardly seen one over the past few years. Now they're getting so desperate they'd pick the bacon out of your sandwich!"

"Beats me why they don't eat all those rabbit carcasses. Out on my land it stinks with 'em, yet nothing seems to be touching 'em now, not even the crows."

"Would you wanna eat one?"

"Why not? In a nice hot curry sauce…"

Some sniggering.

"You don't eat curries, do you? Never tried 'em, don't intend to."

"So, Billy boy. It's the night watch for you from now on then?"

"No choice, have I? I'm losing money. My son'll help, he's fourteen now, you know what they're like at that age. Always looking for something to shoot."

Katie edged a few steps closer.

"Dave got one on Sunday. Gave it to the hunt, a treat for the hounds. Poor buggers have forgotten what fox tastes like. Gotta keep 'em keen otherwise come November they'll be sitting there twiddling their thumbs."

"Don't believe it. Once they get a sniff of one…"

"Katie?"

She was unaware that Ben was stood there waiting. She was unaware of anything except the conversation that she'd just overheard.

"Ready?"

"Yes. Let's go."

She couldn't wait to get away, knew that if she didn't she'd say something she'd regret.

Looking back later Katie decides she's over reacting, being pathetic. A real townie. Sitting in the dark in the bedroom she consoles herself with the thought that in any case they weren't talking about her foxes. The ones raiding the farms must be living closer in to the village, over towards the west. Hers live up on the edge of the moors and well away from habitation. They're safe up there. Safer. But what if they too start to run out of food? Already Katie's noticed she's not seeing live rabbits on her morning walks now, only dead ones. What will her fox eat instead? What will she feed to her cubs? Katie could take them more meat, she'd be happy to do so, but it wouldn't help them learn to hunt, to feed themselves.

But then again it would keep them going for now.

She can hear Ben pottering around downstairs. He thinks it's time she went back to the city, for a week at least, to catch up with some friends, the latest films, to try the new brasserie that's opened along the road. He's right and she will. Soon. She'll probably go back with him next time.

SUMMER

# EIGHT

It's hot, a real heat wave. Hotter than in Spain, or Cyprus, where everyone has gone to find the early summer sun. As hot as New York, and almost as humid. Katie is wearing shorts and a halter top, enjoying the cool of the kitchen floor beneath her bare feet. She's slicing courgettes so fresh it's like slicing through butter. She bought them at the local Farmers' Market from a stall run by a woman in a flouncy skirt with long grey hair, along with other organic goodies: pencil thin green beans, mushrooms, spicy rocket and red Batavia lettuce. It was Guy who told her about the market, bless him.

She's excited. Tomorrow is her birthday, and Andrew is coming down with Tess and the children. She's making a summer vegetable flan, has already prepared a selection of snacks to keep in the fridge. Tomorrow night Tess insists she's doing the special dinner, which means she's probably been cooking all week. Tess loves feeding people: it's the way you prove your love. They once had a young female cat who needed to have liposuction before it could be neutered.

"Don't forget we only have one temperamental cooker and a microwave."

Earlier in the week Katie had been on the phone for hours trying to persuade Tess not to make too much fuss. She was looking forward to seeing them, but she'd never much liked birthday parties, and certainly didn't want to be reminded that she was another year closer to her fortieth.

She walked with the phone across to the window that opened out onto the overgrown garden, the air shimmering under a white sky, watched a gang of blue tits in the bird bath she'd found on its side in the shrubs, their wings shivering, making sprays of droplets that sparkled in the sun. The paving below was getting soaked. Must top up the water, she thought.

"We'll eat outside on Saturday, shall we?"

If Ben and Andrew could somehow manoeuvre the kitchen table out onto the little patio at the side, she would dress it up with a lace tablecloth (she must get Ben to find it and bring it down), and flowers of course. And he could bring those glass globes that they'd had for ages and never used, that you put lighted candles in and hang from trees.

"As long as we don't get bitten by bugs. You wouldn't believe how many insect bites I'm allergic to."

Bet I would, Katie thought. Typical Tess. She still can't understand how Andrew picked her to be his wife.

"I'll dig out the repellent." she said.

*For the first time in weeks I didn't think about you. Now, for a few days at least, I had my other family around, and though seeing them back in London was no big deal (sometimes a bit of a chore if I'm honest) having them come down to visit me in Devon was completely different. I planned things, like showing them around the village, driving up onto the moors to see the wild ponies, maybe even heading off to the coast which everyone says is stunning around here. Hard to believe that I'd been down here months and still not managed to get to the sea.*

*Again I debated telling Andrew about you, but again I had doubts. I could imagine his face, that strange sideways grin he used to give when he was about to deflate my excitement with some cutting remark. I'd seen him do it to the girls, too. Fortunately they take his need to tease no more seriously than a wasp buzzing around the ice cream I'm convinced they're addicted to, turning their backs and flapping a hand whilst continuing to lick. "Oh dad, grow up, will you?" I once heard Tilly say, and then she and Rose doubled up, heads touching, giggling uncontrollably whilst he pretended to be upset.*

*After my initial panic – after the fair – I'd decided you really weren't under any immediate threat, not if you stayed close to your own territory, which the second-hand book I found in a village shop assured me you'd do. It was an old book, written back in the sixties, but I figured fox behaviour probably didn't change much from year to year. It was the assurance I needed, and left me free to at least delay worrying about you, and get on with enjoying my visitors.*

They all arrive together late Friday evening, in two cars, Ben having volunteered to show Andrew the way, knowing how easily he gets lost. Katie stands smiling, holding the front door wide as they file past her, Ben first carrying an assortment of boxes, giving her a passing peck, Andrew next, his arms locked around a plastic crate in which cartons and cool bags are neatly packed, bottles wedged between them. And was that champagne she spotted? Andrew kisses her other cheek.

"You've put on weight," he says. As she goes to deny it he grins. "It suits you."

The two girls follow, rubbing bleary eyes, yawning. Katie crouches down, curves an arm around each of them. Tilly, the older of the two, stands stiff whereas Rose immediately wraps her arms tight around Katie's neck, her hands sticky with perspiration.

"Hey, you're strangling me," Katie laughs, turning them both and pushing them gently into the house. For a moment they're awed by the new, strange surroundings. Soon though they'll be racing around, completely out of control.

Tess is still hauling things out of the car boot.

"Here, I'll take those. Whatever they are."

"Blow up mattresses for the girls. I hope there's going to be floor space for them."

"I'm sure we'll find somewhere," Katie says. "There's always the bath."

Tess probably thinks she's joking.

Back when Katie and Andrew had holidayed on Exmoor, when it was really hot, they were occasionally allowed to sleep outside. Someone would put up a tent in the garden for them – a father or uncle, anyone who fancied the challenge. Someone else would find the sleeping bags that were always brought down but rarely used, and that smelt of damp and mud and – when unravelled – revealed squashed wine gums, biscuit crumbs, the desiccated bodies of woodlice. Andrew was always enthusiastic. Katie would enjoy the adventure at first, when there were lights on in the house still, the sound of adults chatting coming through open patio doors, and she and Andrew would sit there cross legged in their pyjamas drinking cans of Coke. But once darkness fell and Andrew was asleep she'd begin to have doubts. Why was it meant to be such a treat, sleeping outside? She'd toy with the idea of sneaking indoors – if anyone saw her she'd say she'd forgotten to clean her teeth – and finding a nice big sofa, a big safe sofa. Eventually though she'd decide it would be more scary trying to find her way around a pitch black garden that she didn't know very well, than staying put. She'd move a bit closer to Andrew.

Now though – just before she went to bed – she'd sometimes go out onto the patio, stand breathing in the heady concoction of night smells, actually feel comforted by that soft, thick blanket of blackness.

Of course, there's no way Tess would allow the girls to sleep outside. It may have to be the bathroom.

Indoors, the house feels transformed. There are lights on in every room, footsteps thumping overhead as the girls check out the upstairs rooms, the kitchen table groaning under enough food to feed an army for a week. From the bathroom next door to the kitchen comes the shush of running water as Tess braves the shower suspended over the bath that creaks alarmingly when anyone stands in it.

Andrew has already found the TV and is sprawled on the sofa, feet on the coffee table, beer in hand, roaring at a sitcom that Katie hates. She switches it off, picks up his feet and drops them back on the ground.

"When I said make yourself at home, I didn't mean it that literally," she says.

Andrew pats the seat beside him.

"So come and tell me what you've been doing."

There's a crash from upstairs, a scream, nervous tittering. Andrew tilts his head backwards to gaze at the ceiling.

"Later. We've got a whole weekend to catch up," Katie says. The tittering has turned into a wail.

"Besides, sounds like you're needed."

As he passes her en route for the stairs Andrew lightly caresses her shoulder.

In the kitchen Ben is opening wine. It's chilled and she can see he's having trouble gripping the slippery bottle, but he does it. He watches as she unwraps cheeses, arranges them in a circle on a wooden board, searches amongst a tumble of boxes for crackers.

"OK, love?"

Katie nods.

"I wonder if this house ever had a big family living in it," she says.

"Must have at some time. Not recently, though. It had that feeling, didn't it? Not just damp and dirty, but unloved."

"And now?"

"Better. A hundred times better. You've worked wonders already."

He's saying what she wants to hear of course.

"I'm enjoying it."

"Are you? Are you really?"

"More than I ever thought I would."

Someone's tugging at her skirt.

"Rose sweetheart, what is it?"

"Daddy said that a ghost lives in the grandfather clock, and that if you open the door it will escape and do bad things like knock down books and pinch your bottom and turn lights on in the middle of the night. And he said the only way to get it to go back is to put a dish of... angie things?" She waits for help.

"They're fish." Her nose wrinkles. "I hate them."

Katie is inspired.

"Anchovies? Like you have on pizzas?"

"Yes and you mix them with strawberry jam and put them in the clock, and the ghost goes back and you slam the door, and lock it."

"Did he now?"

Andrew and his stories.

"Well, why don't we have a look inside and…"

"It's locked. Daddy said that's to keep the ghost in."

Her round face is open and trusting, her expression half fearful, half wanting it to be true. Trying not to smile, Katie glances at Ben for support. And for a moment she's shocked by his expression, the intensity of his longing as he listens to the ramblings of a little girl. In a flash it all comes back to her: the discussions, the rows, the cajoling, the slammed doors. He'd so love to be a father. Poor Ben, he married the wrong woman.

"Enough about ghosts," she says. "I think it's time you and your sister went to bed, don't you?"

Usually Katie treats her birthday much like any other day. Today – as the girls inform her when they tiptoe upstairs with a bowl of cereal on a tray, a pile of envelopes resting in a puddle of spilt tea – they're here to share it with her. They like birthdays. Anybody's, it doesn't matter whose.

"So we'll all celebrate together, shall we?"

Two heads nod.

First rule, it seems, is that you're not allowed to do anything towards the celebrations. So seeing as she's banned from the kitchen, she decides to take the girls up onto the moors before it gets too hot, in search of wild ponies. Even so the breeze coming in through the rolled down car windows is like a blast from a hair dryer.

At least there's air up on the moors. The flat open space around them is shimmering, so that when she does eventually spot a small group of ponies grazing back off the road, they look like part of a mirage, strange shapes with elongated legs moving under water. Closer to they become stocky animals with soft brown coats, their muzzles the colour of oatmeal, long black manes matching even longer black tails.

"Why do they keep flicking their tails?"

"To keep them cool. Aren't they lucky having their fans attached, so they can never lose them?"

"And to keep the flies away." That's Tilly who knows it all.

"Look!"

From behind a clump of prickly shrubs there's movement, a young foal getting to its feet, all legs, hesitating then wobbling its way across to the others, one of which instantly nuzzles it. Neither of the girls speak, but Rose reaches for Katie's hand and Katie knows what she means.

They head back to the house via the village, calling into the mini market for a few forgotten items, the girls trailing along behind Katie, scuffing their sandals, staring intently as the other customers. An elderly man in shorts and sunhat clutching a large box of Bran Flakes comes in for special scrutiny. Silently Katie beckons the girls to keep up with her.

"Katie, look, ice creams." There's a surprise, she thinks.

"Can we have one, Katie? Please?"

"Isn't it a bit early in the day?"

"Mummy would let us." Tilly was doing the talking, Rose staying silent but looking hopeful. Only six and five years old, and they'd already got their act in place, knew exactly how to use the stick and carrot approach to getting what they wanted.

"If it was a special day, like a birthday or something," she adds.

Katie has lost, and she knows it.

"You two should be politicians."

Three choc ices are added to the basket.

Patrice is behind the till again. For the first time she manages to lift her eyes and smiles at Rose (who smiles back) and then at Tilly (who doesn't).

"Got your family staying for a while then?"

"Yes," Katie says. What's it to do with her? She never usually manages more than three words. "For a while."

Ben has found a hose and is playing with the girls. There's a hosepipe ban in London, Katie isn't sure about here in the west country, but who's going to know? There's a lot of shrieking and laughter and all three of them are soaked. It's good for Ben too, this weekend, she thinks. He needs to be silly sometimes. She wonders what Andrew is up to, can see him way across the other side of the garden. Surely he's not still into collecting insects? He won't find any slugs, that's for sure, not in this weather.

Katie is examining the digital camera Ben bought for her birthday, squinting in the dazzling sun as she tries to read the print on the instruction leaflet. She has one at home, but it's already out of date. There's less chance of picture blur with this one, it has far more pixels, millions more, a zoom, a bigger screen. You can print directly from it. That could be especially useful, well, when she has access to a printer again.

She wonders how they're doing, her foxes, how they're coping with this extreme weather, if they're finding enough to eat.

But no, she promised herself. She's not going to think about them today.

Finally, everything is ready for the dinner party.

The men have smartened up, at least they've both put on clean shirts. Katie and Tess have both changed into dresses. Kate's is a simple black sheath with narrow shoulder straps worn with big beaded earrings handmade in Morocco. She's tied her hair up on top of her head. It's still way too hot for shoes so she's barefooted. Tess has gone for a turquoise wrap-around dress that makes her look soft and cuddly. Andrew must think so too as more than once Katie sees him touch her, rubbing her back lightly, putting an arm around her shoulders. It's only then that it strikes her that she's rarely seen them touching. They'd probably say the same about her and Ben.

The kitchen table too is unrecognisable. It brings to mind a film Katie once saw, a period drama set during a long hot summer in a Swedish country house. The orange flames of the candles balance motionless in the still air.

"It's beautiful, Tess. Thank you. Don't think I don't realise how much trouble you've gone to."

"Katie, I'm loving it. Truly. So – shall we eat?"

It's a banquet. To start, a smoked trout salad with endive and rocket. Next, roast duck in a tangy citrus sauce, baby potatoes freckled with fresh herbs, asparagus, slivers of carrot with sesame seeds. As well as the champagne Katie had already spotted there's a sumptuous red wine. The girls have been allowed to stay up and join them at the table, but though they pick at their food they're too excited to concentrate.

The air cools a degree or two. Around them, the tree lights flicker attracting big white moths that flutter lazily against the glass. Under the table, Ben puts a hand on Katie's knee making her jump. She looks up, catches his eye, and rests her hand on top of his.

Now the sky is almost dark, as dark as it's going to get this close to midsummer. A bird starts to sing, a clear, melodious song interspersed with low trills and warbles. Ben says it must be a nightingale, though he's never heard one before. Andrew says aren't they extinct in the UK? Rose asks what extinct means.

"Coffee, anyone?" Tess is collecting dishes. Andrew says he'll go and put a kettle on. He winks at the girls who nudge each other as he heads off around the side of the house.

*If only I'd known what was about to happen. If only I'd had some little hint. Of course that was the whole point – it was meant to be a birthday surprise, and it was. They'd all done a brilliant job at keeping it secret, even the girls.*

*And anyway, even if I'd known what could I have done about it?*

The first phutt catches Katie unawares, catches everyone out so that they all gaze upwards open mouthed as the rocket zigzags almost silently up into the dark blue sky, higher still, then explodes into a shower of emerald splinters that drift downwards, and are passed by two more rockets heading skywards which in their turn cascade down scattering splinters this time of red and silver.

Fireworks.

And now the girls are jumping up and down, clapping their hands as from around the garden comes one whoosh after another, then what could be a burst of machine gun fire, the sky getting brighter all the time, the noise echoing across the valley.

For the first few minutes Katie smiles with amazement and delight. Then, a thought: the foxes.

"No!" The one word. She's not even sure if she shouted it aloud.

As the whooshes, screeches and bangs grow even louder Katie spins around, confused, presses her hands against her ears, unaware that she's dropped an earring. When Andrew ambles towards them across the patio, the flickering lights showing his smile of satisfaction, Katie runs towards him.

"Stop them, please, you must stop them."

His smile falters, fades.

"Katie, what's wrong? Don't you like them? I thought…"

"Andrew, please."

He holds out his hands.

"How? I can't. It's a linked display. Once you light it, it's off and running."

"But there must be something…"

She takes a deep breath, gives an apologetic shrug.

"No, of course not. Sorry. Ignore me,"

Gradually the display calms, subsides, then − after one final flamboyant burst − it stops. The silence is stunning. A layer of acrid smoke hangs over the garden.

Katie knows her reaction has shocked them all. She doesn't know what to say. Andrew has turned away, is running his fingers through his hair. She glances round and everyone is looking at her.

"I'm sorry," she whispers. As she hurries back into the house she's aware that Ben is following her. In the bedroom she throws herself onto the bed face downwards. She knows she's behaving like a crazy woman.

"Katie, what is it? What's wrong?"

She must pull herself together.

"Love?"

He's waiting. She sits up again.

"The noise. It was horrendous. The foxes will have been freaked, they're so nervous, they'll think they're being attacked or something. The book said any disturbance can drive them away."

"Ah. Right. The foxes."

"I can't help it, Ben. I don't want to be like this, but I can't seem to stop myself."

"I know."

He sits down beside her but doesn't touch her. From outside comes the quiet murmur of voices, Andrew and Tess not understanding, and how could they?

"But you mustn't…"

Katie waits for his words of comfort or advice.

"They'll be fine. They're miles away, probably wouldn't have heard a thing."

"They've got brilliant hearing, and sound carries. Besides, you'd have to be hundreds of miles away not to hear that lot!"

Ben stands.

"Did you know? About the fireworks?"

"No. Not before Andrew started setting them up. But I admit I didn't think about the foxes. I mean, why would I?"

He's right. Why would anyone?

"Katie, love, can we talk about it later? I think we ought to go back outside."

"You go. I'll be right down."

"Don't be long."

"I won't."

Everyone has obviously decided to ignore her outburst. Coffee has been made, an apricot tarte tatin brought to the table with a single candle on it, which Katie blows out slowly. Everyone applauds enthusiastically. Too enthusiastically. And then in no time the girls become drowsy, chairs are pushed back, the job of clearing the table begins, though the dishes are to be left in the kitchen until tomorrow. Ben takes down the tree lights, extinguishes them one by one.

"Leave that one, Ben. I'll take it. I'd like to stay out here a while longer."

Reluctantly he hands it over.

"On your own? You'll be alright?"

"Of course."

She kisses him lightly on the lips.

"Thank you for today."

She steps down from the warm stone onto the scrubby grass.

When the candle dies, she doesn't notice; there's a sliver of moon and it's casting just enough light for her to make out the grey, shadowy world that surrounds her. She sees him approaching even before he drops something light and jangly into her lap. Her earring.

"Wouldn't want you to be lopsided, would we?"

She knew he'd come. Andrew settles on the bench beside her.

"Just listen to that silence," he says.

"It's deafening, isn't it?" She smiles in the dark.

"It's pretty quiet in the daytime too," he adds. "Don't think I've heard a single plane going overhead."

"I suppose we're not on the route to anywhere." She hadn't thought about it. "Have to say I do love it here. More than I expected."

"But there must be some things you miss?"

Katie has to think hard.

"Fresh ground spices, the Tate Modern, my hairdresser. Think that's it. And you, of course."

He runs the back of his fingers down her cheek.

"Yes. Me to, I miss you."

Katie senses someone has come out onto the patio, turns to see Tess silhouetted against the light from the door.

"I'm going to bed, Andrew," she calls in a loud whisper. "Don't you two stay up talking all night. We've got a busy day planned for tomorrow."

"We won't," Katie and Andrew say in unison, smiling at each other in the dark. They wait until they hear her go inside.

"Seeing as we're already in trouble…"

Andrew reaches into his back pocket, gets out a packet.

"I thought you gave it up?"

"I did. I have."

He lights two cigarettes, passes one to her, and though she hasn't smoked for years, Katie takes it. It's about memory lane as much as anything. The sharing. The feel of it between her lips, the way it glows.

It's cooler now, a bat zipping silently above their heads.

"So, astonish me," Katie says. It was the way they always used to start a heart to heart.

"Let's see. The new tumble dryer isn't working. We've had the engineer in three times. It'll probably have to be replaced eventually."

"Fascinating."

"And Tilly's in trouble again, for spitting on another kid's birthday cake this time. She said she thought it was on fire."

"Quick thinking, I'd say."

"Trouble was, all the others then joined in."

He draws on his cigarette.

"And I'm having an affair."

At last. She knew there was something.

"With one of your students, I suppose?"

"Of course. She's twenty-two, blonde, deliciously squidgy. She thinks I'm Tom Cruise."

"Christ, Andrew."

"What? Everyone's doing it."

"Exactly. It's so banal, such a cliché."

"Possibly. But I tell you what, it's great for the ego."

Katie wants to ask him more, all the details, but doesn't. She feels a twinge of something and wonders if it's jealousy.

"So. Are you going to tell me what all that drama earlier was about?"

His change of subject catches her out.

"Nothing. Nothing you'd understand anyway."

"Why not try me?"

He stubs out his half-smoked cigarette.

"I remember how you used to love fireworks," he says. "From midsummer you'd be counting down the days to November fifth. You had pictures you'd cut out of a catalogue on your wall."

Katie smiles to herself.

"I even like sparklers," she says. "In fact we used them in an ad campaign I worked on once, can't remember what it was for. Fizzy mineral water, I think. The photographer complained, said they were a nightmare to shoot."

Katie knows she has to explain.

"I did appreciate the display. It must have been a lot of work too, setting them up. It was all just so… noisy."

"Yup. That's what it says on the box. Noisy."

"And you probably haven't noticed, but sound really carries in all this space."

"So?"

What else can she do?

Katie tells him about the foxes. Everything. She thinks he'll laugh or tease her, but he doesn't say a word, just lets her talk.

"I didn't know you were into animals," he says when eventually she stops.

"I'm not. Or I wasn't before I came here. I suppose living closer to nature can change you."

Andrew stands, links his hands and stretches, sits again.

"So you think the fireworks might have frightened them off?"

"Andrew, it was like being in a war zone. I'm sure fireworks didn't use to be so loud."

"OK, I've got the message."

"Sorry again. I'm an ungrateful bitch. They'll be fine."

A comfortable silence.

"They're so amazing though," Katie says quietly. "Unreal, like something from one of those legends, you know, where ancient forests hide all sorts of strange creatures with too many legs or heads, and babies stolen at birth."

"Is she really that rare? You hear about albino deer and lions, and that trophy hunters pay mega bucks to shoot them."

"Comforting thought. Thanks for that."

She used to think he said things like that on purpose, anything to upset her. Maybe he just didn't think.

"No, but seriously, Katie. Surely you must have checked?"

"How? I don't have my PC with me. It won't work. And besides, I came here to escape all that, find myself, as Ben put it. Not that I knew I was lost. Remember?"

"And three in one family. That must be a statistical first."

She's surprised at the interest he's suddenly showing. He's seeing them from a whole different angle.

"And they know you, they're not scared. Why don't you keep a diary, too? Note the things they do, their habits, food, your thoughts too. It's why women make good naturalists. They're observant, they spot details."

"Really? And since when did you become an expert?"

"Saw a documentary on the box. It was about Jane Goodall and her work with chimps. Brilliant woman."

He surprises her.

"OK, well. I'm already planning to take some pictures. Ben's camera will be ideal."

Katie feels a fizz of excitement.

"I found an old box camera thingy in the house. There were three shots left so I used them, got them developed in the village. All you could see were white blobs. The rest of the pictures were of a Christmas party. A lot of old people in silly hats looking miserable."

A light goes on in the house behind them. Someone still up. Probably Tess. Or could be Ben. After a minute it goes off again.

"Tell you what, the press are always looking for animal pictures, especially ones of freaks."

Freaks. Is that what they are?

"Trust you to spot the monetary opportunities."

Katie yawns. She can't see her watch but it must be two, two thirty. The garden seems especially quiet tonight. The fireworks probably scared everything away.

"I'm off to bed," she says.

"Me too."

Andrew takes her hand and together they edge their way across the dark lawn.

"Katie, this fox thing. I can see why you're hooked. But it's a tough world down here, especially for the wildlife. Don't get too involved, don't let it take you over."

"I won't," she says, knowing his warning is far too late.


Sunday is spent as a summer Sunday should be.

A morning drive to the beach where jeans are rolled up and everyone paddles in rock pools searching for seahorses and other minibeasties with strange names (the girls insist Andrew is making them up!), and finding only limpets and strings of smelly seaweed. Beyond, a flat grey sea sparkles, a single speedboat cutting across the horizon. A pre-lunch drink outside a pub that's heaving with holidaymakers with Hawaiian shorts, blistered red shoulders and panting, over-heated dogs.

Seagulls lurk menacingly waiting to snatch a snack when someone's back is turned.

"First gulls I've seen down here," Ben says. "Think we've got more in London".

"Nasty dirty things. Vicious too."

That's Tess. She catches Tilly's hand, tries to pull her close but the excited girl squiggles free.

On the drive back to the house they detour along a road that winds between craggy rocks, moors on one side, sea on the other, and everywhere kids racing around, many using the dusty lower slopes like ski runs. At the very summit of one of the crags a party of walkers edge along, one behind another, small dark figures against a white sky.

"Hey look, mummy."

Of course Tilly notices them. Of course she wants to be up there with them.

"Can we? Please? I'll be careful, promise."

"No way."

"Why not?" Tilly slumps back in her seat angrily.

"Because I say so."

"It's not fair!"

Katie takes pity.

"Tell you what, girls. Next time you come to visit bring your walking shoes and we'll go up there together. OK?"

Ben is driving. He glances across at Katie.

"So you're planning on staying down here a while longer then, are you?"

"I might do." She feels tricked.

"Thought you missed the city."

"Ben, just watch the road, will you? Our turning is coming up any minute."

Lunch is a salad plus leftovers out on the patio. Then there's washing up to be done, furniture to be scraped and lifted back to where it belongs. A disagreement between the men about Boris Johnson and what kind of mayor he'll make. They agree though that Barack Obama would be the best thing that's happened to the USA. If he gets in, says Ben. When he gets in. Andrew is convinced. Screams interrupt them as Rose tumbles down the steps and cuts her knee. There's ice cream to stem the tears. Ice cream for everyone.

And it's time to go. Sandals are dug out from under the bed, dishes stashed back in crates, sleeping bags rolled. And with final hugs and kisses and promises to do it again soon, very soon, their visitors have gone.

Ben will leave a little later. He's getting the gun down. Andrew's ghost story gave him an idea: why don't they keep the gun in the grandfather clock? Right sized space, and no one would think of looking there, whereas the attic is the first place anyone would look.

Katie nods, thinking how much safer it would be to get rid of it altogether, but she knows he won't, not yet.

She's noticed a couple of innocent looking clouds high in the sky, the first for weeks. Looks like the storm they forecast this morning is on its way. She can't wait; much as she loves the heat she's tired of having no energy. It won't be much fun to drive through though. She wishes Ben would get going. He's only hanging about because he's hoping she'll change her mind and go with him. She ought to, that's for sure. There are so many things she needs to do back in London: go to the bank, dentist, hairdresser. And some she'd really like to do, like catching up with friends. Though they'd rung at first, kept her up to date with the gossip, made plans to meet, she has the feeling they've begun to think of her as a lost cause.

"Come with me."

Ben can't delay it any longer.

"Next time."

"You said that last time. I don't like you being here on your own, Katie. It's not good for you."

"Why? I'm fine."

Katie turns to look out of the window.

"Better get on your way, there's a storm coming."

When he drives out onto the road he doesn't look back, doesn't wave. From far off comes a faint growling that could be thunder. Katie goes inside, shuts the door, and for a moment the house feels like a hollowed out shell, empty, lifeless. But as she walks from room to room plumping up cushions, rescuing a rag doll that's peering out from under a cupboard (Rose's favourite – she must put it somewhere safe), topping up water in the jugs of flowers, the feeling changes to one of comfortable familiarity. Of solitude, yes, but what's wrong with that? Nothing, she decides. In fact she likes it, she likes it very much.

# NINE

They're still there.

Katie had put off going up to the moors, reluctant to make such a long climb in the rain, knowing it would make it not just difficult but dangerous. Walking across the muddy lawn was like trying to walk on ice. There was the other reason too: until she went up there she could convince herself that her reaction to the fireworks had been way over the top, stupid, and that of course they wouldn't have been scared away.

And she's right. She doesn't see them, but she knows they're close by. Some time back she'd figured that their earth was deep inside a thick tangle of gnarled tree roots set a short way from where she usually watched them. First she'd noticed the holes, old rabbit holes probably. Then she'd spotted the more grisly clues left on the scrubby ground out front: a bird's wing, a mangled squirrel, chunks of something dark that reminded her of rats. This time there's a pigeon that has fresh blood trickling from a wound on its neck. A recent kill, then.

Katie waits nearly an hour but there's no sign of the vixen, or her cubs. Disappointed, she gives up, heads for home.

Could they be scared of her?

She'd loved it when the cubs came close to her, so confident that they'd play around her feet. She hates to think of that bond being broken. But it'll be better for them, they must learn that humans are the enemy. If she really cared about them she'd stop coming up altogether. She makes a decision: that's what she'll do. She'd like to see them once more, to check they're alright and take some photos to remind her how exquisite they were (as if she'd ever forget). Then she'll stop.

Besides, she wants to concentrate now on getting the house finished.

Ben probably won't be able to come back down for a while. The Clever Clogs project is getting under way. He has meetings scheduled with the architect, the structural engineer, the company's representative; quotations to go through from a surprisingly large number of contractors who've put in bids. When he rings she can tell that he's on a high. This is the best time, he always says. Right at the beginning when everyone is positive, optimistic, amenable, when none of the inevitable problems have yet surfaced.

His absence means she doesn't have to bother about the state of the house. She can leave opened paint tins in the bathroom, do test patches all over the walls, pin curtain hems on the floor. No point in sweeping or dusting, of course. She needn't bother to cook either; toast is becoming a mainstay these days, with either Marmite or marmalade.

The weather has deteriorated again, the continuous rain making it feel chilly even indoors. Katie has gone back to wearing a sweater, though she still has on the shorts she got used to during the hot spell. She's trying to decide on a colour for the living room walls, something neutral but warm – it's a choice between Calico Kiss and Hessian Heaven – when the front door bell rings, a strong confident ring. There's only one person it can be.

"Guy, I thought so." She tries to keep the irritation out of her voice. Not that she's not pleased to see him, but right now she wants to get on.

"Thought you might need some cheering up. Then again, you Brits are used to this miserable weather, I guess."

Even though he's standing close to the wall he's getting soaked, his shirt sticking to his shoulders. He leans towards her and she realises he expects to be invited in.

"I'm sorry, Guy, but I can't stop. I'm in the middle of… painting." Well, it's almost true.

"Your other half not here then?"

"No, he's in London."

"OK, here's an idea. Why don't you come and eat with me tomorrow evening? I could rustle up a little something, I've got wine and a sofa."

He's casual about it but she has the feeling this isn't a sudden idea at all.

"I'd love to."

"Really? OK, it's a date."

The instructions he gives on how to find his barn sound simple enough. He reminds her of his mobile number in case of problems.

"See you tomorrow then?"

As he gets back into his truck it occurs to her yet again that he's lonely. He may know a lot of people, but that isn't always enough. He's an odd character, a bit of a fish out of water in Devon, she'd think. He can't have much in common with the locals even if he likes a drink with them.

Then again, he's probably invited her over because he thinks she's lonely.

A few hours later the rain eases As the clouds unravel and loosen there are patches of blue overhead, even some glimpses of the sun. Katie's only ever been with the foxes in the mornings, but evenings are said to be a good time to fox watch. And it's such a beautiful evening, too good to spend indoors.

She puts on her boots and a raincoat, tucking the camera carefully into an inside pocket. She catches a glimpse of herself in the hallway mirror.

"You look ridiculous," she says out loud. At least her bare legs are naturally tanned this summer.

The climb is even more difficult than usual. Much of the time she has to hang onto shrubs and haul herself up over rocks made especially slippery by wet lichen. Great swathes of purple heather perfume the air, bees hover, and Katie stands there in breathless admiration.

By the time she reaches the woodland glade it's raining again. There's no sign of the foxes. Even the area in front of their earth looks unusually tidy, with only some soggy black feathers – a crow probably, or a blackbird - lying in the mud. This time they've gone. It's possible they've just abandoned their earth and are still somewhere nearby. But they could be miles away. It's about now that the cubs begin to wander, learning to hunt, gradually becoming independent of their mother. They could be anywhere.

The word that comes instantly to mind is bereft.

She feels bereft. Or is that only when someone dies? It feels like they've died though of course they haven't.

Pulling up her hood, she turns back, deliberately turning her thoughts to other things. She trying to remember what she has in the freezer – hopefully something she can take along to Guy's tomorrow, she can't go empty-handed – when she sees them. Instinct makes her drop to the ground. They haven't noticed her. Partially hidden by grasses they are far too intent on sniffing the ground, dabbing at things and then getting bored and moving on. One of them lifts its head and she thinks she's been discovered, but then it races across and hurling itself high into the air lands on top of the other cub, the two of them starting what could be a dance, a circling movement, making noises that remind her of the yowls of cats. And then they're off again. Even in the short time since she last saw them, Katie can see changes. They're growing up.

Slowly she edges forwards, keeping low. She reaches for the camera. Though it's very quiet to use, she's concerned that the cubs will hear it. The whirr of the zoom is the main problem, but she needs it as she daren't go any closer. The automatic flash might disturb them too. She has to take the risk. Holding the camera close, about to click it on, she hears a slight movement to her right, and there is the vixen looking straight at her, the raindrops on her white fur making it sparkle, like snow. Not a snowman, but a snow fox Katie thinks. And then, don't run away, please please don't. Never again will she get a chance like this.

When the vixen turns and pads gracefully down through the undergrowth towards the cubs she thinks that's it, any second now they'll all be off, swallowed up by the greenery, gone. But as the cubs run whimpering towards the new arrival, babies again, still needing to know that mum is there for them, just for a little longer, Katie breathes a sigh of relief. For this moment in time – be it only minutes, only seconds even – she's been accepted, she's part of the family. She lifts the camera to her eye and starts shooting.

Guy's instructions are spot on. Katie – who'd allowed herself time to get lost – arrives early. She still can't get used to the difference it makes not having to contend with cars, white vans, bikes, buses. And traffic lights; she can't remember when she last saw a set of traffic lights. The front door opens before she's turned off the engine.

"Welcome. You found it OK? Come on in."

She only has time for a glance at the outside but it's enough.

She loves it with its grey stone and slate walls, ivy draped over the roof like a blanket, two wooden barrels alongside the red front door filled with orange and purple flowers. She wouldn't have had him down as a flower tub type.

"It's wonderful," she says. "A dream to work on, I'd imagine."

There's music playing, a violin, Brahms she thinks though she could be wrong.

"If you're into DIY, I guess."

Inside, it's white walled and basic. Still, he seems to have everything he could need: a long table, two benches, a sofa and an armchair set facing each other, some rugs. In the kitchen area is a cooker very much like the one she has, that Ben keeps promising will be replaced soon, just as soon as he gets time to order a new one. Through the windows set high in the walls she can see the tops of trees shuffling about in the breeze.

"I can't imagine anyone being unhappy here," she says.

He glances around as though seeing it with her eyes.

"I'm certainly not. The last occupants didn't complain either, far as I know. They used it as a holiday home."

He pours her a drink without asking, leads the way across to a picture on the wall. She can feel the cold of the stone flagged floor through her sandals. It's a photo of a herd of cows. Or bulls possibly, she's not sure.

"Pure bred Devon Reds. Splendid animals, gentle, strong, look at the width of those chests. They're bred for beef but the cows are like milk machines, they never run out the stuff."

Katie sips her wine. She tries to imagine the barn full of cattle.

"I sleep upstairs," Guy says now, pointing to an open staircase leading to a balcony area. "And the bathroom – should you want it – is through that door at the end there. Right, tour over. Let's eat."

He won't let her help with the cooking, which he says is virtually done anyway. He tells her to make herself at home.

She hesitates, then crosses to a drum kit that looks familiar. "Is this the one you got for your friend?"

"Yup. Kevin. Did I say he lives on a farm? Seems his family don't appreciate the gift as much as he did."

Pans clatter, steam rises from pasta as it drains.

"He's here a lot. Comes over to do odd jobs, helps me with this and that."

Guy stirs the sauce. Using oven gloves he takes two plates out from where they've been warming in the oven. Katie tries to imagine how Ben would cope with making a meal for a guest.

"And if he wants to practise into the early hours, there's no one round here going to complain. Besides, he's not at all bad at it."

He reaches for a pot of basil, carefully chooses some leaves. "If you really want to help you could clear the table."

Katie collects together the newspapers that are everywhere, piles them neatly, glancing at headlines and realising with a shock how little she knows about what's going on in the rest of the world. She's becoming a recluse. Guy obviously still cares. From the way the papers have been folded, the edges worn, she can see they've been read from front to back. Even the crosswords have been filled in.

"The cheese!"

She's left it in the car, hurries out into the dusky evening to retrieve it from the passenger seat. As she turns back she senses movement on the other side of the hedge, someone on the road, and yet no-one passes the gate, nor emerges beyond the wall in the other direction. She was probably imagining it.

Guy has placed a candle in the centre of the table, and changed the music to guitars playing flamenco. They eat their pasta sitting opposite each other on the benches, Guy insisting she has a cushion. After a bit she can see why.

"This bolognaise is delicious," she says, feeling she has to say something complimentary, trying to decide what's in it. Lamb? Beef?

"Road kill," he says, glancing up at her over his twirling fork. "My speciality. But you already know that."

Katie's stomach churns. The food in her mouth thickens and refuses to go down her throat. She reaches for her wine.

Guy gives a small dry laugh.

"Hey, Katie sweetheart, I'm kidding you."

"It's not, is it?"

"I bought it at the butchers, I swear. Having said that, I can't understand why people are so reluctant to eat road kill. The animal's had a better life than those poor sods reared in factory farms, it contains no chemicals or growth hormones or God knows what else."

He tops up both glasses.

"There's a restaurant in the US specialises in road kill. You have to book weeks in advance to get a table."

Guy pushes a dish of wafer thin tomato slices towards her.

"Here, help yourself."

Katie is still concentrating on swallowing. Lately she'd found it difficult to eat meat of any kind, unless it was highly disguised. Too many trucks full of animals on the roads. Too many anxious faces and pitiful eyes peering out.

"Ever had tomatoes cooked with cream and sugar?" he says. "My mother used to make them for breakfast on special days. Boy, were they good."

"I bet." Katie wishes he'd stop talking about food. "So how come you're living over here anyway?"

Her question sounds abrupt, but he doesn't seem to notice.

"It's a long story. Long and boring."

She's not letting him off that easily.

"So tell me the shortened version. Leave out the adjectives."

Guy smiles. His smile never looks comfortable, she thinks, as though he needs more practice.

"I married an English woman. Girl. She was eighteen, I was twenty-nine. A cradle-snatcher, isn't that what you Brits say?"

"Not really a big enough age difference. How did you meet?"

"Through Romeo and Juliet. The ballet, that is. I was dancing Tybalt, nephew to Lady Capulet. It's a fantastic role. Lots of sword fighting, a violent drawn-out death."

He jabs at the air with his fork.

"She was in the corps."

"You're a dancer?" That explains the loose limbed way he walks, his graceful hands, long supple fingers.

"Was. For fifteen years. Then I broke my ankle, had an operation, it didn't heal, so I gave up the stage and took up teaching. Bored yet?"

"And your wife?"

"Went off with a younger man, a musician, played… I don't know, clarinet or something. Wilma, her name was. Imagine marrying someone called Wilma. Selfish, ungrateful little bitch. But sexy, God was she hot in the sack."

He glances down.

"Good. A spotless plate. Can't stand women who pick at their food."

His plate is still half full, she notices, but now he's gathering things together, piling them up.

"Shall we move to the squidgy seats? Tell you what, you stash these over by the sink, I'll go get us another bottle of wine."

Katie has lost track of time. The candle had burnt out, the standing lamp on the other side of the room providing just a small circle of light, leaving the rest of the room in shadow. The music stopped a while ago; instead, a couple of owls seem to be having a conversation somewhere close by. Guy is sprawled at the end of the sofa with one ankle resting on his other knee, she sits alongside him with her legs folded under her. Both are now barefooted.

Two empty wine bottles stand on the table. Another, half empty, is on the floor beside Guy.

"And so you, Katie Tremain, what are you hiding from?"

"Hiding?"

"Come on, everyone knows that people who come to live down here are running away from something."

Katie hadn't thought of it that way. But he had a point.

"I don't know. Failure, I suppose. My career stalled, my confidence evaporated, I lost track of the purpose of my life. Of the purpose of anything, come to that."

"Sounds familiar," Guy says. "But then, you don't seem like a loser to me. You've got looks, money, talent. I've seen what you're doing with that house, don't forget. And a very nice husband who obviously cares about you."

"He may care. But he doesn't like me much. And he certainly doesn't trust me."

"Ah. Now you've got me intrigued." Katie pulls a face.

"It was all so long ago – we hadn't been married long – and I thought I was pregnant. Ben was thrilled, but I wasn't. The timing was all wrong, and I wasn't sure I wanted kids anyway."

Katie could hear that voice he'd used: calm and sensible, yet with a hint of desperation; trying so hard to make her be happy, to convince her that this would be the best thing they'd ever done together, making a beautiful baby. That financially he could cope, that she could pick up her career later, lots of women did these days, that no way was she resigning herself to a life of potty training and baby talk.

"Anyway, I wasn't. Pregnant, that is."

"So problem solved?"

"Not quite. We'd discovered a fundamental flaw in our perfect marriage. I still don't understand how we never discussed it before."

"OK, it's important but not major, is it? Not if you love someone."

Katie empties her glass and Guy picks up the bottle and refills it. Somewhere in the back of her mind she wonders how she's going to drive home in this state.

"It wasn't just that, though. Something else happened…"

His phone starts ringing.

"Shit. Excuse me."

He lopes across the room and retrieves it from a jacket pocket. Katie glances at her watch. It's gone twelve. Still she's grateful for the interruption. She was about to say far more than she should.

"Yes. Yes. Yes. I'll let you know. Go away, will you?"

He drops the phone onto the table as he returns to the sofa.

"So, where were we?"

"About to go onto a new subject. Foxes, for example. What's your opinion of them? I mean, do you like them? Loathe them?"

Guy raises and drops his eyebrows.

"Yup, that sure is a change of subject."

And not the best of ideas either, Katie realises. Still it's too late now. Guy sips his drink, pauses, empties his glass.

"No, sorry. Nothing. It seems I don't have an opinion." He tips his head. "Any special reason?"

"I've seen some on my walks, that's all. A vixen and her cubs. I'm just… well, curious I suppose."

"Kevin's your man. He's in his twenties, I guess, yet he's lived his whole life on Exmoor. Never left it. Can you imagine? There isn't a thing he doesn't know about foxes, or any other wildlife come to that."

Guy's fond of him, she can tell. She'd intended to ask if he had any children of his own; somehow she doubts it. But this isn't the moment.

A yawn catches her unawares, so big it makes her eyes water. She doesn't have a chance of stifling it.

"You're tired," Guy says.

"Tired, and very drunk."

"OK, listen. You have three choices. You can sleep right where you are, or in my bed upstairs and I'll sleep on the sofa. Or we could get you home to your own bed. What d'you think?"

There's no question about it.

"But can I get a taxi round here?"

"Not a taxi, but Kevin would take you."

"Kevin? Would he mind?" It seems too much to ask of someone she doesn't even know.

"I doubt it. He likes to help. Besides, I already warned him he might be needed."

Katie uncurls her legs, links her fingers and stretches her arms above her head. She'd started some work on the garden today, digging out brambles, and aches mildly in every joint.

"If you're sure."

Guy picks up the phone, walks away from her as he talks. The conversation is brief.

"He's on his way."

"I hope you didn't wake him?"

"He never sleeps. The young don't, do they? He was up at the crack of dawn for hound training, probably worked on the farm all day. This evening – what did he say he'd got planned? – helping a friend clear a pond? He'll be out with the hounds again in a few hours. He'll cope. Trust me."

"OK."

She's put it off long enough: she has to brave the toilet which is as primitive as she expected, though clean. She keeps a careful eye on a couple of very large spiders on the ceiling.

"So what's hound training?" she asks as she comes back into the room.

"It's when the pups are taken out to learn what fox hunting's all about."

"How do they do that?"

Guy is filling a kettle.

"No idea. Fancy a coffee before you go? I'm going to have one."

She shakes her head.

"And why the early start?"

"Best time to find things to practise on I guess."

Suddenly she understands.

"Like fox cubs, you mean? That's what you're talking about, isn't it? Cubbing?"

She's confused.

"But I thought you said Kevin likes animals?"

Guy spoons granules into a mug.

"No, I didn't. What I said was there's nothing he doesn't know about them. Slightly different thing."

And now Katie can feel herself growing more sober by the minute. There is no way she's going to sit in a car next to someone who goes cubbing. She'd seen a documentary once, filmed under-cover by a journalist who'd infiltrated the hunt; it was ages ago but she could still remember it. The inexperienced dogs being hyped up to chase the cubs, to rip them apart, to get a taste for fox. The terrified cubs – their mothers driven away or shot – racing around in circles, yelping, having no chance of escaping, none. The shouting, the cheers, the chaos. Almost worst of all was the one timid pup who seemed to have no killer instinct, was all legs and waggy tail and just wanted to play. He'd been shot. A single bullet in the back of the head.

"Guy, I've changed my mind. I'll sleep here, save putting anyone out, no problem."

She drops back down onto the sofa, grabs a cushion and tucks it under her head, puts her feet up. Not that she's sleepy anymore. She's too angry to sleep.

"Ring him please, will you? Say not to come." She sits up again. "And anyway, I thought hunting with dogs was against the law."

"So is driving too fast, buying computers off the back of lorries, downloading child pornography."

"So? What sort of an answer's that?"

He looks around for the phone.

"It's how people live down here, Katie. The whole place revolves around hunting, has done for centuries, and it's not going to stop, whatever the law says. Either accept it or go back to the city where the nice, kind bunny huggers live."

It's the first time he's been tetchy with her. Even as he's opening the phone they hear a car pulling up in front of the house, the purr of an idling engine.

"Too late, sorry," he says with a small shrug. "Your taxi has arrived."

He walks with her to the door, hesitates, then before he opens it he puts his hands on her shoulders, turns her towards him.

"Katie, thanks," he says quietly. "You don't know how special it's been for me to have your company this evening."

He brushes a strand of hair back from her face.

"I've really enjoyed it. Please don't let's fall out."

She's behaving like a child and she knows it. She kisses him on the cheek.

"So have I, and we won't."

Outside the only light is a wedge of yellow from the open door behind her as she walks to the car, an old Suzuki 4x4 that she climbs up into with difficulty. Guy follows her, bends down to smile at the driver.

"Thanks, Kevin. I owe you."

He turns back towards the house, one hand raised in a wave.

For the ten minute journey, Katie doesn't say a word. She can't, it would be like turning on a tap. Kevin doesn't speak either, obviously not into small talk. Grudgingly she accepts he's probably half asleep. The car smells of stale cigarette smoke and manure; she fumbles in the dark for the right button, determined not to ask him, relieved when the window slides down and night air rushes in. He seems to know exactly where he's going. As they reach the house he swings the wheel and the car turns into the yard, leans across in front of her and opens the car door. The overhead light comes on and she sees him for the first time: a nice enough looking young man, strong chin, dark floppy hair. There's a strong smell of mouth freshener; he must have used it just before he came to collect her. He gives her a hesitant smile.

"I'll wait until you're safely inside," he says. Soft voice, with the Devonian accent she's getting used to.

"There's no need."

But he waits.

She has difficulty getting the key in the lock, then it's stiff to turn. She can feel his eyes watching her. Once inside she slams the door and stands there with her back pressed against it, waiting for him to go, longing for him to be as far away from her as possible. Something is scratching her foot; she switches on the light, looks down and finds a thick clump of mud and straw stuck to her sandal.


Katie has made up her mind: this obsession with the foxes must stop. There'll be no more wandering in the woods searching in vain for a glimpse of white fur, no more lying awake nights worrying about where they are and how they're doing. No more writing up her observations in that pretty pink diary Andrew had sent, insisting she start using it right away; she'd enjoyed it, in more ways than she'd expected, but that too was about to stop.

Time too to stop procrastinating and get on with the house. There was no way she wanted to still be living there in the winter. It would be freezing, full of woodlice, miserable. She'd also be missing out on the winter social scene in London for the second year running. People really would think she'd died. Besides, she'd had an idea for her next project, a brilliant one, absolutely right for her. If she put it off for too long the excitement would fade, the doubts set in.

She has the radio on, two experts discussing the pros and cons of wind farms, both convincing. All the doors and windows are wide open, She's wearing shorts again, one of Ben's old vests, and is about to start painting the bathroom.

Barnstaple yesterday was a nightmare. She'd hated it: pavements heaving with bored children and bare-chested dads loitering outside stores whilst mums checked out the summer sales; with parking wardens prowling up and down, notebooks in hand. On-road parking places were non-existent. There were signs to car parks everywhere but either she couldn't find them, or they had FULL in red lights over the entrance. Then she'd got lucky. Just as she was about to give up and go home a car swung out from the kerb without warning, forcing her to brake hard. Raising a hand in thanks she'd shot forward into the vacant space. She had one hour to find inspiration.

She was surprisingly successful. At a tiny back street flea market she'd bought an old cupboard with squat bowed legs that she intends to paint a soft, muted green and put in the bedroom. She also found a length of faded calico, perfect to hang in front of shelves in the kitchen, some unrecognisable but dramatic looking dried flowers. She spotted a damaged log basket on a skip, decided it could easily be repaired, hauled it down and hurried off. And then there were the paint samples she'd bought for pennies, their names alone made her mouth water: Gooseberry Fool, Barley Sugar, Nutmeg Cream, Raspberry Crush. Inspired, she's decided to paint the bathroom in stripes, like in Haiti where people aren't afraid to play with colour. She doubts they've even heard of Magnolia.

On the patio outside the back door she's noticed a whir of activity, winged ants circling, crossing paths, climbing over each other, and then a few at a time lifting gently off the ground, going higher and higher until the air is sparkling with them. She ought to shut the door, doesn't want them coming inside. But even as she watches the birds start to swoop down, summoned to the feast by some silent bell, picking them off in mid-flight, a couple of robins dropping down to the ground to clear the stragglers.

She thinks of her little garden back home. The birds she sees most often are the parakeets that seem to be taking over. They're flamboyant, noisy. City birds then. And these are their more restrained country cousins.

The phone distracts her. It's Guy.

"Just checking," he says.

"That…?"

"That you're OK, of course. You sound a bit short of breath."

"That's because I hurried to pick up the phone."

"You knew it would be me."

She's never quite sure if he's as arrogant as he sounds.

"No. I hoped it would be Ben."

"Ah. Right. On the subject. Of Ben, that is." He hesitates and Katie has the feeling yet again that he's planned in advance what he wants to say.

"The other evening, I kind of felt you wanted to talk about him, about you and him, and I cut you off. I'm not good at all that relationship stuff, but I could be a listening ear, if that helps. If you need one, that is. Any time. No charge."

She has to smile.

"It wasn't you, Guy. It was me. Sometimes it's best to leave these things alone, not keep getting them out, turning them over, poking at them. You know what I mean I'm sure."

"Well, the offer's there."

"Thanks. I'll keep it in mind."

"Do."

But how could she talk to him about it? To anyone?

There was nothing to talk about. Nothing happened. It was a misunderstanding, that's all.

Pregnant one day, and then her periods started and relief quickly turned to panic. Why had she told Ben? A stupid, stupid thing to do. She'd given him hope and now she was going to snatch it away from him, and he'd be so disappointed. Worse, he'd be devastated. Probably in a foul mood for months.

As soon as she'd realised she wasn't pregnant she'd made an appointment to have another test, one that had been in the back of her mind for the past year. She'd read an article about the growing number of women having a premature menopause, the symptoms, the problems it can cause. She had a niggling feeling that she might be one of them. It would explain a lot. She found the thought depressing, and also – bizarrely – embarrassing, as though it was her fault, that she'd failed in some way. But the article said things could be done to help. A simple blood test would tell her.

Ben had found the appointment card from the clinic. For some reason he'd decided that it was for a termination, that she'd gone ahead without telling him. Or was at least considering having one. When she'd denied it he said he didn't believe her. She'd been shocked. Gradually her need to convince him of her innocence had turned from hurt (how he could believe she'd do that, and behind his back too?) to anger (how dare he accuse her of such a thing!).

She'd told him to ring the clinic, they'd confirm everything she'd said. Had insisted, even giving him the name of the doctor she'd seen and her patient number. She had no idea if he ever did. For a while they'd avoided the subject, hadn't spoken about that time, what happened, what it meant, what they could or should do next. It felt dangerous to even touch on the subject again. Well, there was just the once, when they'd both had a drop to drink.

She still couldn't decide if that had been a good thing, or a bad.

There had been nothing wrong with hers; the blood test confirmed all was normal. Another false alarm.

Outside on the patio there isn't an ant to be seen. Katie can't imagine that even a single one made it through that flurry of hungry birds and their pecking beaks, but some must, otherwise ants would be extinct by now.

It seems like ages since Ben was last there. He's been bogged down with a couple of on-going jobs he needs to visit regularly, to keep on schedule, and of course the new project which seems to be taking over his life right now. He doesn't mind, he says. It's what he's being paid for. When Katie and Ben do get to chat on the phone their conversations are usually brief; often she can hear machine noises in the background, or hammering. He always ends by dropping his voice and saying he loves her, but it's so much a habit now that Katie doubts he even realises what he's saying. She imagines him in a crowded room, the meeting stopped for refreshments, someone passing him a coffee and him smiling his thanks at the same time as he's declaring his love. Or he's casting his eyes over a delivery document, checking quantities, noticing there are only half as many steel beams as he'd ordered.

Still, he'll be there with her this weekend and Katie is looking forward to it. She's determined to make it special for him, for them both. There's a pub along the coast that the local newspaper said is under new management and doing Mexican food on Saturdays. Fajitas, nachos, chili. She'd missed them. And there's a panoramic view of the sea from the terrace.

She'd like to get Ben out walking too. All that sitting in the car in traffic jams breathing in fumes, blood pressure soaring, it can't be good for him. She doesn't want him to be one of those statistics the government keep bringing out.

More women under thirty taking up smoking. More children being injured by conkers. More men in their forties dying of heart attacks. She's thought about suggesting the coastal footpath which all the tourist literature says is stunning, but also steep and craggy. Do they want to work that hard? Or there's that stretch of the river she'd discovered months ago but still hasn't found time to explore properly. It's beautiful down there. Wild, untouched.

She tidies, cleans, polishes, picks flowers from the garden and blackberries from along the road where they're already growing fat as bumble bees, even though it's not yet September. They're too beautiful to cook. She'll serve them with clotted cream.

She takes a pile of bedlinen, towels, and most of her clothes, to the village launderette. It's the only way she has of getting so many things cleaned at once. Back at the house she lugs them out into the garden and pegs them to the lines she's looped between trees, squinting in the dazzling midday light. She recalls her mother saying the smell she liked best of all was that of sheets dried in a summer breeze. As she collects them to take and put on the bed, Katie holds them up to her face; they're warm and smell of blue skies and wild flowers and sunshine. Now if you could just bottle that fragrance.

Ben has more grey hairs than when she last saw him, she's sure of it. He looks hot and tired, has his shirt sleeves rolled up. He's come straight on from a meeting, didn't bother to change, just got into the car, found some music on the radio and drove without stopping. It was worth it to miss the Friday evening exodus, he said. And at least he'll have a few extra hours there in which to unwind. It's good for him, this place, Katie thinks. Good for both of them.

She makes tea and then gets him to follow her – mugs in hand – so she can show him what she's been doing since he was last there.

"D'you think this works? It's a lovely warm colour, but does it clash with the curtains?"

"I found this screen in a junk shop in the village. If Rachael's not keen on it we could find a spot for it at home."

"Right, advice please. I'm going to tile along the back of the sink in white but I want to put in a few patterned tiles to lift it. I love this art nouveau one, but this is nice too. And this one – or is it too twee?"

He gazes at them, his brow furrowed.

"Which do you think Rachael would choose?"

Ben rubs a hand over his face. She should let him go and take a shower, get out of that suit.

"Must say I'd expected her to come down long before this," Katie says. "To make sure she's happy with how things are going, what I'm doing."

"The tulips," he says, coming to a conclusion. "She says she has complete faith in you."

"That's amazing, seeing as she's only met me once."

"In me then."

"What you mean is she doesn't care. All she wants is for the house to be tarted up so she can get shot of it quickly."

"You're probably right."

Katie's disappointed. It's illogical, of course. She knew what the deal was right from the start. She's getting a thrill out of doing up the house, she's learning a lot, her confidence is growing. So what if she's been used to getting feedback, which more often than not amounted to praise. She doesn't need it. She knows her own mind, what she's aiming to achieve and if she's succeeding. Sod Rachael.

"The tulips it is then," she says, stacking the tiles and putting them back in their box. "Are you hungry? I've made sandwiches, thought we could eat them in the garden."

"Perfect. Give me ten minutes."

When he joins her outside he's wearing shorts, his legs startlingly white. He's also carrying the gun. She'd almost forgotten about it. Obviously he hadn't.

"I've been talking to this guy," he says. "He belongs to a gun club, gave me a few tips."

She'd thought at first he was going to say he'd found someone who'd be interested in buying it.

"On how to shoot straight, you mean?"

"These look good. I'm starved." He takes a bite of sandwich, a bit of lettuce sticking out of the corner of his mouth. "Straight-ish anyway."

Katie has a thought.

"Of course, strictly speaking the gun isn't yours to do anything with. Surely, as the house now belongs to Rachael, so does everything in it?"

Ben doesn't reply..

"And if it's really in such good condition and worth as much as you think, she'll be wanting to get it off to a buyer as soon as possible."

He takes another sandwich.

"So maybe you should take it with…"

"Katie, stop."

He puts down the crust, takes both her hands in his.

"Stop being annoyed about everything. The gun, I promise you, will be gone soon. Just let me indulge the little boy inside me for a short while, will you? Please? I know it's pitiful, but I bet you'd find most men are the same."

Katie shrugs. She can't argue with that.

"And stop being angry about Rachael. No-one said she was a kind, caring person, and she's certainly not doing any of this for your sake, or mine. Does it matter? You seem to be having fun playing with the house, and I have a rural retreat to escape to whenever I can get the time."

She knows he's right. About everything. Why is she getting so worked up? She glances up at the pink sky, takes a deep breath.

"You know, London seems like a lifetime ago," she says. "A dream. Being here is the reality."

Ben looks straight at her.

"Is that good?" She smiles.

"I think so."

He lets go of her hands, leans back.

"I must say you're looking so much better than when we arrived. Kind of softer round the edges. Bit of a tan."

He grins.

"I like your hair longer too," he says. He's always trying to persuade her to grow it.

"Don't count on it staying this way. If I could find a good hairdresser – any hairdresser – I'd get it cut."

Especially if it's going to get hot again, she thinks as she picks up the plates and heads indoors. Ben follows her.

"So," he says, leaning against the door frame, hands in his pockets. "I don't suppose you've got any empty cans handy?"

"If you want to go through the rubbish you might find a couple."

He wrinkles his nose but then heads for the bin.

"I'll only stay out ten, fifteen minutes at the most. Til the light goes."

Sunday evening. Ben had planned to leave for London tonight, but he's going to go at the crack of dawn tomorrow instead. For both of them it's been a good weekend. They've relaxed together in a way that they haven't for years, rediscovered the pleasure of doing absolutely nothing. Neither of them wants it to end, not yet. Now they're sitting in the kitchen, have decided they really must go for this walk they keep putting off. Already the evening is drawing in, the air cooler. Ben hesitates, seems unsure whether or not to say what's on his mind.

"You haven't once mentioned the foxes, Katie."

"Haven't I?"

"You said on the phone that you'd tracked them down again, taken some photos. You sounded thrilled. That was a few weeks ago."

Katie knows she's going to have to say something yet suddenly she's reluctant.

"I haven't seen them since."

He waits.

"It's unlikely they're still around anyway," she goes on. "The cubs were growing up fast. They disperse round about now. Go their own way."

Not entirely true. She thinks of last time, the enthusiasm with which they'd welcomed the vixen back, like excited puppies. They're part of the dog family of course.

"It's a shame. I'd have loved to see them," Ben says. "Just once. I know, if I'd been with you they probably wouldn't have come anywhere near us. But I'd have liked to give it a try."

She hadn't realised he felt like that. She'd never thought to ask him.

"They've gone, Ben. I'm sure of it. Last time I went up to their earth there was no sign of them. It felt strange. Abandoned. I didn't like it."

"Would you show me the place then, at least that? Where you used to sit and watch them?"

He doesn't understand. How can he?

"I can't. I can't go there, Ben. I'm sorry."

He looks disappointed.

"It's up to you."

She slides back her chair.

"But there's another walk I'd like to take you on. A surprise. You'll enjoy it, I promise."

The river is slow now, trickling over the rocks. A rough path follows the curves of the bank, so narrow that they need to go single file, getting tangled up with brambles, having to look down all the time or they're in danger of tripping. They stop to watch a small dark brown bird with a white bib that's bobbing up and down on a flat rock in the centre of the river.

"I think … now wait a minute, that couldn't be a dipper, could it?" Ben says.

"Whatever makes you think that?"

She's teasing and he knows it.

Further on a bigger bird, black and sleek, dives into the river and disappears, seems to be under for ages and then reappears some distance away.

"And that is…?"

Neither of them has any idea.

"Next time we'll bring a bird book."

It's getting darker, but still they walk on. This is heaven, Katie thinks. And so quiet, and so unspoilt. Why had it taken her so long to come back to Exmoor?

"Katie?"

Ben is walking behind her, and she stops, turns. He steps off the path and heads towards the thicket of bushes and trees that runs parallel with the river, threading his way across ground lush with ferns and bracken, stepping from one moss draped stone to another. He stops, beckons, and she follows. It's dark beneath the canopy of leaves. The air is buzzing and flickering with insects; there's a green smell, moist and heavy.

"D'you think it's like this in a rainforest?" Katie says.

Ben touches a finger to his lips as though to say don't speak. When he reaches towards her and lifts her tee-shirt up over her head, she smiles, goes to protest, and then – as he unfastens her bra – she feels the cool evening air on her breasts, her nipples tightening, and she no longer wants him to stop. He bends and circles them with moist lips, first one, then the other, his lips so hot that they almost burn. Now he takes off his own sweater, and even in the shadows she can see he's put on weight, his body soft and pale, yet when he pulls her closer she can feel the muscles in his arms, the strength that's still there beneath the fleshy padding.

He kneels, unzips her jeans, eases them down over her hips.

"Ben, someone might be..." she starts to say, but it's too late, he's lifting her feet one at a time, and now she's completely naked and he's nuzzling her, gently, insistently, and she rests her hands on the top of his head and closes her eyes.

When he pulls her down beside him she no longer cares about the possibility of passers-by, about the rough ground grazing her back or the prickling of the drying grasses. She wraps her legs tightly around him, arching her hips, hardly breathing, watching the patterns of the leaves overhead shuffling, overlapping each other then sliding free, moving with the breeze, with the feather light touch of a bird that settles briefly on a branch then flies off. There's something so natural about sex in the open air, so right. It's exciting, liberating. She remembers other times, sand beneath her back, the smell of gorse. She remembers sobbing uncontrollably though she's not sure why. She remembers...

There are voices, close, on the other side of the river. It could be children; she'd noticed some when she was here before, fishing, drinking lager from cans. Ben's face is tucked into her neck, his breathing heavy, and at first she thinks he doesn't hear them. Then he hesitates, then stops moving, and they freeze. His body is heavy, they're both sweating. Katie can hear a heart thumping – she's not sure if it's hers or Ben's but it's so loud that she's convinced it will give them away. Now there are footsteps, boys running past, chasing each other and yelling as they go, a glimpse of bobbing heads beyond the shrubs, a splash as something heavy is tossed into the river. A rock probably. They stop in a giggling cluster and Katie thinks for sure she and Ben will be spotted, and she can't think of anything more embarrassing. But then with a thump of boots they're off again, their voices fading. And then they're gone.

Ben starts to shake and for a moment Katie thinks something is wrong until she realises he's laughing. What starts as a chuckle becomes uncontrollable, and then contagious so that Katie starts giggling too.

"God, I thought we were about to have an audience," he says, rolling away from her onto his back, flinging an arm up over his head. "Still, I suppose they might have learnt a thing or two."

"You're joking. They already know it all."

And now Katie wants to get some clothes on. Quickly.

"Ben, I can't find my bra anywhere. Where did you throw it?"

"Don't panic. Here."

Now he too is dressing.

"It's OK for teenagers to screw behind the bushes," Katie mutters, pulling on her sandals. "They probably haven't got anywhere else to go. But a respectable middle aged couple…"

"You know, I think that's the first time we've ever made love outdoors in a public place, isn't it?" Ben says.

"And the last. I don't think I can cope."

"Don't tell me you didn't enjoy it too?"

He pulls her close, gives her a kiss that lasts longer than either of them expect.

"I hated it."

"Liar," he says.

They walk home with their arms looped around each other's waists.

In the morning Ben tries not to disturb her. He tiptoes around in the half light, doesn't make coffee, doesn't want to crash around in the kitchen. He'll get one at a service station on the way. Just before he goes he kisses her lightly on the top of her head and although still half asleep, she mutters something, he's no idea what but takes it as a goodbye.

When the phone rings she's sound asleep again. The phone, it seems, has been left downstairs. She glances at the clock as she pads out into the hallway; it's not yet six in the morning. Who'd ring at this time? Then it hits her: there's been an accident, Ben has been hurt, or killed even, his body trapped still in a mangled wreck. No, they'd have had to get it out to find his wallet and contact details, otherwise how would they know to ring her?

"Hello?"

Even to her, her voice sounds small and frightened.

"Love, I'm sorry to wake you. I had to tell you."

"Ben? Are you alright?"

He ignores the question.

"I've just seen them."

"Who?"

"Your missing cubs."

Now she's wide awake.

"Where?"

"You remember where we first saw the vixen, alongside the road? Not far from there. A mile or so further on. They were in a field on the other side of the hedge, I thought it was dogs at first."

"Are you sure it wasn't?"

"Yes. I got out of the car and walked back. I edged as close as I dared then I stood absolutely still and peered through the hedge. They were on the other side of the field, but I could see them clearly. Two little white foxes playing tag."

Katie sits down, the phone pressed tight to her ear. She wishes she'd been with him. She'd said she might go back this time, had again put it off. If only, if only.

"Did they look alright to you?"

"They looked beautiful."

He sounds thrilled.

"And healthy, and certainly happy. I'm no expert, but to me they looked as though they're doing just fine."

"Any sign of the vixen?"

"No. Sorry." There's a lot of crackling and she's not sure if he said anything more.

"I don't expect she was far away," Katie says. "She's been such a good mother."

The line is getting worse, and she hopes he isn't driving at the same time as he's talking to her. Better not to ask.

"Ben, thank you for telling me."

"You're very welcome, love. I thought you'd like..." He's gone for a few seconds. "...worrying about them, will you?"

"I'll try. I promise."

But she's hardly put down the phone before the doubts start. They've gone the wrong way; she'd hoped they'd have gone in the other direction, along the ridge of the moor where it's woody, the land steep and unsuitable for most kinds of farming which means it's virtually uninhabited. They're growing too bold, playing in an open field like that. Too careless. And where was the vixen? Was she really nearby?

Katie goes out into the garden. It seems to draw her whenever she needs to think. She deadheads some roses that have somehow managed to fight their way through a thick mat of ivy, their lemon petals floating downwards as soon as she touches them. A robin drops at her feet, pecks half-heartedly at the ground, flies up to a nearby shrub and sits re-arranging its feathers. The sun is rising in a soft blue sky and another beautiful day begins.

The important thing is they're fine right now. That has to be enough.

# TEN

She's walking in the front door, just back from the village with a few groceries to tide her over, and wine of course, the cheap red in the box with the bull on it that she's resigned to now, even beginning to enjoy. Somewhere her phone is ringing. She finds it down the side of the sofa.

"Where the hell have you been? I've been trying to reach you for hours."

"Andrew?"

"Don't you keep your mobile with you?"

Katie flops onto the sofa. The room smells of paint, and already she can feel her throat tightening. Still, not many more walls to do. She should go and open the window but she can't be bothered.

"Not much point. Can't get a signal most of the time, unless you're on the top of…"

"Ok. Skip the excuses. Listen."

"And why aren't you in France anyway?"

Andrew's groan says more than words and Katie has to smile.

"We're off tomorrow. Today we're cleaning the house from top to bottom. Don't ask why. So it's nice and welcoming for any squatters who might break in, I guess."

"You should be used to Tess's ways by now. Bet the girls are excited."

"They're sulking."

"Why?"

"Because I won't let them take every single toy they own. The car's already bursting. Can't remember why we thought a camping trip to France sounded such a fun idea. What were we on?"

"Watch it. You're turning into a miserable old codger."

"Not so much of the old!"

The sound of scampering feet on the polished wooden floor, then giggles.

"Tilly has something she wants to say."

"Fine. Put her on. Hi, Tilly love."

"Bonjour."

"You speak French? Clever girl. D'you know any more words?"

Silence. Then whispering.

"I know one." It's Rose now. "Merde."

Katie can see Andrew nodding encouragement. Will he ever grow up? Next, two very loud and moist squeaks.

"That's us sending you kisses," Tilly informs her.

A rustling, and she's back with Andrew.

"D'you really think you should be teaching those sweet little girls to swear?"

"It's OK in a foreign language. Anyway, Katie, listen. Your foxes."

She sits forward.

"I've been doing some research. Albinos in the wild population are very rare, only a few ever recorded in the UK. Those that have been spotted were mostly in the north, though I think there was one down your way, Dartmoor or close. It's all down to a genetic quirk."

Katie can't resist.

"Much like yourself, then," she teases. "And those eyes? They're like pearls."

"As there's no eye pigment, you're actually seeing straight through to the blood capillaries at the back of the eye."

"It's a strange effect, makes…"

"But Katie, wait. For a white vixen to even survive long enough to breed is unlikely. Like it virtually never happens. For her to meet and mate with a dog fox with the same recessive gene, extraordinary. To produce two white cubs – I was going to say it's like your chance of winning the lottery, but it's less. One in ten million, the experts say."

Katie can't take it in.

"They really are that unique?"

"That's what I was told."

Suddenly she's suspicious. "Who told you? Andrew, I asked you not to tell anyone about them. You promised."

"Wait a minute. There's a conservationist guy I know through the college and I put it to him as a hypothetical case. You know, what if..."

"And of course he wouldn't wonder why you were asking."

"Possibly. Not necessarily. Does it matter?"

Katie's confused. She'd have felt thrilled to have spent time with her fox family even if they'd had normal genes and red fur. But the fact that they're so unique makes her feel even more privileged. At the same time she's aware of a shadow in the corner of her mind, something sinister, a threat she can't quite make out.

"So did you take some photos?"

"Yes. Not as many as I'd hoped, but some. They're not bad. I used the zoom."

"Any with the whole family together?"

"A couple. It wasn't easy, they were pretty skittish. Why?"

He pauses.

"Have you any idea what a shot like that would be worth?"

He's back on that again.

"I don't want people to know where they are."

"You wouldn't have to say."

"Come on, Andrew, if I submitted it to any paper worth its salt they'd have their spies sniffing around here before I'd cashed the cheque."

"I could submit it on your behalf."

He's thought of everything.

"You think they'd be put off that easily? Besides, they'd want someone to authenticate it. You know how nervous they are about hoaxes."

"We'd find a way round it. Katie, I reckon they'd pay thousands. And who was it saying how hard up she is now she hasn't got a proper job?"

"I don't know. It doesn't feel right."

"You'd be making people happy too. Baby animal pictures are like porridge, they give everyone a nice warm glow inside."

"But they trust me," she says, knowing she's beginning to sound defensive. "I'd be exploiting that trust."

A sigh.

"OK, I'm not going to bully you."

Now she feels bad.

"Let me think. You'll be away for two weeks, right? Let's talk again when you get back."

"Fine. Whatever you say."

"And meanwhile…"

"Katie, the boss is pulling faces at me. I have to go." Is he annoyed? She can't tell. Disappointed, yes.

"Andrew, I do appreciate it," she says. "You know, everything you've done."


Katie is putting off the moment. A bumble bee is trapped inside the window, bumping gently at the glass but its buzzing indicating it's getting angrier, more frustrated by the minute. She's tried opening the top of the window and scooping it up on a piece of paper but it falls back down just before she can tip it through the gap. Bees don't sting, do they? she thinks. That's wasps. So cupping her hands she tentatively traps the fuzzy ball first against the glass, then between her palms where it vibrates gently as she hurries out to the back door, then into the garden. She opens her hands. Now the bee goes quiet, probably shocked to find itself almost free. Then it lifts into the air, and is gone.

She feels ridiculously pleased with herself.

And now, at last, she gets out the camera, pulls a chair close to the window and flicks through the shots she took that evening in the rain, stopping every now and again, knowing what she's looking for but having trouble finding it. Amazingly, out of probably thirty or so shots, there are only three that fit the bill. In one of them the vixen is sitting so far back you can hardly see her, whilst the two cubs are in opposite corners of the shot. In the second they're playing, one crouched low, the other rearing up, the vixen close but far more interested in giving herself a wash than watching her cubs. It occurs to Katie that though she obviously cares and will defend them to the death, she's had enough. She's brought them up alone (what did happen to her mate?), she's done a brilliant job. Now she wants her own life back. And she deserves it.

The third one is The One. In it the vixen is standing looking directly at the camera, eyes half closed. Both the cubs are on her left side, (which is the camera side), crouched slightly below her, suckling. They didn't get much of a meal. After what seemed like seconds the vixen had pulled free, snapped at them in a half-hearted way, turned and walked away. For a moment the cubs had hesitated, exchanged puzzled glances, then one had scampered off after her, the other following, and the moment was over. It was probably one of the last times they were suckled.

If she was to submit it, this is the one that would get the front page treatment. It might even get onto the local TV news, national TV, a wildlife magazine or two, some specialist websites. If she submitted it.

## ELEVEN

How often, when something terrible happens, do people say they had a premonition? They might not have recognised it as such at the time, but looking back it's obvious. The feeling, in the middle of the night, that an adored but deceased parent was standing at the foot of the bed. The black cat that appeared on the doorstep, stared with orange eyes and then seemed to simply vanish into thin air. The tomato ketchup stain that, when studied carefully, was obviously a map, or a bomb, or a face. All of them warnings of something sinister to come.

Afterwards, Katie couldn't recall having any such hint. How had she missed it?

Or could it simply have been that things were going too well? Happiness is like a bauble made of fine glass, exquisitely beautiful but very, very fragile. One sharp tap is all it takes to reduce it to a handful of spiteful, brittle shards.

Ben is back, just for one night. He nearly didn't come at all but his schedule is getting fuller by the minute, and with such a heavy workload coming up he might not make it back again for some weeks. He's worried about the economic situation, the looming threat of a financial crisis that will affect everyone, muttered about the possibility of the project coming to a halt. He didn't need to add that, of course he he'd be devastated.

She agrees he needs a break if he's going to stay strong. Some quality air, a nice meal, a walk even. He said on the phone he wants to talk to Katie properly. That with the house coming on so well she – they – have to start planning what to do next. He's got some ideas.

Now he's sitting in the living room with the local newspaper which he'd picked up as he came through the village. He likes to read what's happening locally. Though none of it means much to him, it makes him feel as though he's stepped into one of those Sunday night TV dramas set in a rural community. Comfort food for the brain, he calls them. Katie can see him from where she's working in the garden, still tugging away at the brambles, beginning to accept that it's a losing battle and she's going to have to resort to chemicals. The sunset is like nothing she's ever seen before, stripes of pink, plum, gold and grey, like an Indian sari.

"Ben?"

She stands in the doorway, licks her finger and then dabs at a scratch on her arm. "Come and look at this sky."

He lifts his head but doesn't move. His face is all wrong.

"Ben? What is it?"

He hesitates, sighs. Then he folds the paper, folds it again as though reluctant to let go of it. When he passes it to her one particular story is on top.

"I'm sorry, love," he says.

She steps inside, takes the paper from him.

## RARE FOX CUBS KILLED BY YOUTHS

**Two albino fox cubs were killed yesterday evening outside the Queen's Head public house near W – on Exmoor, kicked and beaten to death by four youths. Distressed witnesses, who were watching the cubs in the playground of the village primary school opposite whilst drinking outside the pub, said they didn't stand a chance.**

**The youths, on two quad bikes, had been coming along the main road when they spotted the cubs, who were especially visible even at dusk because of their dazzling white fur. The bikers swung in through the school gates and chased the now terrified cubs around in circles before cornering them up against a far wall.**

They then dismounted and either kicked or battered the cubs to death, using some met posts that had been stored nearby for use as part of a new fence. After throwing the two small, shattered bodies over the wall into the undergrowth they got back on their bikes and left.

"It was absolutely pointless brutality," said Mr. Fred Bayley, 61, on holiday from Cheltenham. "You had to look away. You could hear the poor little things yelping and screaming."

His wife, Mrs Liz Bayley, 60, said "There was blood all over the place. I hope someone is going to clean it up before the children start classes again."

Another visitor, Mr. Tony Reynolds, 53, from Birmingham, who is staying with his son and daughter-in-law, Dave, 27 and Suzi, 26, who live near Minehead, said that as the youths were coming out of the playground he went across and asked them why they did it.

"They said foxes are vermin, doesn't matter what colour they are, and that they were doing the local farming community a big favour. They were hyped up, shoving each other and laughing."

On hearing about the killings, a local conservationist, Mr Edgar de Vries, 42, went immediately to the spot. Despite an extensive search of the shrubs and undergrowth by him and other volunteers only one body was found. Though it was badly damaged, with its skull smashed and most of its bones broken, he could confirm at once that it was an albino cub. A few metres away was a large patch of dried blood, but no sign of another body.

"I would imagine it was in better condition than the first one, and that someone took it, probably intending to get it to a taxidermist. Make no mistake about it, this is a tragedy. For a vixen to produce two white cubs is almost unheard of. These must be two of the rarest creatures in the world, and now they are dead. Of course, even their bodies are extremely valuable. There will be collectors willing to pay a fortune to own a stuffed albino fox cub. I am surprised this one too was not taken as even its fur, made into some kind of accessory for example, would be highly desirable to many people."

As the killing of foxes is not illegal, a police official confirmed that they will not be taking any action.

Katie's legs start to shake, her head feels light and there's a buzzing in her ears. She crouches down on the floor hugging her knees, bends her head and rests her forehead on them, closes her eyes.

"Katie, are you alright?"

Now Ben is kneeling beside her, he's wrapping something around her shoulders, the throw from the sofa.

"You look awful, Katie. Don't faint on me, please."

She tries to lift her head, the buzzing becomes an angry swarm of bees. Not a good idea then, not yet.

"I won't," she mumbles.

"What can I get you? Some water? Have we got any brandy?"

She reaches her hand towards him and he catches hold of it.

"Christ, you're freezing. Katie, let's get you…"

She manages to lift her head.

"Ben, stop flapping. Just leave me for a bit."

"You've had a shock. I'm so bloody stupid, I should have realised."

"Please."

He stands, unsure what to do.

"Katie, I'm sorry… I'll see if I can find…"

She senses him leaving the room, has no idea where he's going. She doesn't care. She just wants to stay here on the floor and shut her eyes and forget there is any world outside this room with its vase of purple and bronze dahlias, its framed Charles Renee McIntosh print, with its snuggly sofa and four Calico Kiss coloured walls; with doors and windows you can shut tight and lock, so you need never again have anything to do with the vile, ugly, brain-damaged bastards who think they have every right to destroy the things you love for no reason other than for fun.

It's the next day and Katie's anger has a new focus: she now hates herself.

"It was all my fault."

"And how d'you figure that? They're wild animals, Katie. They're free to go where they choose, it's how they learn about life. So they chose the wrong way. How exactly is that down to you?"

"I'd made them too tame. They thought they could trust human beings."

"Rubbish. You said yourself how they'd changed over the past month, how they were suddenly much more wary."

Katie can't stay still. She paces the carpet, arms crossed tightly as though needing to hold herself together, frightened of what will happen if she doesn't.

"Bet they were after the dustbins. Isn't that what always happens when natural food supplies run out? Like bears in Alaska in winter, coming into town."

"OK. Stop. That's enough. I know you're only trying to help but..."

How can she explain?

Katie goes out of the room, slams the door. Upstairs she throws herself onto the bed. Her anger is fizzing inside her and she doesn't know what to do about it.

She knows what she'd like to do.

She'd like to meet the four youths on the quad bikes. She imagines them drinking outside the same pub, draped along the wall where a lot of the youngsters congregate.

She'd go up to them and smile pleasantly, an unremarkable middle aged woman passing the time of day. They'd probably nod hello, exchange looks, smirk? She'd say she'd heard how they've been clearing the area of vermin, thought she'd like to thank them personally for what they've done. Then from behind her back she'd produce the gun, Ben's shotgun, only with the end of the barrel sawn off so that the shot would spray wider and do maximum damage. Their eyes would be blank, not yet understanding. Maybe one of the brighter ones would catch on quicker than the others, would lick his lips nervously, mutter something like, hey, what's this about? Or would say shit, put his hands up in front of him, as though they'd be enough to protect him. She'd shoot the one sitting closest to her first. She'd have to be quick to get the others. She might get another one full on if they froze, but more likely they'd freak and run and she'd have to shoot them in the back. They'd fall heavily, face down, maybe try to crawl along the ground away from her, from this mad, murderous woman. Their shirts would be peppered with lead shot, little red flowers patterning the denim, or plaid cotton.

It helps, imagining it.

What's worrying, what really frightens her, is that she thinks she could almost do it.

Her phone is ringing downstairs. She hears Ben talking, a brief conversation. A pause and then his face at the door.

"That was Guy." Ben comes into the room. "I thought you wouldn't want to speak to him right now."

When she doesn't respond he crosses and sits on the side of the bed, but he doesn't touch her.

"Come back to London with me. Even if you come back down here in a week or two. You need to get away from this place for a bit."

Katie rubs her eyes which she knows are red and sore. She didn't sleep last night.

"I keep thinking about the vixen, wondering what happened to her, if she's OK."

"Katie, you're going to make yourself ill if you go on like this. She's probably fine. Why wouldn't she be?"

"Because her babies have just been murdered, possibly?"

She's said it before she can stop herself, regrets it immediately but it's too late. Now the words hang there, like a spider's web, waiting for the lightest touch to trigger the entrapment mechanism. If he says one word, if he dares bring up the subject again, if he even looks at her in that hurt yet accusing way that he'd cultivated back then, not speaking, not needing to... she'll scream.

The seconds pass, become minutes. Ben stands, walks to the window and rests his forehead against the glass. It's getting dark already and she can just make out his reflection though she can't see his face. He'll be off soon, his things are already in the car. His shoulders are sagging and she knows he's exhausted too. Exhausted with his work. Exhausted with driving from London to Devon, Devon to London, London to Devon. Exhausted with trying to help her through this. She swings her legs off the bed, goes to him and winds her arms around his waist, pressing the side of her face against his warm shoulders, linking her hands in front of him. After a moment he picks up one of her hands and kisses it.

"I'm sorry Ben. I'm being a real pain. You're right. Give me half an hour and I'll be ready."

"Good girl."

He sounds instantly cheerier, goes off to check what's in the fridge, to make sure they don't leave anything that will rot or curdle in their absence. He'll check the rubbish bin too, and bring in the few bits of washing still out on the line. Katie can't recall when he was last actually volunteered to do domestic chores.

She looks everywhere for her overnight bag – it seems like a lifetime ago she unpacked it – and finds it eventually on top of a cupboard in the bedroom. She switches on the light, opens drawers and turfs out handfuls of underwear, some tee-shirts, bits and pieces which she doesn't sort through, just drops them into the bag. From the top of the chest of drawers she scoops up some bottles: skin lotion, make up remover, realising she's hardly used them. She won't bother to change, no-one is going to see how scruffy she looks. They'll go back in Ben's car, he'll drive. They'll sort out later what to do if – when – she wants to come back down to Devon.

It's dark outside now, the air absolutely still and so humid it could almost be raining, though it isn't, not yet. A slow, determined tapping at the glass turns out to be a large brown bug that Katie thinks might be a hornet, though she's far from sure. Slowly she pushes the window up to shut it, slides the bolt across.

She picks up the diary, is about to drop it into the bag, then changes her mind. She has to search for a pen.

*Were you there when they killed your cubs? Did you watch them from a hiding place under bushes nearby, crouched, shivering, listening to your babies yelping yet not knowing what to do to help them? You wouldn't have run off and left them to their fate, I'm sure of it. But I can't imagine you attacking their attackers either.*

*I don't think you were there.*

*They were getting bigger and bolder every day, more fascinated by the world around them, more daring, and that was how it had to be. You needed to get your own strength back, to recover from having to bring them up on your own, to feed them and nurture them. A single parent family, that's what you were, and you'd done a brilliant job. The time had come to let them go.*

*But you knew they were dead, didn't you? Later, when you'd have expected them to re-appear and they didn't, did you get a twinge of concern? Give that muffled little bark that always brought them straight back to you? Did you search the places you'd found them before, checking the territory you'd carefully marked out so that they'd know it was theirs?*

*If you'd gone close in to the village you'd have picked up their scent, followed it to the school. You'd have found the blood, the smell of their fear. You'd have known then that they were gone.*

*I'd picked up another second-hand book in Barnstaple. (Or third or fourth hand, by the state of it – I wash my hands thoroughly after handling it.) It told the story of a vixen and her cub, up north somewhere, the vixen hand reared but then released. When – as so often happens, it seems, with foxes – her cub was shot the vixen stood on a jagged outcrop, her silhouette just visible against a black sky dazzling with stars, stood there and screamed for her lost cub, a high-pitched sound more like a human scream than that of an animal. The listener counted the screams. There were three hundred and seventy-two.*

*Did you release three hundred and seventy-two screams into the night?*

Ben is waiting patiently in the kitchen, or maybe not so patiently. When she comes slowly down the stairs he's on his feet instantly.

"Ready then?"

"Ben…"

"Let's get a move on, can we? I've got a crack of dawn start at the site tomorrow. Where's your bag? Is it still upstairs?"

"Ben, I can't."

"Can't what"

"Leave."

"For Christ's sake, Katie."

"I can't go without knowing if she's OK. I just can't."

He pushes the chair under the table, snatches his jacket from the back of it.

"OK. Fine. Whatever you want. But I'm off."

He doesn't kiss her, doesn't say another word. The front door clicks shut, she hears the car engine turn, the angry spin of wheels on gravel. Yet again he's leaving in a temper: it seems to be happening more and more often.

She wonders why. Is it really all her fault?

During the evening her phone rings again and again. She ignores it. Later she deletes the message telling her she has seven missed calls.

AUTUMN

Ben is sulking. He's says he's sorry, he doesn't have time to talk right now. That she obviously doesn't remember what it's like to work under pressure, the struggle to find time to do anything, buy bread, shove things in the washing machine Put out the rubbish even; he missed the collection last week and now the contents are stinking. There's a hint of accusation in his voice. Because she's not there to shop and cook and care for him? When has she ever done that anyway?

He says it's all because of the new job, the toy manufacturers. The building will be fantastic when it's completed; it may even win awards. It will win awards. Right now it's rapidly becoming a nightmare. He says when he gets five minutes to himself he'll ring her and they can have a proper chat, as long as it isn't about her bloody fox. It depresses him, all this drama about one wild animal. It depresses her, Katie says.

"My point exactly," Ben snaps. He makes an effort, softens his tone. "You were doing so well down there, Katie, enjoying getting the house together, getting yourself together. Now it's like you're sliding back down the hill again and I can't catch hold of you."

"That isn't the fox's fault."

"So whose is it then? Mine, I suppose."

"No, Ben. That's not what I'm saying."

He's sulked before, mini sulks that usually last no more than a few days. Sometimes – when Katie was distracted by work, for example, or they were having an especially manic social life – she'd hardly even noticed them. Only once before had he retreated deep inside himself, rarely speaking, not touching her, not meeting her eyes so that she'd have thought he was having an affair if she hadn't known better. Ben wasn't any good at lying, hopeless in fact. He couldn't have an affair.

It was then - one drunken evening, when she'd asked him what was wrong, insisted he needed to tell her before she flipped completely - that he'd finally opened up.

"OK. Tell me the truth. Do you want to have children? Like, ever? Or is it just that you don't want to have them with me?"

She was caught out. This was not what she'd expected them to be discussing.

"Don't be ridiculous."

The wrong reply. Hurt had flickered briefly across his face.

"It's not ridiculous. It's a conversation we should have had years ago. It's important. It matters."

He'd hesitated.

"To me anyway."

She wanted to be honest yet what could she say?

"That's not fair Ben. I don't know how I feel, not at this moment. My work is... well, you know. I love it. I'm good at it. And why are you bringing this up right now anyway?"

He'd signed.

"Because you asked me what's wrong."

She'd crossed to look out of the window, mesmerised by a flock of gaudy parakeets stripping their mimosa tree of blossoms, as they did each year. She didn't want him to see the tears in her eyes. He was right, of course he was and she was being selfish yet again. He moved to stand beside her and she could see his reflection in the window.

"I'm sorry Ben. Right now I can't answer your question. But if you're forcing me to say something then... then I suspect I have some kind of maternal instinct missing. Probably something wrong. Unbalanced hormones, or some psychological damage I suffered but have long since buried. I know I'm letting you down, but..."

"You don't want kids."

"No. Not yet anyway."

"Maybe never?"

A loud bang from the road startled the parakeets and she watched as they rose like a cloud, circled and were gone. She'd turned to him, wrapped her arms around his waist, pressed her face against his neck.

"But I do want you. I love you. You're so kind, and funny, and… you're just my other half. I need you to be complete. It's that simple. And I hate myself for disappointing you and wish…"

It had been alright.

He'd sighed, said no, it was good that she'd been honest. He was sorry that he hadn't believed her when he'd found her clinic appointment card. That he was an absolute shit to have said the things he said, that he'd been cruel and stupid, and that he wouldn't have blamed her if she'd left him. No man has a right to be that insensitive, he'd said.

"It hurt most that you didn't trust me," she'd said quietly.

"I know. I do know."

He'd stopped speaking for a few long minutes. She'd waited. Then he'd said he still didn't begin to understand how she felt about children, but that was no excuse. He was sorry. Would she forgive him? Please?

She'd stayed close, letting him hold her in a grip so tight she could hardly breathe, aware that something had happened to him, something that had made him recall that terrible time. She waited for him to say more, but he didn't. She realised she'd probably never know what it was.

Then, once again the subject had been dropped.

Suddenly the air smells different, as though it's autumn even though the trees are still heavy with rustling leaves, the days unseasonably warm. Katie thinks how it must be like this every year, one day it's summer, the next the thermostat has moved on a notch and it's autumn, but people don't notice. She never noticed before. She loves it, being so close to nature that she's aware of the subtle little changes. She'd like to talk to Ben about it. She'd like to talk about other things too, but he's increasingly difficult to get hold of. He hasn't answered her last three calls. She leaves another message.

"Ben, be honest. Are you angry with me? I don't know why you would be but, well, it's been lovely the way we've been getting on together lately. Like way back. Please don't spoil it. Or don't let me. I know this fox business is irritating you, but I can't just walk away from it all, not yet. But soon, I promise you that soon I'll…"

She'll what? She has no idea. She tells him she loves him and ends the call.

There's something in the local newspaper, an item at the bottom of page two that Katie nearly misses. Her eye had been caught by a story with a bold headline about teenagers in rural areas using horse tranquillisers as drugs, and she wonders how anyone would even come up with the idea of trying such a thing. Or dare to. Do they really find their lives so tedious that they can treat them as carelessly as used burger boxes?

Underneath is the article.

It says that following the recent item about the killing of two albino fox cubs, two young men – who wished to remain anonymous – had reported shooting an adult white fox last winter. Though they knew they had hit it, the fox had headed for the river, and disappeared. Despite an extensive search they never saw it again, and came to the conclusion that it had died, probably swept away by the river. At the time they were unsure whether it was a fox or a dog, and it was only on reading about the cubs that they became convinced that it had been a rare albino fox.

Conservationist, Mr Edgar de Vries, said it seemed very likely this would have been the mother of the cubs he'd investigated months ago. Since there have been no sightings of her he assumed she was either dead or had moved on.

Dead or moved on.

If only Katie knew. If she could just find the vixen's body. She'd be devastated, she'd cry buckets, but then she too would be able to move on. Or rather, move back to London; there wasn't much more she had to do at the house, and it was time to get on with her real life. But if anyone had shot, or snared, or battered to death the vixen, they wouldn't have left her body there to rot or be eaten by crows. No way. They'd have taken it, that's for sure.

Katie remembers a trip with the family, another holiday on Exmoor, another of those grey, rainy summer days when everyone – even the adults – is bored and desperate for something to do. She'd been about six years old. An aunt had been flicking through a guidebook, found mention of a museum up on the moors that sounded vaguely interesting, so everyone had grabbed plastic macs and umbrellas and piled into the cars.

From the moment they stepped into the dusty damp smelling room Katie had gone quiet. She'd taken hold of her father's hand. They'd filed past glass cabinets full of what she at first took to be toys: kittens wearing frocks, little trousers and hats, kittens sitting at tables or playing tennis, fluffy little creatures with dead glass eyes. Every now and again her father had lifted her up so she could see better.

"Aren't they cute?" he'd whispered. There was something about the place, an eerie stillness that made you keep your voice down and tiptoe. Like in church.

A guide, a middle-aged man with a completely bald head, had tagged along behind their little group, no doubt delighted to see some customers.

"Taxidermy was very popular with the Victorians, of course," he said. "People would have their pet dog or cat stuffed and mounted to keep under a glass dome as an ornament in the parlour."

He gave a big smile.

"Wild animals too. Things they'd shot or trapped. Though it took a skilled taxidermist to remove the flesh and bones if the skin had even the tiniest tear. And birds – everything from robins to eagles, hawks. Owls, of course. Owls were always very popular."

An uncle approached him, glanced at Katie then bent close to ask a question. The guide shook his head.

"The kittens? Oh no, I doubt they were killed specifically for use in the tableaux. Feral cats have always been a problem on farms, they still are. Breeding like – well, feral cats. There were no doubt plenty of little corpses available for the asking."

Katie can still feel it, the shock when she'd realised these were real kittens.

"Aren't they pretty?" the guide had said, bending close, pointing. "See that one with the straw hat and the basket of flowers?"

She turned, pressed her face into the nearest warm leg. Refused to look. Stuffed dead kittens, it was horrid. She'd kicked up such a fuss that she'd been taken out and made to sit in the car. Of course Andrew had been fascinated, wanted to stay behind and ask all sorts of questions.

She imagines her snow fox, stuffed, lifeless, displayed in the study of some stately home. No, she'd be much too valuable, too rare. More likely she'd be locked away in a safe, to be seen and admired by a privileged few.

Would she be given pink glass eyes?

One more week. Katie makes herself a promise. She'll go all out to find her for one more week. Seven days. Then she'll give up, switch off, go back to the city knowing she's done everything she possibly could.

In the end it's Guy who makes the impossible happen for her.

"Katie, talk to me," he says. "You did promise you'd let me be a listening ear, remember?"

He's called round, kept his finger on the doorbell until she had no choice but to open the door. As she does, he walks straight in.

"I have doughnuts," he adds, waving the bag at her. "You have coffee, I hope?"

Katie is tipsy. It's three twenty in the afternoon, a soft autumn day, the world outside a misty haze of bronze, rose, and purple heather, and Katie is indoors with the curtains pulled drinking vodka tonics. She's shattered from her early morning and evenings walks, climbing higher than she's ever been before, seeking out new places, her eyes sharp for a giveaway glimpse of white fur, which she never sees. And that's the worst thing of all: the sense of failure.

"Did I? I don't remember promising anything?" she says to his back as he heads for the kitchen, fills the kettle with water and then looks around for mugs. She follows him, reaches into the bag. The doughnuts are still warm, sugar getting under her finger nails. It's the first thing she's eaten all day and she finishes it quickly, digging into the grease-stained bag for another.

"OK. Here we go."

He links a finger through two mug handles, picks up the cake bag with his other hand, heads across to slump down onto the sofa. Katie follows him obediently.

"So? I'm waiting."

Katie is aware that she's about to say more than she should, that alcohol is loosening her tongue. Alcohol and disappointment and the feeling that she needs to share this with someone, someone who'll understand. Is Guy the one? She actually crosses her fingers, takes a deep breath.

"You know the white fox cubs that were killed, their story was in the paper?"

"I read it, yup."

"And you may remember I said I'd been watching a fox family?"

"Sure. When you came over, right?"

He stops munching, swallows.

"Was that them? You actually saw them?"

"The vixen – their mother – is white too. Obviously if she's spotted she's going to be shot. It's dangerous enough out there for your average fox, but one that's worth a lot of money…"

"A lot? Katie my sweet, that beauty'll be worth a small fortune."

He's sitting straighter now, all attention.

Has she made a mistake? Can anyone be trusted when money is involved? Guy seems to live comfortably so presumably he has enough. And he's not at all materialistic, not in the way her city friends are; replacing their kitchen and their car every year, buying things just to show they can afford to do so, things they certainly don't need and often don't even like.

But what does she really know about him?

"So. I was in the village the other day," Katie goes on. "I overheard a couple of women talking about a white fox, some story about an uncle who'd seen it from his window but by the time he'd got his gun and raced outside it had gone. No-one had believed him."

Anyway it's too late, her secret is out. She can't take back her words.

"Until now, that is. Now that there have been the couple of bits in the local paper. Soon everyone will be out there looking for her. Give it – what? – a week, two at the most and she'll be dead."

Guy sits back on the sofa.

"Christ" he says, running a hand over his head.

"I have to find her and catch her, Guy," Katie says quietly. "I've no idea how, but I have to do it. And soon. So? What d'you think?"

He sighs, gives a quick apologetic smile.

"Sweetheart, when I offered to help I was thinking more along the lines of talking through marital problems, or putting up shelves, or…"

"I've got no choice, Guy. She'll hate it and she'll hate me. But at least if I have her safe I can talk to people, conservationists, wildlife experts who'll maybe have some idea about what to do next."

He tips his mug to get the dregs.

"Katie, it's not easy, you know, catching a fox. Sure you can shoot or snare them, but to catch one alive…"

"But it's possible, isn't it? It can be done, can't it?"

"And then there's the small problem of actually finding her, of course."

Guy stands now, walks to the window. Katie is suddenly feeling very sober.

"I won't let her be stuffed and put on display, Guy. I can't. It's obscene, grotesque."

Somewhere her phone has started to ring. She ignores it, wishes she didn't need it, always going off at the wrong moment. It stops. After a bit Guy turns back to face her.

"There's one person who could do it. Possibly. He's the only person who'd stand a chance anyway."

Katie waits.

"Kevin."

She can't believe he said that.

"Kevin? You're not serious? Someone who works for the hunt, who ideas of bit of fun is to go cubbing, who thinks wild animals exist simply so that his…?"

She manages to stop herself.

"I know. I know how you feel, Katie. Then again, I've already told you he's not your average farmhand."

"No way."

"You won't find anyone else."

"Then she'll have to take her chances."

Guy comes back, sits beside her.

"Her chances aren't good, Katie. You said it yourself. Getting Kevin to help – if he will – at least tips things in her favour. Slightly."

"But he kills foxes," Katie mutters.

"You're right. But we'll ask him not to kill her, OK?"

"And you think he'd be prepared to have a go? Really?"

"Yes."

It feels as though someone has lit a match in a huge black cave: there's a tiny glimmer of hope.

"And you'd trust him to keep it a secret, between the three of us? Not to tell anyone else?"

"Sure. In case you didn't notice, he doesn't talk much anyway."

There's one thing puzzling Katie.

"But why, Guy? Why would he do such a thing for me?"

Guy gives her a long look, then stands, picks up his mug, scrunches up the doughnut bag.

"He wouldn't," he says as he heads out to the kitchen. "But he'd do it for me."


Though she'd like not to have to go into the village, Katie is always running out of something. She thinks if she lived here permanently she'd buy a huge freezer and go shopping once a month, or better still order on-line and get everything delivered. And she'd keep chickens, grow a few vegetables, and cut herself off from the rest of the world.

Meanwhile, she's in the village again, trailing up and down the mini market aisles, debating the nutritional value of a sad and yellowing lettuce that's come from Spain, some blotchy apples from New Zealand. Trouble is, it's them or nothing.

This time there's a different face behind the till, a skinny lad with a nose ring who doesn't even acknowledge she's there as he taps in her purchases. He's talking to the person behind her, another lad clutching a six pack of lager between heavily tattooed hands. Katie tries not to listen, why would she be interested in anything they have to chat about? But they're so close to her. And now an odd word or two catches her attention. There's a journalist who's been hanging around, says he's writing a feature on albino animals, is trying to track down the boys who killed the white fox cubs. He's willing to pay for a successful tip-off. Generously. He's left his card behind in case anyone can help, has any contacts.

"If only," nose ring mutters as he drops coins into Katie's hand. "The crap pay I get here, it's criminal."

Katie wonders if she's blushing. She feels as if she is. She can't wait to get back to the house.

There are two phone messages waiting for her.

One is from Ben. He says he's sorry he's been so hard to get hold of lately, things aren't going as well as they should be. Nothing to worry about. He says he's wondering if she's had any news about her fox. HER fox, she notes, can't help but smile. He says he does understand, and he'll try not to nag, it's just that he wants her back in his life. He'll do his very best to get down to Devon soon because they really, really need to talk.

The other is from Guy.

"I've spoken to Kevin. He's already onto it. There's this eccentric old biddy lives out towards the top, close to the moors, keeps all sorts of animals. She's been losing chickens over the last couple of weeks to what she says is a white dog. She's glimpsed it a couple of times, says it seems to have a limp. She's asked Kevin if he'll go out there and shoot it. If it is your fox he says he'll try and trap it instead. No guarantees, of course. Hey, who knows, it may even be a white dog!"

It's not, Katie is sure. She knows, deep down inside. It's her fox.

Instead of the excitement she'd have expected, it's relief that she feels. Overwhelming relief. Everything is going to be alright.

She goes out to the shed. It's almost dark now, but she takes the torch. She wants to get started clearing things, throwing out as much as possible. When she goes to the skip tomorrow she'll stop off in Barnstaple and buy one of those big metal dog cages. She hates the thought of keeping a wild animal in a cage, it goes against everything she believes in. But at least she'll be safe.

# THIRTEEN

*You were absolutely petrified, weren't you?*

*Pressing yourself against the back of the cage as if convinced you could disappear through it if you just pushed that bit harder. And so small. And thin. You'd definitely lost weight since I last saw you. Kevin said the old lady was right and that you were limping, most likely because of an infection in an old wound, from a fight or a shotgun possibly. That was probably why you were going for easy pickings rather than hunting. even though it was riskier. Not that there's much left to hunt anyway. The rabbits haven't come back. They won't, for years. If ever. The few that somehow built up an immunity are picked off by birds of prey the moment they put their twitchy little noses above ground.*

*Even so it took nearly ten days for you to be brave (or desperate?) enough to go into the trap. I was giving up hope. The old lady was getting tetchier by the minute, saying she didn't care whether Kevin shot you, caught you or kissed you to death, she just wanted you gone. You stole from her again that week, which didn't help. You ignored the trap with its gift of fresh meat, and killed two more of her pedigree flock, all of which have names. I suggested to Guy that I offer to pay for them but he said no. It would be suspicious, and anyway, she might choose to live like a penniless hermit but she's loaded. I said I'd like to pay Kevin for his help and* he'd shrugged, said that was between me and Kevin. Trouble is, I can hardly bring myself to speak to him. He's given me the one thing I most wanted in the world, and yet still I hate him.

It's a bizarre situation.

Kevin caught you for me, volunteering his time, his patience, risking getting bitten (and laughed at, for sure, if any of his mates knew what he was up to... or worse, if they knew what you were worth!) Then he brought you here, carefully transferred you into the cage I had ready with straw and water. I said it was the biggest I could get, more like a run, but I could see he disapproved.

He gave me advice. To leave you alone, let you settle. To get one of those small plastic carriers people use for their pets and tuck it at the back of the cage so that you've got a bolt-hole, somewhere you can hide yourself right away from prying eyes. My prying eyes, he meant. And he was right, he understood you. You use it all the time.

To somehow get hold of some antibiotics for that infection. He thought it unlikely any local vet would let me have them without seeing you, and that I might do better through London contacts. Or possibly I could get some from a doctor instead, or maybe already had some, tucked away and forgotten in a bathroom cabinet?

He even presented me with a dead magpie that he'd spotted alongside the main road, one wing flapping sadly as he held it out. You'd like it, he said. He said at the *hunt kennels they have plenty of meat: road kill people bring them, diseased livestock that can't go into the food chain, surplus calves, shot because it costs more to feed them than a farmer will get when he comes to sell them, which doesn't make sense to me. I can get as much meat as you want, Kevin said. Just ask. When I said don't worry, I'll buy what I need from the butchers, he'd given a single nod.*

*It was then that he'd said there was one other thing he needed to point out, and briefly he'd actually lifted his eyes to mine, though only for seconds – I'd already noticed how his gaze is always sliding off to one side or the other, though whether it's because he's shy or shifty I'm not sure. Anyway, he said he has no idea what my plans are, but that I mustn't keep you caged for too long. You're a wild creature. You'll die. Before I could stop myself I said not as quickly as you'd die if I released you. You'd be shot, or torn to shreds by dogs, or caught in one of the snares that are everywhere, chewing your foot off and then limping away to die of gangrene or blood loss. That shut him up. He shrugged, then jumped back into his van, started the engine, leant out of the window.*

*"And don't give her a name," he said.*

*Had he been reading my mind? How else can I talk to you?*

*"We only give names to the ones we're going to keep round 'ere. Means you own 'em. You don't own her. Never will."*

*As he pulled away. I called out thank you but I don't think he heard me.*

*Why do I hate him so much? And the people he works for, the people he mixes with? Why do I suddenly feel this need to stand up for the rights of all living creatures when, let's face it, up until now my only contact with animals has been when I grill or stir-fry bits of them?*

*At the same time I'm so grateful to him for what he's done, I have no idea where to begin to thank him. It's too enormous, my gratitude. Words aren't enough.*

*Talk about being screwed up.*

*And of course he's absolutely right. Andrew is going to help, he's promised. He has connections. He's going to put the word out, see if we can't find you somewhere to live where you can be both free and safe, or at least safer than you are here. Not with a collector, of course. Not in a zoo, definitely not in a zoo.*

*Be patient. We'll find the right place.*

*Meanwhile, I wish you weren't so scared of me. It's natural, but I hate to see it. I remember those days when I sat beneath the trees with you and your cubs, and you'd yawn and lie down and stretch out with your head across your paws, eyes almost closed, not quite but almost. Relaxed. Trusting.*

*Now you won't even eat in front of me, will you? I open the cage door a fraction, slide in a chunk of meat and drop it onto the floor, then I retreat to the back of the shed and I wait. Mostly you won't even come out of the little carrier. If you're out of it, you stay at the back of the cage. You look at the food, and at me, and back at the food, and you refuse to move. I've only to go indoors for a few minutes and next time I check the food has gone so I know you want it, that you're probably ravenous, but you won't eat if I'm there. At least you are eating, I suppose. That's the important thing.*

*I'm amazed at how white your fur is, even in the dim light inside the shed. It's luminous. And longer than I realised. It looks very soft too though of course I haven't touched it. What would you do if I tried? Back away? Snarl? Bite me?*

*I like to think you'd let me, but I doubt it. Maybe, one day.*

*Sometimes, when I'm with you, I try to imagine what people would think if they saw me now, London people, people I've worked with, worked out with at the gym, people who know me as a woman who dresses stylishly, would never as much as open the front door without touching up her perfume. Here I stand with my hair like a frizzy wig, no makeup, wearing one of Ben's old sweaters and jeans with mud and God knows what else on the knees, that won't zip up properly because of my new eating plan of doughnuts, toast and wine. And I don't care. That's the thing that would shock them. It shocks me. And it's not a negative thing, like when you give up. It's a positive thing, like when you discover you don't need to do something any more, you've broken free. How comes I've changed so much in such a short time?*

*And is it a good thing? Or bad?*

## FOURTEEN

Katie would have been pleased to see Ben even if he'd been empty handed. But when, from the back of the car, he produces gifts she's delighted. As well as a box full of food goodies there's an ostentatiously large bunch of yellow and white flowers from her favourite florist where they wrap them in brown paper and tie them with string, and somehow make them look as if they cost a small fortune, which they do.

"And…"

He rummages around in his jacket pocket.

"… antibiotics."

"Fantastic. How did you manage to get them?"

Katie snatches the little brown bottle from his hand.

"Don't ask."

"From a vet?"

He gives her a look as he peels off his jacket.

"It's freezing in here. Why don't you put some heating on?"

"Because there isn't any. Remember? Turn on the oven and open the door. So where did you get them?"

"Katie, I'm sworn to secrecy."

"Come on. Tell."

"OK, this guy I know, his dog had just started a course of antibiotics, but he didn't need them any more."

"So the dog's alright now?"

"No. Dead. He got run over. The guy was devastated."

Ben gives a shrug. He's pleased with himself.

"That's sad," she says

"Isn't it?"

Ben rubs his hands together.

"So when am I going to get to see this freak of yours?"

"Later. I feed her in the evening. I'll stuff a pill in with the mince."

"Mince?"

"She needs building up."

"As long as it's not our dinner she's having."

Dinner; she hasn't even thought about a meal yet. Food is way down her list of priorities. Of course Ben will want regular feeding for the few days he's here, so she's going to have to focus her mind.

"I thought maybe pasta at the pub tonight?" she says.

Ben is on the phone again. Katie is beginning to hate that Mozart ringtone. She suggested he switches it off, lets it take messages for a bit, but he says he can't, might be something important. Katie thought one of the reasons he'd come down was so that they could talk. How can they do that when he's forever pacing back and forth muttering into the mobile that seems to be permanently attached to his ear?

"If you're going to spend the whole time on the phone you might as well not be here," she says. Even to her it sounds like she's whining.

"Give me a break, Katie. It's a complicated job."

"All your jobs are complicated."

"Not like this. A grown-up architect would help instead of a sulky little girl."

"The architect's a woman?"

"Anyone can come up with stunning concepts. The skill is in coming up with ones that'll work without bankrupting everyone involved."

"And you think women…"

"For God's sake, it's nothing to do with her being a woman. It's because she's crap at her job."

It's later and yet still he's wound up, a scowl on his face. She should be sympathetic but instead his mood is catching.

His phone starts again. It's lying on the kitchen table next to a cut glass dish of blackberries she'd picked this morning, before he was awake. He glances at it. She doesn't say anything. He turns away then, unable to stop himself, snatches it up. After just a few words he closes it, drops it back on the table.

"Have you worked with her before?"

"Anita Rogers? No. And I won't bloody work with her again."

"Is she young? Attractive? I mean… well…"

Katie has no idea why she asked him that. It's irrelevant. She's never had any doubts about him and other women. And if it's because he's alone up there in London then that's her fault anyway, her decision to be here. She feels herself flush.

Ben crosses to the open doorway and stares out, hands shoved deep into his pockets. The late autumn air has a fusty smell of mushrooms about it. Katie has found a number of different varieties growing in damp, dark corners of the garden, out of the sides of logs and even living trees. She hasn't dared eat any of them.

After some minutes he comes back into the room.

"Katie, it really is time you came back to London. I don't know what's going on in your mind, but you're worrying me."

"I will. But I can't until I get the fox sorted. I'm going to have to…"

Mozart again. This time both of them look at the phone.

"Leave it, let it ring," she says quietly, knowing there's no way he'll be able to.

"I'd better just…"

"Ben, please."

"It could be about an order that's gone missing."

Before he can move Katie snatches up the phone and throws it at the wall, following it with the dish of fruit. There's glass and blackberries everywhere. From under a chair, Mozart plays on. She can feel Ben's eyes on her back as she hurries from the room.

When Guy turns up late afternoon with a bulging black plastic bag and drops it on her doorstep Katie feels a moment of panic. She has no idea what's inside, but she's sure she's not going to like it.

"I won't come in," he says. "Here, from Kevin. He got them from a chicken farm, said your fox'll be needing feathers and feet and stuff to keep her digestion working properly. You've got a freezer, haven't you?"

"A small one."

"Just dump what won't fit in," he says, opening the truck door. "As far away as possible, I'd suggest."

 He climbs in.

"I'll call you."

She stands there on the gravel, waiting until he's out of sight before reluctantly untying the string and peering inside. It could be a bag of small balls of bright yellow wool. It isn't. It's crammed full of dead chicks. She shuts it quickly. There's no way she's going to be able to handle them, it's too revolting and too sad. Anyway, the fox is doing fine on mince. She'll get Ben to offload them somewhere on his drive back to London. She lugs the bag across to the shed, tucks it just inside the door. The contents settle as she lowers it to the ground, and for one chilling moment she thinks she hears a chirp coming from deep inside it.

So does the vixen who's lying stretched out along the back of the cage. Her head shoots up, ears erect.

"You're not having them so forget it!" Katie says, more loudly than she intends. The vixen hunches back into the shadows. As she crosses the yard in the thickening dusk Katie's aware of blackbirds squabbling in the bushes, jostling for the best positions for the night. Usually they make her smile. Today she wants to shout shut up.

"I've been feeding the fox," Ben comes in carrying a small cardboard box, puts it by the door as he takes off his bodywarmer.

He washes his hands by the kitchen sink, shakes them dry.

"What with?"

"The chicks. She likes them. When I dropped one in for her she shook it and growled. Reminded me of a terrier I had once. He'd kill anything. Loved him to bits."

"I wasn't intending to give them to her."

"Why not?"

"Because…" Because what? The only reason is that Katie doesn't want to handle the tiny bundles with their dead eyes and stiff legs and curled up feet, doesn't want to be reminded where they come from, that they're only babies. OK, she doesn't want to face reality.

"They must be better for her than the stuff you buy. More natural anyway."

"And how comes you're such an expert all of a sudden?"

Ben shrugs. Since her outburst he seems to be trying not to upset her. He's even – a couple of times – let the phone take messages. She's aware of him watching her out of the corner of his eye.

"Did you see that bit about albinos in the local rag?" he says.

"I haven't had time to look at it yet."

"It's interesting."

He finds it, opens the page, sits at the table and reads to her as she chops vegetables for a bean stew. The cooler evenings always make her fancy thick, warming stews.

"OK, it's an inherited condition that affects pigmentation... etc. OK. Recorded cases include blackbirds, robins, jackdaws, pythons, badgers, giraffes, tigers. There was a white hind on the Quantocks, found in a ditch, probably killed by a poacher. Snowflake, an albino gorilla lived in Barcelona zoo, was very bad tempered. Can you blame her? Albino hedgehogs are common."

"And foxes?"

Ben glances up.

"Yes. Guess it was your girl that gave them the idea for the article. It talks about the cubs killed locally. And the vixen too."

He hesitates.

"It says there's a theory that she might still be in the area."

Which is just what Katie doesn't want to have to think about. What if people start asking questions? Sooner or later someone is going to track her down. And then what?

A chirping sound makes them both jump.

"Shit. I forgot," He goes and picks up the box, peering inside. "This one is still alive."

Together they look at the chick half hidden by straw. When Katie tentatively touches an outstretched leg it twitches.

"Poor mite. It doesn't look very good, does it?"

"Nor would you if you'd been gassed and then squashed into a bag with a lot of your dead mates."

"I can't believe it's survived."

"He. It'll be a he."

Kate makes up her mind.

"Right. I'll get some water. And what might he eat? Bread crumbs?"

Another chirp. At least he hasn't given up, not yet.

Katie turns away.

"So are you going to pour us some wine then?" she says. "Unless you can find anything stronger."

She checks the box before she goes to bed. The crumbs haven't been touched. The chick is on its side, dead.

*Did you sense that I was getting anxious? Was I passing it on to you, my feeling of a net closing in, and decisions having to be made, none of the options appealing? None of them right. Was that why you snapped at me?*

*That morning I'd decided I was being ridiculous about the chicks, so I took a couple of the soft feathery balls out of the bag and dropped them in for you. You were on them in an instant, a few quick crunches and they were gone. I held the next one out and eventually – after a very long pause during which you debated the wisdom of coming closer – you actually took it from my hand. Snatched it from my hand anyway.*

*I was taking liberties, I understand that. I was in the wrong. But I can't tell you the thrill it gave me, winning your trust at last. Of course, when I dropped that one accidentally I should have left it. How could you understand I was only going to pick it up for you? You're a wild creature and you thought I was after your food. We both reached for it at the same moment. You snapped.*

*You caught me on the outside of my right hand, the little finger and down the side. It was just a small wound, not deep, but your teeth were sharp as a razor and it bled for quite a while. I watched the blood ooze and then trickle down as far as my wrist. I forgave you. It felt more like an initiation ceremony than anything else.*

*I should have known, of course. I should have realised it was a bad omen.*

The slight toothache Katie has had for weeks is getting worse. And they've run out of milk. Again. It goes so quickly when Ben is there; she's never known anyone drink so much tea. After feeding the fox she decides to drive into the village. It's early but the mini market should be open and she's sure she's seen paracetamol on a shelf behind the till. She'll be back before Ben is awake.

It's even quieter than usual in the village, the few late season holidaymakers dawdling over their fried breakfasts, children crouched in front of the TV, still not ready for school. Though the bakery isn't yet open the smell of warm bread wafting on the cool, misty air is irresistible. Katie peers through the door and eventually a young girl comes over and unlocks it, says they'll be opening soon anyway, so come in. She buys a brown, crusty loaf with seeds in it, then notices the cheese and onion baps and gets half a dozen (she can freeze what they don't eat).

In the mini market Patrice is painting her fingernails green. She looks up, almost smiles.

"Been reading about this white fox, have you?" she says as she drops Katie's few purchases into a carrier. Katie nods, sorts through her change.

"Would have thought you might have seen it, you living out there on the edge of the moor?"

"No such luck," Katie says, scooping her bag off the counter. "Nearly forgot. Some paracetamol too please."

She feels a moment of panic. Why did Patrice say that? Does she know something? But she can't possibly. She was just making small talk.

Once she's back in the car and on the road the feeling fades. Katie switches on the radio, flicks through the stations, settles for Stevie Wonder. She takes the familiar curves in the road steadily, tapping her injured hand on the wheel, aware of a slight soreness, nothing worse. She notices with surprise that the hedges on either side are beginning to thin, yet she still thinks of it as late summer.

She glances at her watch; Ben will be up by now, hopefully making coffee with the fresh ground he brought down with him.

As the deer steps out in front of the car she presses lightly on the brake, and the animal is safely across in a couple of bounds, and through a gap in the hedge. She thinks how sleek and shiny and new it looked.

She sees the second one too late, its face turned towards her, unperturbed, unaware – or aware too late – that it is about to be hit, thrown up onto the bonnet where it will smash against the windscreen and then slide off to one side and be tossed back into the hedge.

Katie slams on the brakes, skids briefly before coming to a halt.

At first all she can hear is her heart thumping. Then she hears the familiar tic-tic-tic that she's learnt to recognise as a robin.

She doesn't want to get out of the car. She wants to turn the clock back five minutes and not have this happening. She wants to be still in bed with Ben's warm body beside her. She wants to be back in London, never having come to Exmoor. She wants just to be somewhere else.

She takes a deep breath, opens the door of the car, steps out. The deer is now on the side of the tarmac, though when she approaches it tries desperately to get up onto its front legs and drag itself away. One of its back legs is shattered, white bone sticking out from the flesh in a couple of places. Along the side of the animal's body there is a huge gash from which blood is seeping, and maybe something else, Katie can't bear to look. The only sound is the robin's agitated call which is getting faster; then with a flurry it's gone.

"I'm so sorry," she whispers. "I didn't see you."

The deer falls back, panting, eyes rolling. Katie thinks she's going to be sick. She leans against the side of the car, puts her head down. The world spins, then steadies. When she looks up the deer is still watching her, and as she takes a few steps again it starts to struggle, its movements frantic but pointless.

It's going to die, there's no way it can survive such injuries. Katie thinks she should kill it, stop the suffering, the look of accusation in its soft eyes, but what can she do? Hit it with something? She looks around for a rock or a stick, knowing there's no way she could do it even if she found a weapon. Drive back over it? But it's lying too close to the hedge, she'd have to pull it out into the middle of the road. She can't do it. If only someone would come. She glances around at the now familiar landscape, at the fields, hedges, the road a ribbon of tarmac. She's never once met anyone on it, been grateful as it's so narrow.

She'll have to go and get help.

Shaking, she gets back in the car, praying it will start, aware that she shouldn't be driving with such a badly cracked windscreen, but what choice does she have? The engine kicks in. Slowly she drives the short distance back to the house.

Ben is in the kitchen.

"Ben, I've hit a deer and it's… it's a mess, blood and bone…we need to find a vet, there must be…"

Katie feels the hysteria bubbling up even as Ben grips her upper arms, forces her to sit, makes her look at him, makes her tell him slowly and clearly what happened and where it happened.

"Doesn't sound like a vet will be able to do much," he says.

"No, to put it to sleep. To kill it. If you could see it, Ben, it's in agony…"

His face is now as ashen as hers. He stands up, turns away, runs his fingers through his still spiky hair.

"OK," he says, turning back to her. "You stay here."

"I'll come with you."

"Katie, I know the spot you mean. I'll go alone."

"But you need me to…"

"I need you to make a strong coffee, and then drink it. I won't be long."

Katie puts her head down on the table, wraps her arms around it, closes her eyes. She hears him running upstairs, then coming down and crunching across the gravel to his car. The door slams. He's gone. She wants to do as he says and make coffee but she can't move. She feels exhausted, empty.

It seems like no time and he's back.

He stands in the doorway looking as though he's shrunk, as though suddenly his clothes are too big for him. He rests the gun against the wall.

"What happened? Did you…?"

He nods, checks the kettle for water and switches it on. Katie is stunned. She never would have thought he could do that, shoot a beautiful young animal. It's what people around here would do, of course, Guy and Kevin, farmers, hunters, bored teenagers. Without a second thought. But Ben, a man with a sentimental streak as big as a football pitch? A man who rescues mice from cats, for God's sake?

She hates him for it. Yet she's proud of him too. And relieved.

"Ben," she says, moving closer but not touching him. "I'm sorry, that must have been awful for you. I don't know how you could… it was such a pretty creature, so alive one moment and then…"

He takes two mugs from the draining rack.

"It's in the car boot," he says. "Your friend Guy could probably sell it to a pub, or give it to the hunt for the dogs. Or of course there's the fox."

Her response is instant. "I'd like to bury it here, in the garden. Can we?"

Ben nods again. She realises he doesn't want to talk, and neither does she. She thinks of the warm bread, the cheese and onion baps still in the car, going to waste.

It's drizzling by the time they find a place in the garden suitable for burying such a large animal. Katie helps clear some of the tangled undergrowth, but Ben insists she leaves the digging to him. Watching through the window she can see that he's getting soaked and that the digging is hard work, harder than he'd expected, but he won't stop, not even for a short break. She takes him water and he downs it in one go. It's as though he's punishing himself.

She takes a throw off the sofa to wrap the deer in. Ben won't let her look at it again. He says it's a male, probably a youngster.

Next he rings a garage in Barnstaple who promise to get someone along straight away to replace the windscreen, check the car over. He says accidents involving deer are on the increase. If you ask him, the reason is that since the hunting ban their numbers are going up and up. Tell your wife not to upset herself about what happened, he says. She's done us all a favour.

Ben passes on the message.

"Too many rabbits, too many deer," Katie says. "This is the countryside, isn't it? Like, the place where animals are meant to live?"

Ben shakes his head but doesn't reply. Then he says he must be off.

"So early? But Ben, you look exhausted. And you haven't eaten all day."

"I'm alright."

"At least leave it an hour or two."

"It's better I go now, Katie."

She has to ask him. "Are you angry with me?"

"Why would I be?"

"I don't know. Because of the deer?"

"It was an accident. They happen."

"But you seem to always be…"

"Katie, love, I'm sorry, I really haven't got time for this."

He's changing into dry clothes, throwing things into his bag, anxious to go. Katie sits on the bed, knees drawn up, watching him.

"I thought we were going to talk," she says quietly. "About us, the future. I thought that was one of the reasons you came down."

Ben snaps the clips on his overnight bag. He looks straight at her. There's a look of defeat in his eyes.

"What us, Katie? What future? Right now it feels as though we've stalled. There's no point in trying to get things started again until you come back to London, and you've obviously got absolutely no intention of doing that. Not yet anyway. So what's there to talk about?"

"That's unfair."

"Look, Katie love, I've been thinking. Why don't I just leave you alone for a bit, let you sort yourself out? With so many problems at work it's not easy for me to get away at the moment, and when I do it doesn't seem to accomplish much…"

So he's opting out, abandoning her.

"Fine," she says. "That's fine with me."

Ben leaves shortly afterwards. Before he goes he tells her he's sorry, but she doesn't know what for.

Katie lies awake for a long time thinking about the deer. She thinks too about the one that got away. Was it the mother? A brother or sister? How was it managing on its own? And why oh why hadn't she stopped completely when it crossed instead of driving on?

Next morning she's cleaning out the fox's cage when she hears the phone going through the open front door. She ignores it. As usual the fox has tucked herself away in the smaller carrier, licking her mouth nervously, which saddens Katie but at the same time makes her job so much easier. Quickly she sweeps out the soiled straw, replaces it with fresh, tops up the water bowl. She's got used to the strong, distinctive smell that seems to permeate everything. In fact, she's beginning to like it. She enjoys cleaning the cage too; it's something she can do to help make life more tolerable for her reluctant guest. Even though Kevin said foxes are not particularly into cleanliness, not like badgers who are constantly tidying up their setts.

What did he know about her snow fox?

She doesn't get around to checking her phone until later, convinced it was Ben who rang. The message is actually from Andrew who, as usual, is speaking much too fast, and she has to listen to it half a dozen times before it sinks in.

"Katie, am I bloody brilliant, or what? That eco-journalist I told you about, Jessica Bourne, remember? She's made contact with someone who'll take your fox. He sounds perfect, a big-name serious conservationist, got a great reputation - seems everyone in the business is full of praise - and three hundred acres of land, and he'd be able to… hold on, this is ridiculous. Ring me and I'll tell you everything. Soon as you can, OK?"

WINTER

# FIFTEEN

Katie takes a taxi from Paddington, concerned she doesn't have enough time to get to her appointment by underground. It would only take one of the all too frequent signal failures somewhere along the line, a delay of fifteen minutes, and she'd be late. Mr Neru has done her an enormous favour, fitting her in at the last minute, so his receptionist stressed. Nowadays Mr Neru is one of the most popular dentists in town. Footballers, celebrities go to him. Miss your slot and who knows when you'll get another chance to see him. Besides, Katie really can't face the underground. She's never much liked it, with its stark lighting and stale air, crowds swarming up and down like ants. Now, having got used to being surrounded by open moorland, even the thought of it makes her hands sweat.

"Here we are."

The driver's voice is distorted by the barrier. She puts the money onto a tray that spins round, then back round with her change. Everyone is so nervous, she thinks. Probably with good reason.

Her visit to the dentist isn't as bad as she expects. A broken filling is the cause of the toothache that's been nagging for weeks now. Mr. Neru removes it, replaces it with a new one, and she's impressed by machinery that quietly whirrs and buzzes and sprays her with a fine fountain of water, nothing like the clunky implements of torture she'd so dreaded when she was a child. He's given her an injection and half her face is numb. As she tries to smile her thanks to the receptionist, the girl beckons her close and whispers to check in the mirror, and when she does she finds a delicate trickle of blood emerging from the corner of her mouth, making her look like a vampire.

Out again on the grey, drizzly early afternoon street, she's unsure what to do next. Having decided she wouldn't feel like travelling after her treatment she's arranged to stay in London overnight. Ben, bless him, offered to take her place in Devon and look after the fox. Then tomorrow she'll get the train to Taunton, he'll meet her and drop her back at the house before he drives up to London for a late meeting.

It isn't just that the fox needs feeding. It's having someone there – and lights on and a car outside – so that the place looks occupied. Though Katie has never actually seen anyone hanging around, she's sure she's heard voices, more than once. It could be kids, of course. But what if it's snoopers? Everyone is talking about the fox now. And after Patrice's comment, Katie can't help but worry. Whenever she leaves the house she covers the cage with a blanket and padlocks the shed door.

Soon the fox will be gone, right away from the area, safe at last. And no longer her responsibility. Katie's counting the days. Six to go. She tells herself she's looking forward to it all being over, this drama, wishes she'd never got involved but can't see that she had any choice. She's lying of course. Even those moments when she gets down onto the dirty floor and stretches out alongside the cage – the two of them only feet apart – watching the gentle rise and fall of the sleeping fox's body, make her tingle. Often she adjusts her breathing to match that of the fox. Her fox.

Her fox without a name. Katie's thought about calling her Precious or Snowy or Daisy, or something, but it seems wrong: it implies ownership. This beautiful wild being may be confined at the moment but she's a free spirit, she always will be. She must be.

Clipping her way along the hard grey pavement feels strange, dazzling with so much of everything: traffic, shops, bright lights, bustle. The stream of planes droning overhead surprises her; she'd forgotten how low they flew as they came into Heathrow. And how noisy they were. No-one even looks up though, oblivious to the world around them as they march along, many of them looking at their phones as they weave their way through obstacles, none of them walking at her slow pace. Most don't even glance at a blank eyed young man sitting on the pavement wrapped in a duvet, propped against his knees a piece of cardboard. HELP ME GET TO MY DEAR MUMS FUNERAL TOMORROW, it says. Katie's gone past but stops, is trying to find some coins when she hears a mobile phone ringing. The young man shuffles around beneath the duvet. Next thing he's chattering and laughing as he clambers to his feet, scoops up his things and hurries off, still talking.

Suddenly Katie feels an overwhelming desire to go home. She gets a taxi again and once settled on the slippery back seat, gets out her mobile. There's no answer. Unusual for Andrew to have it switched off. She doesn't leave a message

By evening she feels as if she's never been away. At first the house had struck her as luxurious but unlived in, unloved. Then she recalled Ben saying he'd organised for a cleaner to come in, which explained a lot. Now she's scattered her things around, her shoes are in the middle of the floor, there's music playing and she's opened some wine. And it's her home again. As she tries Andrew's mobile once more she checks herself in the mirror. Her face looks slightly swollen on one side – probably from where she bit the inside of her cheek – but apart from that she looks fine. She pushes her hair back then lets it fall forwards again. She's beginning to like it longer.

Still no answer. This time she leaves a message.

When he returns the call it's getting close to midnight. "Katie, I'm on my way home. What's wrong?"

"Nothing. I'm in London and I thought we might…"

"Why didn't you say you were coming up?"

"I didn't know. Dental emergency."

She can hear the frustration in his voice. She feels it too. A pause then he laughs.

"OK, here's an idea."

It's the first time they've met at a 24-hour supermarket. It's the first time she's been in one so late at night, and she's amazed to see so many people walking around filling their baskets.

Andrew buys some cans of Coke, a jumbo pack of crisps.

"And now?"

"This way."

He leads her towards the café area at the far end which is closed, a rope across the entrance, chairs on the tables. The floor is wet and smells of disinfectant, but there's no-one around.

"By the window, I think, don't you?"

They climb over the rope, take down a couple of chairs.

"It's nice here," Katie says, meaning it. At least it's warm and private. She pulls the tag off her Coke, takes a swig. Through the window she can see people going past, still, at this hour on a weekday. If anything the traffic seems even heavier than it had been earlier.

"Thanks for putting me onto Jessica," she says.

"Is it all sorted?"

"Almost. Fingers crossed. I'll be relieved when it's over. So will Ben. He thinks I'm obsessed."

Andrew lifts an eyebrow.

"OK, I am obsessed."

She opens the crisps, takes a handful.

"I can't help it. I hate their attitude to wildlife down there. It's beautiful countryside but there are some ugly things going on, especially where animals are concerned. Unless they can be eaten or chased or used for target practice they're… I don't know. What's it to do with me anyway? I'm just visiting."

Andrew glances around and then pulls a miniature bottle of rum from his pocket, tips half of it into her can, the rest into his.

"Don't think urban foxes do much better," he says. "There are so many of them now. Too many. There was this news item, this woman had a whole family shot – said they'd attacked her cat or something. Fair enough. But she made sure to film the massacre and now there's a website you can go to and watch the foxes being dispatched. Punished. Whatever."

"That's sick."

She sips her drink, pulls a face, sips again.

Outside, two boys – hardly in their teens – are racing past, notice them and bang on the glass, shouting and jeering. Katie looks away.

"I don't remember seeing any foxes when we used to go down to Exmoor, do you?" she says.

Andrew laughs.

"I had other things on my mind. So did you. Especially that last summer."

Katie hesitates.

"We've never really talked about it, have we?" she says.

"What's there to be said?"

"Do you never even think about it?"

Andrew shrugs. "Sometimes. I try not to otherwise I'd be forever trying to manoeuvre you into dark corners."

"It was illegal, what you did, you realise that? I was barely fifteen."

"But willing. You can't deny it."

Katie thinks back to the first time, one of those chilly summer evenings.

"Not at first I wasn't. You frightened me. We'd been swimming in the sea, d'you remember? I couldn't stop shivering. You wrapped a towel round me and said to take off my wet costume, and then you spread your towel on the sand between the rocks and said come and sit down. And then you went for it."

Katie had looked away as he took his trunks off. When he laid himself on top of her she'd felt she couldn't breathe, and as he'd shuffled and grunted she'd actually started to push him away, not sure whether to laugh or cry out. It had hurt, when he'd entered her, but it was exciting too. And afterwards, when he'd got his breath back, and had started to run his cold, slim fingers over the small mounds that were her breasts, and then down between her legs, she hadn't wanted him to stop.

"It was a good summer, that one," Andrew says.

"It was."

She gives a small laugh.

"We were at it all the time."

"In the barn, on the beach, on walks. I'm surprised no-one got suspicious, us going off together on any excuse, staying away for hours."

"Coming back exhausted."

"Coming back scratched to buggery by the gorse," Andrew says. "There was that dell we found, remember? Sandy ground, overhanging trees, a ring of gorse bushes."

"I still think of you when I smell gorse," Katie says.

They couldn't get enough of each other, not just having sex but exploring each other's bodies, from the souls of their feet to the tip of their ears. They'd used their hands and their lips and their tongues, never embarrassed, amazed by the things they were discovering, about themselves as well as each other. And the sounds, especially the sounds: the little gasps, the gurgles, the sound of their bodies sucking at each other.

"It was sheer luck I didn't get pregnant," Katie says. Though afterwards – when they both went back to their respective lives in different towns and she missed him and craved his touch – she'd thought at least if she'd been pregnant they'd have been together again. No-one would have dared try to keep them apart.

It would, of course, have been a disaster. Unthinkable on so many levels.

The following spring his father had died and he and his mother didn't come to Exmoor. Katie had moped, kicked stones, not caring or unaware that she was worrying everyone.

And then he was at university and everything changed.

Now he runs his finger up and down her wrist.

"D'you ever fancy having a tumble, you and I? For old times sake?"

She's never sure if he's serious or not.

"No thanks," she says. "I'm happy enough with the memories. Besides, what about your bit on the side, the one you can't get enough of?"

"Ah, yes. In its dying stages, that particular relationship."

His smile holds a hint of regret.

"So Tess will have you back home evenings for a while?"

He nods.

"Poor Tess. She deserves better than you."

"So she tells me."

Another quick smile. He's still as infuriating as he always was.

They are both unaware they have company until he coughs.

Though he's trying to look officious, Katie thinks he can't be more than twenty-two, twenty-three, standing there in his dark shiny suit, a dazzling white shirt no doubt washed and ironed for him by a proud mum.

"I'm afraid you can't sit here," he says. The corner of his mouth twitches. "This area is closed."

"Come on, what harm are we doing?" Andrew says pleasantly.

A couple of shoppers slow down to watch. One, an elderly woman with wild grey hair and wrapped in a blanket, begins to titter. The young man clears his throat again.

"Sorry. It's against the rules."

"Promise we won't tell anyone if you don't."

"That's not the point."

Andrew stretches back in his chair.

"And the exact point is…?"

Katie recognises that look; he's a nasty little boy again, tying a can to a dog's tail, or blocking the path of a stream of ants. Waiting for the reaction.

"Come on, Andrew, it's time we went anyway."

She pushes back her chair, catches his sleeve and pulls him to his feet.

As they emerge into the cold night air a siren approaches, screams at them as it passes and then fades, the police on their way to some drama or other.

"Andrew," she says as they walk along, both looking out for a taxi. "You do trust this Jessica woman, don't you?"

"You're not back on that subject again, are you?"

"I mean, tell me again how you found her?"

"Through a guy I used to work with. Katie, all I can say is these people are experts, they believe in conservation and animals' rights, and if there is any way to give your fox a decent life, they'll know about it. No guarantees, I'm afraid."

"She sounds genuine enough, when we've spoken on the phone."

"There you go then." He steps back as a taxi draws into the curb beside them. "Let's share, shall we? I'll drop you off first."

He holds the door for her, gives a mock bow.

"Don't suppose you've thought any more about selling some of your foxy photos?"

"You don't give up, do you?" she says, laughing, but she doesn't answer his question.

She still can't understand. A fox is vermin unless it's white – a freak of nature, if she's honest - and then it's so valuable people are prepared to do just about anything to get it, and it has to be locked away for its own safety. Why can't all foxes be considered special? Or at least, why can't they all be left to get on with their lives?

Early the next morning Katie remembers she was going to go through her bank statements. She knows there are at least a couple of queries that need to be sorted: a bill she thought she'd already paid but doesn't seem to have, a direct debit problem. Ben said he'd put everything together in an envelope, but he didn't say where.

She's going to be late for her train if she doesn't hurry. In the hallway, already pulling on her coat, his words come back to her: not in an envelope, but a pink folder he'd received as part of a promotion. He couldn't believe any professionals worth their fees would choose pink for a mailing shot to men.

Should be easy enough to find.

His office desk, as usual, is a tip. She pushes papers aside. She tries a couple of drawers. Then, just as she's about to give up, she notices the small blue envelope. Not pink, obviously not the one she's looking for, so why does she open it? She doesn't at first. She holds it, turns it over, hesitates. And then she does.

Inside is a single photograph. It shows a woman with a small boy and seems to have been taken in a park. The woman is vaguely familiar; Katie has a good memory for faces. Didn't she work for a company Ben worked for some years back? As a secretary or assistant? She was Polish, went off to see her family and returned with bottles of mind-blowing vodka – wasn't there a bison on the label? – for everyone.

But it isn't the woman who holds Katie's attention. It's the boy. Round faced, he has light brown eyes framed by very long lashes, a hesitant smile that could be due to shyness, or to a stubborn determination not to smile. Beneath his short trousers his legs are a dazzling white.

She's seen a virtually identical photo of another small boy, a photo taken much longer ago. Glancing at the time, she stuffs the photo back into its envelope and slips it into her pocket. She'll give up on the pink envelope for now.

She catches the train, just, and collapses into her seat. For the first ten minutes she manages to resist getting the photo out again, but then the urge is too strong. And again she's reminded of the photo upstairs somewhere in an album, slightly faded now, but still clearly a photo of Ben.

What a coincidence, she thinks.

Whilst searching for something else he'd found her clinic appointment card, misinterpreted it and came to entirely the wrong conclusion. And they'd never quite got over it.

And now she'd done the same thing, and was in danger of jumping to a conclusion that was almost too incredible to believe. Incredible, unlikely, ridiculous.

But it could be true. She could be right.

That little boy could be Ben's son.

# SIXTEEN

Even though it's only mid-afternoon, all the cars have their lights on, their reflections on the wet road making Katie squint. It's one of those early winter days when dawn and dusk seem to merge and it hardly gets light at all. No wonder suicide rates peak, though imagine living somewhere like Iceland or the Arctic where there really is no daylight for months on end. Then, come summer, there's no night and insomnia is the problem, everyone getting baggy eyed and ratty with each other.

She couldn't think which was worse.

She's keeping her mind busy, keeping it distracted from the things that are happening in her life right now. Trying to keep herself sane.

She's taken the drive steadily, using the motorway whenever possible so as to avoid uneven surfaces or winding roads, only too aware of her precious cargo, not wanting to frighten her any more than was necessary. In fact, after some initial scuffling during which – Katie could see in her mirror – the plastic carrier box twisted and then moved half way along the back seat, everything had gone quiet. Katie likes to think of the fox curled up with her nose under her tail and sleeping, but probably she's frozen with fear. Wild animals can die of fear, can't they?

"Don't you dare," she mutters.

She's due to meet this Jessica Bourne and her colleague at the Michaelwood Service Station on the M5. It's a long drive from the house, from Devon, but she doesn't want them to know where she lives, nor where the fox was found, none of the details in fact, and Jessica agrees. There, the fox will be exchanged, and then driven on up north, up to Scotland, where her new life will start. Katie feels she's been in limbo waiting for this moment. Now it's almost here and she's relieved and grateful.

And yet. Letting her go is going to be a wrench. It feels like a betrayal, too. As though after tricking this wild creature into trusting her she's now just getting rid of her. Passing her on to a life where she's going to be cared for and admired, and safe at last. But no longer free.

Katie's going to miss her company too, she knows that.

Every morning when she quietly opens the shed door and watches the fox get to her feet, yawning, stretching like a dog, her fur such a sparkling white it looks unreal, Katie gets a thrill. Like a very mild electric shock.

With her gone, the house will be dead. Still, Katie's time in Exmoor will soon be over too, she'll be moving back to London. Or on to somewhere else? Right now she's not sure. She can't think.

One thing at a time.

As she slows, indicates left and pulls onto the slip road into the service station, a huge lorry edges alongside her, its wheels so close she could touch them, and she thinks again how dangerous roads are nowadays. Roads are one of the biggest destroyers of wildlife, she's read. Especially foxes. Wouldn't that be ironic, her snow fox ending up squashed flat by a juggernaut?

She parks where they have arranged to meet, in the furthest corner from the bright lights of the main building with its cafes, winking fruit machines and shops. There's only one other car there, an old Ford that looks as though it could be abandoned. Jessica will be in a plain red van. They have the use of a wildlife ambulance but don't want to draw any attention to the vehicle. The more anonymous the better.

Even they, it seems, are nervous, wary.

"See the trouble you're causing," Katie says, turning to look at the carrier. She can just about see some tufts of fur through the slots.

"You're worth it though," she adds. "You deserve a second chance. Or is it a third?"

She's half an hour early. She climbs out of the car to stretch her legs but has no intention of leaving it, or even letting it out of her sight. Once the exchange has been made she'll go and get a coffee before she starts the drive back. The wind is icy, gusts tug at her coat and hair, and she's pleased to get back to the warmth inside.

She switches on the interior light, gets out the photo again. Is it Ben's child? She can't believe it and yet it looks so much like him. And anyway, why would he have the photo in the first place? She still finds it hard to imagine him having an affair without her knowing. Of course he had plenty of opportunity: he was often away from home, had no set routine. And besides, Katie had her career too. Maybe all the signs were there and she'd just been too distracted to notice them. Maybe her distraction, her never being there were why he'd been tempted into an affair in the first place?

But no, she still found it impossible to believe. Deception wasn't in his nature.

She's remembered the woman's name. Marta. She thinks her surname is something like Nowak, can recall her joking about it being as common as Smith in Poland. So it would be easy to check. If not easy, possible.

Katie glances at the car clock. Twenty past four. They're twenty minutes late but it's not surprising. What is surprising is that anyone gets anywhere on time. Though she's trying hard not to keep the noise down, she switches on the radio and tunes into a local traffic report. There are major hold-ups at Junction 10 on the M6, emergency roadworks affecting rush hour traffic. Would they be coming that way? She realises that just as she didn't say where she was based, neither did Jessica. Secrecy seemed to be a major part of the arrangement, and with good reason. Yet now she isn't so sure. How much does she really know about these people? Is she doing the right thing? How the hell can she know?

When the red van comes towards her, pulls across and then reverses to park a few bays along from her, the relief she feels is like a warm shower. At last. She's getting herself in a state for nothing.

She'll give them a few minutes then she'll go across and introduce herself.

When the van door opens she reaches for the car door handle, then hesitates. A young boy jumps out followed by a slightly older one. Then from the back of the van come two more children, and a man. The driver emerges. It's a woman with very blonde hair and a loud voice, calling them all to stay with her, and that if anyone runs off they can find their own way home. The party heads towards the main building, one of the girls skipping ahead excitedly.

It's not Jessica.

Katie doesn't want to know the time. The later it gets the more worried she gets. But eventually she has to check. Five fifteen.

She has Jessica's mobile number somewhere. Why didn't she think of it before? And where the hell did she put her phone? Finally she finds it tucked in the folds of a road map. She doesn't want to give the impression she's getting impatient, but it would be good to know where they are, why they're so late. She dials.

"The number you are calling is unobtainable at the moment," says a voice that might have been real, might have been electronic. "Please try later."

Katie dials it again, more carefully, in case she got it wrong. The message is the same.

She'd like to go to the loo, she's desperate for a hot drink. But she doesn't dare leave the car.

There's movement in the back, long limbs trying to readjust. Poor creature. Katie had been concerned that the carrier was too cramped to keep the fox in for so long. She wishes she'd bought a larger one. She'd intended to but the week had passed, and she'd been thinking of other things. A poor excuse.

It's still very quiet up that end of the car park, most people reluctant to walk so far to the facilities. She switches off the light and the radio, and the doubts creep back in. There's a saying – Chinese, possibly? If you save someone's life you're responsible for it. Which makes her responsible for that creature in the back. And yet she's planning to just hand her over to a complete stranger. What if they have her killed and stuffed and sold to a Russian oligarch? Or sell her to a zoo? What if they use her as a breeding machine, mating her with a genetically suitable male so she'll produce more and more pretty white fox cubs they can sell at ridiculously inflated prices? And now she shudders: what if they use artificial insemination?

She reaches for a bottle of water, sips, balances it back on the seat beside her. And then notices the blue envelope poking out of her bag. She can't resist picking it up, holding it over her lap and shaking it. A flurry of pieces of paper, what once was a photograph. She'd got so tired of looking at it – of being angry, confused, hurt, then angry again – that she'd torn it up, dropped it in the bin; then spent ages sifting through the vegetable peelings, cellophane and corks to collect them.

Now she picks up a piece the size of a fingernail. It shows a bit of a small podgy knee, scratched on one side. Had he fallen? Had an animal caught him unawares? On the back is a smudge of tomato puree.

Enough.

She stuffs them back in her bag. That's another decision she has to make. But not now. Right now she has other things to worry about.

Like, what is she doing here? What the hell is she thinking of?

If you can't trust the person you're closest to, the person you've shared your home, your dreams, your toothbrush, everything with for years, how can you trust anyone?

A deep breath.

She'll give them another half hour.

Until seven anyway.

They could have been delayed for all sorts of reasons, and not been able to ring her to let her know. Jessica's phone might not be working even. But then wouldn't he have had one, her colleague?

At seven fifty-nine Katie starts the engine, edges slowly around the still half empty car park and back out onto the dark road. She's tired, hungry, tired of sitting. She feels let down. But for now at least – until she can figure out what to do next, which she has to do, and has to do quickly – they're still together, her and her snow fox, and heading home.

## SEVENTEEN

The sheet of paper looks unexceptional, slightly off white, not too heavy but not cheap either. It could be a letter from the local council, or from a building society. Attached is an invoice.

It has taken the detective a week to carry out her instructions. Actually, it probably only took him an hour or two, a couple of phone calls to the right places, but he has to justify his fee. And of course, being a professional he knows exactly where to go for the information.

Under the word CONFIDENTIAL the double-spaced text is centred, typed with no errors, clearly set out. Someone has taken the effort to make it not just easy to read, but professional, its contents not to be questioned.

MARTA WHEELER (prev. NOWAK)
Age: 43
Work: various, mostly office work, currently unemployed
Married 4 years ago to
DAVID WHEELER
Age: 41
Work: company accountant
One son: STEFAN
Age: 9 years
Below that is an address and phone number.

That was all that Katie had asked him to find out, and now she has it there in front of her, in black and white. She's been carrying the letter around with her for days, re-reading it as though convinced there is more information hidden between the lines, something she's missing.

It answers the one big question; or at least, there's enough there to convince her that it does. Ben must be Stefan's father. Unfortunately that then leads to more questions, so many more she doesn't know where to begin. And despite his enthusiasm, the elderly ex-police detective with the moustache, and obvious sense of humour (who else would call their business The Snoop Dog Detective Agency - Commercial, Private and Matrimonial) can't help with any of these.

Outside the house the garden is looking sad and defeated. Even the assorted birds who come to the seed and fat balls she puts out each morning seem to be depressed, rarely singing, either eating voraciously or pecking viciously at any new arrivals. She'd thought two sparrows were going to kill each other, rolling over and over in a ball of brown feathers, like tumbleweed. Sometimes a sparrow hawk zooms down and tries to snatch a bird off the feeder, sending everything scattering in panic. Yesterday – as she stood at the kitchen window waiting for the kettle to boil – he caught a chaffinch, dropped it, scooped it up again.

Katie knows she isn't coping well.

Since the fiasco with Jessica Bourne she seems to be in a daze, like the morning after a night of heavy drinking. She doesn't feel good. Her head hurts, she doesn't feel like eating though knows she should.

Fiasco is an unfair word. Of course it was no-one's fault and she should feel sorry for Jessica and her friend, their van being written off by a silver BMW that jumped the lights, both of them ending up in hospital. (Or to be accurate, it was the fault of the BMW driver, who got away with cuts and bruises). Jessica is still not home, though her doctor says she's doing well and should be out soon. Accidents happen. Being angry with them for letting her down is not just unfair, it's illogical. Seeing it as a sign that she should pull out now, while she can, that she was insane to have agreed is – according to Andrew – real insanity. He thinks she's finally flipped and he's furious, asks what's the point of him trying to arrange anything for the fox if she's going to throw in the towel first time there's a hitch.

Trouble is, she can't seem to think clearly about anything these days.

It's because of the letter. No, the contents, though of course they don't really prove a thing. This could all be a figment of her overripe and fetid imagination.

The obvious thing would be to talk to Ben, but she can't. Not yet, not until she knows what it is she's talking to him about.

A crisp sunny morning is the sign she's waiting for. What better day for a drive up to London? She'll go and see Marta, that's what she'll do. She'll come back the same evening, and Ben won't even need to know.

When she arrives she has difficulty finding somewhere to park, decides to use a pub car park, then thinks she'll have a drink first. She needs it. It's a Tuesday lunchtime, and she's assumed Marta will be home and alone. But she's just as likely to be out, or to have company in which case Katie will have made the journey for nothing. She should have checked first. She should have rung. Still, she'll do it now.

Sitting at a round table in the corner of the almost deserted pub, Katie starts on her second whisky. They're tiny, pub measures. The first one has done nothing to help.

She gets out her phone.

"Yes, who is this?" The accent is slight but unmistakeable.

Katie has already worked out exactly what she's going to say, has even scribbled it on the back of a beer mat.

"Hello, this is Katie Tremain. Ben's wife." She waits a few seconds for her words to sink in. "I'd like to talk to you, preferably this afternoon. Are you free? I could come over right away if that would suit you."

There's a long pause. She can hear a voice in the background, a radio announcer enthusing about the US elections – she'd forgotten, the US has a new president and everyone's very excited - also a whirring sound that could be a washing machine.

"Yes. In one hour. You have my address? Good."

The phone is replaced.

Katie goes straight to the Ladies. She brushes her hair, touches up her mascara and puts on perfume, her favourite red hooped earrings. She looks at herself and sees someone ready to go out for the evening. She needs to feel confident, but has she overdone it? She rubs at the lipstick, finds a paler colour. She drops the earrings back in her bag. Then she thinks, what does it matter anyway what she looks like?

She leaves the car in the pub car park – hopes the owner won't object (and that her car doesn't get towed away or clamped) - and goes to the house on foot. The street is quiet, lined with old trees, its terraced Victorian houses well maintained. Number thirty-one has four bells, so presumably it's divided into flats. The one labelled Mr and Mrs Wheeler is at the bottom; ground floor flat then. Nice. Hopefully with a garden for Stefan. With the blinds rolled up and no curtains it would be easy to peer inside, but Katie turns the other way. She takes a deep breath, tries to relax her shoulders. The door opens almost as soon as she presses the bell.

"Hello, I'm Katie."

What's happened to her voice? She manages a small dry cough.

"We met a couple of times, I think. When you worked with my husband?"

She could have said with Ben, of course. MY husband. She's emphasising the point, and feels embarrassed for doing so.,

"Yes. I remember you. Come in."

She stands aside for Katie to enter the narrow hallway.

There's a slight smell of vegetables. Sauerkraut possibly?

"I thought one day you'd come."

She leads the way into a room at the back with a window looking out onto a small garden. Though a reasonable size it feels cluttered, with fussy flowered wallpaper, an excessive number of armchairs, a Christmas tree in a corner that hasn't yet been decorated though there are boxes of tinsel and garlands on the table. A black cat shoots out from behind a cupboard and jumps onto the window sill where it sits cleaning itself.

Marta is wearing cord trousers and a blouse, her short heavy hair tucked behind her ears. She looks relaxed and Katie is both annoyed and envious. She clears what looks like sports gear – Lycra clothing, socks, dirty trainers – from a chair and indicates that Katie should sit. She crosses to a door, peers in and quietly pulls it shut.

"Stefan is sleeping," she says, lowering her voice. She gives a small smile, the first hint of nervousness. "He's off school today, has a very bad cold. Would you like a coffee?"

For a moment Katie is thrown. She didn't expect him to be there, Ben's son. She doesn't want a drink either, this isn't a social visit. She wants facts.

She shakes her head.

"I want you to tell me about the affair," she says.

"Affair?"

"That you had with Ben."

Marta, who has been standing, sits down in a chair opposite. She looks confused.

"No, you don't understand. There was no affair."

Katie wishes she'd taken her coat off. The room is stuffy, the heating on high. She feels uncomfortably hot.

"But Stefan is Ben's son, am I right?"

Marta hesitates then nods, and Katie feel for a moment as though she's been punched. She'd suspected it, deep down inside she'd known it, but having it confirmed is still a shock. She feels stunned.

"He is a very special boy," Marta continues. "Kind, funny, he works so hard at school. I brought him up on my own, it was what I wanted, he was no trouble at all. Until I met…"

Katie holds up her hand.

"Stop. Please. I want to talk about Ben. About you and Ben. If you're saying you didn't have an affair, then what was it? One amorous drunken night together? You were unlucky and fell pregnant from a one-night stand? Is that what you're saying?"

Marta has interwoven her long, slim fingers, gazes down at them now as though lost for words. Katie can see how Ben would have been drawn to her; she isn't beautiful, nor even pretty, but she has a grace about her, a quiet dignity.

"I don't understand," she says.

"I'm the one who doesn't understand," Katie says now, suddenly angry again. "I'm the one who's just discovered that the man I've shared my life with for all these years, who I love and trust – trusted - has a child that I know nothing about, that he's never mentioned, that…"

"He hasn't told you? About me? About Stefan?"

Katie sighs. Suddenly she wants to close her eyes and block out the whole world, forget everything. She wants to be back sitting in the shed with her fox watching her lick her paws clean, one by one, that soft licking sound, the foxy smell that at first she found hard to take but that she's come to love.

"No," she says quietly. "So you tell me."

Marta stands and walks to the window, as though it's easier to talk with distance between them, though for Katie it makes it even more difficult to hear her soft voice.

"When I worked at the office of Ben's company, I liked him. He is a nice man, he has time for everyone."

Katie can feel herself begin to bristle. Is this really what she came to hear?

"Sometimes we had a drink together. I was concerned, but he laughed, said you wouldn't be waiting for him with a meal ready, that wasn't your style. That you had a career too. He admired you very much, I think."

Marta reaches out to the cat and it pushes it bony head into her hand, purring loudly.

"I'd never intended to stay in England. I was engaged to be married to a soldier back home, what you call a childhood sweetheart I think? I came to study the language for a year only. But it was a mistake. He wrote and said he'd met someone else. Your Ben was very sympathetic."

Yes, too sympathetic. If she's going to say he was only comforting her…

"So suddenly I was over thirty and had no prospect of getting married, and I was frightened. Frightened that I would never have a child. You understand? That I would never meet another man to love, or that if I did it would be too late."

There is a sound from the room next door, someone moving about. Marta turns to look briefly in that direction.

"I couldn't bear that. All I've ever wanted is to have children, lots of them, a big family like the one I came from. But to have grown old without producing a single child, not one son or one daughter, that would have made my life unbearable, pointless. Ben understood."

He would, of course. He'd understand better than most men, far better than Katie ever would.

"So you and he…"

"Yes. He found the clinic. He helped pay for the treatment. He is a kind, generous man, your Ben."

"A clinic?"

Katie's head is beginning to spin. Does she mean… what? That he donated the sperm?

Her confusion must show on her face.

"You didn't know?" Marta says. "Ben didn't tell you that he was helping me?"

"No."

"But I don't understand."

"No, neither do I."

"He said…" Marta hesitates, stops stroking the cat and instead folds her arms. For protection, Katie thinks. They're both of them nervous. She tried a smile but it feels stiff, wrong.

"He said … I don't know but I'm sure it's true, yes? He said you didn't want any children."

She's nervous, waiting for Katie to say how terrible, how could he say such a thing, that doesn't every woman yearn to be a mother?

"That's true."

The words are too stark; some kind of explanation seems to be needed. She has no intention of giving one of course.

Marta nods.

"David, my husband, he's a good father to Stefan. He loves him as if he were his real father. There were problems – I think I cannot have more babies – but David doesn't mind. We have each other, and we have our Stefan, he says. That is enough, more than enough."

A voice calls from the room next door, husky, snuffly, and again Marta glances towards it but doesn't move.

"You would like to meet…?" she starts to say.

Katie shakes her head.

"What about Ben? Does he… I mean, has he ever met Stefan?"

"Once. When he was only a baby. I send him pictures sometimes, but he doesn't reply. I remember he said – how did he put it? – that it would be enough for him just to know that he was a father."

The boy calls again, louder He's obviously used to his mother being there instantly when he needs her.

"Please wait. We'll talk some more. I'll make tea."

She hurries into the other room, the door swinging closed behind her. Katie can hear the two of them chattering in hushed tones – it sounds like they might be speaking Polish – then a giggle from the boy.

The cat looks at her with yellow eyes, blinks and turns away.

Katie stands. She goes out into the hallway and out of the front door, and along the quiet tree lined road, her high heeled boots clipping on the pavement. She'd done what she'd set out to do: found out the truth, because she was sure that it was true, everything Marta had said. She'd never go back there again. Never meet Stefan, Ben's son. Would she talk to Ben about him? Right now she isn't sure, can't think straight, all she wants to do is get as far away as possible from that cosy room with its smug feeling of contentment.

She's been walking for nearly ten minutes before she realises she's going in the wrong direction.

## EIGHTEEN

The frost is a surprise. During the night Katie had got up to dig out an extra blanket, so she knew it had turned colder, but still she doesn't expect to be greeted by a garden that looks as though it's been lightly sprayed with silver when she pulls back the curtains. It's a welcome surprise. It's Christmas Day, and she loves frost. She's always preferred frost to snow. When it snows the world disappears, as though someone has spread a blanket over it. Frost does the opposite. It makes you able to see things you'd usually miss: a delicate spider's web looks as though it's been crocheted in white silk. A smoke tree is topped with white spun sugar. A skeleton of dried bracken could be a bird's feather.

She'll think of the frost as compensation for being alone.

Pulling on trousers, socks, a sweater and a body warmer, she heads downstairs. She switches on an electric fire, and the radio which is playing a carol service from a cathedral in Yorkshire. She sings along with O Come All Ye Faithful – proud that she can remember the words, probably last sung when she was at school – as she pours juice.

She makes plans. She'll have some porridge done her favourite way, with banana and cinnamon, then go and clean out the fox's cage. She might have a walk down to the river, it seems criminal not to get out on a day like this. Later she'll cook herself something special (she's no idea what exactly, it will depend what she can find in the freezer, or what tins are in the cupboard). She'll open a bottle of wine and watch television. Not so very different from most people's Christmases really.

Unless there are children in the house, of course, and then it's a different occasion altogether. Like in Andrew's house. Like in Marta's house.

Does Ben ever think about Stefan? Surely he must do. Is he ever tempted to send him a gift at Christmas? Maybe he does. Birthdays too.

She hasn't told him about her visit to Marta, not yet. She will do. But first she has to get things sorted in her mind so that she knows what she wants to say, finds the words, the right words. She'd read once that the average person knows 20,000 words. She'd been amazed. So many word to choose from, and yet how often was she at a loss when it came to expressing herself, especially when it was something important?

Anyway, lately she and Ben seem to be speaking different languages. It's like they need a translator. Which was why they'd agreed about Christmas.

She wonders what he'll be doing right now. It was a last minute mutual decision to spend Christmas apart. Ben said he was worried about work anyway, about the looming financial crisis: interest rates cuts, talk of a recession, job losses. Hard times. He said he wouldn't be good company and she agreed.

He's staying in London and said he'll probably sleep all day. Or will he go to one of the many clubs that are always open, 24/7? Or be invited by a work colleague to join his family festivities, someone who feels sorry for the poor man, abandoned by his wayward wife at Christmas when no-one should be alone? She doesn't care what he does. She's happy to be here without him, without anyone. It feels strange though, her first ever Christmas on her own. Few people actually opt to be alone at Christmas, do they? Not unless they're grumpy old codgers of the bah humbug variety. Or loonies living a back-to-nature life on a mountain top, cut off from the world, who probably haven't even noticed the date.

Through the window she can see that the surface of the bird bath is like glass, small fluffed up birds edging around the rim, pecking, looking confused, trying again.

"That's never going to melt on its own. Wait, I'm on my way."

She checks that there'swarm water in the kettle, pulls on her boots. When she opens the back door the cold makes her gasp. She can't believe that they can survive up here on the moors, these tiny sparks of life, that any living creature can come to that. It's too bleak. Too hostile. Inhospitable, that's the word.

But then they do.

Katies not alone, of course. She's got the fox. Later she takes a folding chair into the shed, adds a cushion and sits there as the pale sun arcs up and over the house, briefly crosses the floor of the shed, far too weak to add any warmth. Sits watching the animal who's so disrupted her life. She finds her endlessly fascinating, could watch her forever. Even when she's curled up asleep, her flanks gently rising and falling, sometimes twitching her pink nose. It's like meditating, watching a sleeping fox, Katie thinks. Didn't Tess once say that about watching a sleeping baby?

She loses track of time, only knows that her feet are numb and that she should go indoors soon or she won't be able to walk on them.

But first, feed time. At least she's getting used to handling the dead chicks. She can even look at them now. They weigh nothing, their feathers sometimes coming loose so that she has to brush them off her skin. Wide pale pink beaks. Their eyes are mostly closed or just slits, inside them a dull grey film that was once a bright little eye about to discover the world.

Not for long, according to Kevin. The males are gassed within a day, he said matter-of-factly when she'd finally found the courage to ask.

"No use to anyone, are they?"

"But so why can't they be kept until they're bigger, and then they could be eaten. At least they'd have had a bit of a life."

"Different breed. The ones you eat bulk up in no time. Weeks. Specially bred to get fat, they are. These tiddlers are just a nuisance."

Katie had thought that heart-breaking. She still did.

For the past few weeks she's not eaten an egg, nor chicken. Not much meat either. She hadn't really thought about it before, all that suffering. Of course her going without didn't make any difference to the animals. But it did to her. It just felt right.

"Here you are, sweetheart," she whispers, opening the cage door just wide enough to slide her arm inside. The fox is already alert: she recognises the sound of the plastic bag being unwrapped, the rattle of the cage door, knows what comes next. Slowly she edges forwards, and for the first time Katie notices her tail give a small flick. Of recognition? Anticipation maybe? In an instant she snatches the food and backs into a corner, her pale eyes still on Katie as she crunches it quickly, then swallows.

"Another one?"

Katie can't think of a better Christmas gift that having a wild fox take food from her hand.

It gets dark early, a damp mist descending, blocking out the stars and the moon. Katie decides to light a fire. Since they opened up the fireplace they've had a couple of log fires, mostly with Ben in charge. Fire making, he said, is a man's job. She'd laughed, teased him about being macho, especially when it had taken three goes to get the flame to take. But it's not that easy. Now, after a couple of bad starts - one of which fills the room with smoke – she finally succeeds. She leaves the television on despite the fact that she hates it all: the special editions in exotic locations of comedy series that everyone is already bored stiff with, animated films about puppies and little girls, old films that re-appear every Christmas. Mindless rubbish. Background noise. Yet how many families will spend the day slumped in front of the box watching one programme after another?

When the phone rings she's fallen asleep on the sofa, oblivious to the raucous studio laughter filling the room. The fire has burned low, a few pale flames flickering along the top of an almost burnt out log balanced on a mound of ash that's still glowing, just. She glances at her watch. It's late, nearly eleven. As she tries to remember where she last saw her phone, riffles amongst  papers on the coffee table where the ring tone seems to be is coming from, she knocks over a wine bottle. It rolls, the last trickle of wine making a puddle that drips over the edge onto the carpet. For some reason this strikes her as incredibly sad.

She spots the phone.

"Hello?"

"Katie? It's me, Ben."

As if she wouldn't recognise his voice.

"Just... checking that you're OK, I suppose."

"And why wouldn't I be?"

"Why wouldn't you be. Right. So have you had a good day?"

"Yes. Fine. And you?"

"Yes. Not that I've done anything. Anything special that is."

She thinks he's going to say more but he doesn't. There's a very faint sound of movement and she imagines him sitting down on the sofa, probably putting one leg up across the seat in that way that he does.

"Once I can get things a bit more sorted I should be able to get down there, at least for a few days," he says. "That's if the weather holds of course."

Is she meant to be pleased? Grateful?

"They keep talking about snow."

He's waiting for her to say something.

"It's up to you." She keeps her tone non-committal.

"I know. I know, love." He sounds sad, and she's torn between feeling smug – as though by coping perfectly well on her own she's taught him a lesson - and longing to be with him, snuggling close, cherished and safe.

"Ben, I've making some toast."

"OK, sorry, love. Don't let it get cold."

He knows she lives on snacks, bits of this and that, has nagged her so many times about not eating properly. How the tables have turned, she thinks.

"Katie?"

She nearly doesn't hear him.

"What?"

"This isn't right, love. None of it. We shouldn't be…"

"Ben, I can smell it burning and it's my last piece of bread."

"Go. I'll talk to you soon. Bye, love."

She sits there holding the phone for some minutes. Then she rouses herself.

Toast isn't a bad idea, but there's no bread left, nothing in the freezer except a container of dead chicks. Tortilla chips, didn't she see a packet in the cupboard? And she'll open another bottle of wine, put some more logs on the fire, the smaller drier ones so they'll catch quickly.

For the briefest moment she thinks she's going to start crying. No, no, no. If she does, she'll never stop. But she holds on long enough to rip open the bag, and the crunchy spiciness of the chips swished down with a few sips of Chardonnay – stocked at the mini market especially for the festive season, Patrice said – is enough to revive her. She'll sit up a while longer. It's Christmas after all.

Before she goes to bed she takes the three parcels out of the bottom of the cupboard, all of them wrapped in the same silver paper with its holly and mistletoe design. She unpeels the sellotape, removes the paper and scrunches it into balls. She tears up the gift tags she'd written in a silly moment of optimism when it'd seemed Ben might come down and they'd have some kind of reconciliation. She drops the paper and pieces of card into the fire, puts the shirt, the book and DVD of British Wild Birds into a carrier bag.

Next time she's in Barnstaple she'll drop them off at a charity shop.

And then, during the night, Katie hears the noise again: a triple bark followed by an unearthly scream so loud it makes her blood run cold. She's heard it a number of times over the past week. At first she'd decided it was a visiting animal, maybe a dog fox who's scented out the vixen, who wants her to know he's waiting and he's interested. But now she's not so sure. It could also be her fox, her snow fox calling for a mate. It's a painful sound, full of longing.

"Soon," she promises. "You won't be in that cage one minutes longer than you have to be."

But the fox wants more than that. She wants her freedom. She wants a place where she can live without fear of being shot or trapped or chased with dogs. She wants clear water and lots of warm, fat bunnies with which to feed her young. She wants what every living creature wants and deserves: a right to a life. Which means she wants the impossible.

Katie puts her pillow over her head and wills herself back to sleep.

## NINETEEN

Everyone is still going on about climate change – the experts, politicians, the media – but Katie thinks the weather today is exactly what you'd expect of a January day: the sun is shining in a crisp blue sky, there are a few flecks of cotton wool low on the horizon, the air just cold enough to make your nose tingle. As she comes in from taking out the rubbish, she thinks yet again how welcoming the house feels these days, bright yet cosy, more like a home every day. Not just a home, her home. Not for much longer though.

She kicks off her wellies. Most of the jobs she'd so enjoyed listing as she sat at the kitchen table on her first week here are finished. She's waiting for the go-ahead from Rachael to have some heaters fitted – electric panels as there's no gas this far off the beaten track – and a couple more mundane jobs completed, like having the boiler serviced, and tiles replaced on a corner of the roof. By spring it'll be ready to go on the market.

The phone rings. Katie pauses before picking it up.

"Hello?"

Though no-one answers the line doesn't go dead; the silence sounds somehow grainy. Katie has the feeling it's an overseas call, but surely a mobile wouldn't be affected by distance? Though the signal here on the moors is hopeless, completely unreliable. But then who'd be ringing from overseas, apart from possibly a friend on holiday (she can think of one in particular who always manages to have the most dramatic stories he can't wait to tell… but then why wouldn't he speak?) This is the third time over the last few days that it's happened.

"Listen, if you've got something to say, go ahead. Say it. If not…"

There's a click.

It worries her. It can't be someone who's misdialled, not again and again. So why keep on ringing? Unless, of course, the intention is simply to unnerve her, to frighten her. But why? And how would they have got hold of her mobile number in the first place?

This new insecurity annoys her. After the first few months here she'd come to feel so safe that she's often left doors and windows open, even when she's gone out. She wouldn't dream of being so casual in London; there they lock and double lock everything, leave the burglar alarm on permanently. But here it feels unthreatening. Felt. Past tense. Last night she'd closed all the curtains, carefully checked that she'd locked every window and door before going to bed.

The early evening local news on TV catches Katie's attention. A reporter is interviewing people on the eastern side of Exmoor about the problems they're having with foxes. Hungry, with reduced natural prey available, they're turning to farm animals. The grim expression on the reporter's face makes it clear this is serious. One farmer has lost a couple of new-born lambs to foxes (though he does agree they could have been dead when they were taken). An elderly woman with fluffy white hair claims to have irrefutable proof that her missing cat, Daisy, has been killed and eaten by a fox. And a man with an oddly familiar face shot four on his land last week, blaming the problem not on a shortage of food but overpopulation now that hunting foxes with dogs is illegal. The camera closes in on the four bodies neatly arranged side by side. Wasn't he at the summer fair?

The phone again.

Katie is about to pick it up when the reporter adds that there has been no recent sighting of the rare albino fox that locals are convinced is still living in the area.

"And there won't be," she says. The phone stops ringing before she can reach it.

She's in the kitchen when she hears footsteps on the gravel outside. An animal crossing the yard? It sounds too heavy. The kids back? Unlikely.

Katie hesitates. The gun comes to mind. If she's going to have to go out there, wouldn't she feel safer holding a gun? But she has no idea how to load it, how to hold it even, and of course she'd never pull the trigger. It might at least give the impression she meant business? But no, she couldn't.

If only Ben would do what he'd promised and get rid of the thing.

Before she can change her mind she marches to the front door, flings it open, and in the light from the hallway sees that someone is over the far side of the drive bent and fiddling with the lock of the shed door. He looks up.

"Katie?" She doesn't recognise the voice. He moves towards her and instinctively she takes a step back.

"It's me. Kev. Kevin."

The feeling of relief is brief.

"What are you doing?" He can't have missed the accusation in her voice.

He comes closer. He's holding something small, furry, and limp in one hand, a torch in the other.

"It's a squirrel," he says, holding it out as though for Katie's approval. She glances at it, looks back at his face.

"I can see."

"Spotted it in the woods. Thought of your fox. And knowing how squeamish you are…" Katie's confused. Why does he keep bringing her dead things? It's almost like he cares about the fox. Or feels she doesn't care enough about this very special gift he's given her?

"I didn't hear your car."

"I left it out on the road. Planned to just drop this off and go without disturbing you."

He gives her a hesitant smile.

"She'll love it, your girl."

She's a suspicious, ungrateful bitch. She knows it. She thanks him for the thought, invites him in, but he has to get back to the farm for his evening meal. He'll just... he indicates the shed. If that's alright with her? How can she say it isn't, that she doesn't want him anywhere near her fox? Doesn't want anyone near her?

Andrew rings later with news. He's found a couple more places. One is a wildlife park that specialises in rarer breeds, has a good reputation, and though obviously the vixen wouldn't have freedom they'd do their best to ensure she has as natural a life as possible. There's also a zoologist in the US who collects albino animals and birds. True, they're exhibited, but only to a limited audience, and the conditions in which they live are said to be excellent. They'd pay for transportation, of course. In fact one of them would come over and travel with her.

"You didn't tell them where she is?"

"No way."

"Or give them my mobile number?"

"Katie, you're getting paranoid. Listen, these places sound good, but I have to tell you Jessica has been back in touch. She said she's left messages but you don't return them. She's on your side, Katie. She said once she's mobile again…"

"Let me think about it."

"Do that, Katie. Do it soon. You need to make a decision."

"Wherever she goes she's going to be considered a freak, isn't she?"

"Sweetheart, she IS a freak."

"I suppose."

She hates him for saying it, but he's right. He's usually right, which is why she wants to talk to him about Stefan. She has to talk to someone, because every time the whole strange episode comes into her mind it's as though the lights go off, she goes blank, seizes up. She has no idea what she feels. What would be a normal reaction? Hurt? Anger? Guilt?

"OK, I will. I promise. Listen Andrew, there's something else. When I was in London at the house I found this photo and…"

"Katie, sorry, my other phone's going. Think about what I've been saying, will you?"

She promises she will, and she does. She thinks about it all night. Trouble is, she doesn't like any of the options. In the wild – certainly in this area – the fox wouldn't last five minutes, especially now the media are onto her. But what sort of a life will she have in captivity? Katie recalls once when she was coming home from school with a group of friends, ambling along the high street, pausing as they often did outside a pet shop. In the window two gerbils in a cage were mating. Everyone thought it hilarious. They jeered, banged on the glass, the boys shoved each other and made appropriate hand movements. Katie had been upset. She'd felt really sorry for the gerbils. She'd pictured herself marching into the shop, scooping up the cage and taking them off to a tucked away place where they could do whatever they wanted, with no-one peering and laughing at them ever again.

Guy is on the doorstep, his jacket collar turned up, hunched against the northerly wind that has been tormenting the trees and battering at the windows for days now. He thought he'd better come check on things, seeing as she never rings, never returns his calls. He stamps his feet, looks over her shoulder, and she realises she's going to have to invite him in.

They pull the sofa closer to the log fire that Katie has taken to lighting in the day now, as well as the evening. The room is transformed. Guy says he can't believe it's the same room they sat in all those months ago, getting to know each other over a bag of doughnuts.

Katie laughs.

"And how's your queen of doughnuts these days? Haven't seen her in the shop lately."

"She's gone to India. On her own. Backpacking."

Katie is shocked. She'd never have taken Mary Morgan to be the adventurous type.

"Wow. Good for her."

They talk. They sip their coffees. They listen to the wind.

Guy puts down his mug, stretches out his long legs.

"Gather Kevin called in the other day."

"Yes. I… I was a bit off at first. Sorry. Didn't recognise him in the dark."

Guy gives a shrug.

"No problem. Said the fox is looking great. Thick coat, no limp now. So you got hold of some antibiotics?"

"Yes. Well, Ben did." If she's going to say it, now is the moment.

"Guy, about Kevin."

"He's wondering what you plan to do next."

"Why? Does he have any ideas?"

I bet he does, Katie thinks. She still can't believe he gave the fox to her. He may be shy, not very worldly, but he's not stupid. He'll know that she's worth a lot of money. If he didn't before he certainly will now. He's probably kicking himself for passing her to Katie in the first place. If he could only persuade her to let him take her back.

Not, to be honest, that he's ever suggested that.

"Doubt it." Guy looks directly at her, won't look away. "But you know you must do something"

"I do. And I'm going to. There are a couple of options I'm checking out right now."

"Really? What kind?"

Katie hesitates.

"I'll tell you more when I have all the details."

She hadn't told him about Jessica, had planned to announce the news afterwards, when it was all over.

"Sure. Whenever."

The fire crackles as a log shifts. There's a mini explosion of sparks, but they fall safely onto the hearth. Guy turns to stare into the flames.

"You think I'm wrong, keeping her in a cage for so long, don't you?" Katie says.

"I think you're wrong putting her in a cage in the first place."

"If I – if we – hadn't caught her she'd be dead by now."

"So?"

There's a sudden gust of wind that rattles the window, and they both jump. Guy glances back, then tries again to get Katie to look at him, but she won't.

"She's a wild creature, Katie," he says. "They don't survive long out there, none of them. Foxes rarely get to have a second birthday party. That Mother Nature is a cruel bitch."

"It isn't all down to nature, though, is it?"

Not when there are so many other risks to be avoided, she wants to say, but knows he'll have answers, be defensive. That he sees rural life through different eyes.

What about the man-made threats? Guns blasting at pigeons, hares, squirrels; sometimes barrages of them now that it's the season for shooting pheasants, those silly creatures so unfit they have to be freaked into making their first and only flight, many of their bodies simply left to rot. Traps. She'd heard on the radio that's it quite common for

farmers to trap badgers – even though they're protected –
then throw them onto the road so that it looks as though
they've been killed by cars. And cars, of course. Without
warning the deer's face flashes before her, that second
before she'd ploughed into it, its big brown
uncomprehending eyes. She still has nightmares. Thinking
about it, it's a wonder anything survives out there.

"You find it irritating, don't you, my… my obsession
with this fox?"

"I guess. In a way. Not so much irritating as perplexing.
You're an intelligent woman, yet here you are locking
yourself away in the middle of nowhere, scared of every
little noise, cutting yourself off from everyone, your
friends, from your husband too it seems. And for what?"

Katie knows he's right.

"I can't explain it, Guy. Don't think I haven't tried."

"I have to say she's exquisite. I've never seen such a
beautiful animal."

She shakes her head.

"Yes, but it's not that. It's more to do with getting close
to her. She let me share her world. You can't imagine how
precious those times were, sitting there with her and her
cubs. So now she needs someone on her side."

"And you're volunteering?"

"Reluctantly, yes. One of the things I loved most about
her was her quiet confidence, her self-sufficiency. I hate
being responsible for her. I hate seeing what she's
become."

Guy puts out an arm and for a moment she thinks he's
going to hug her. Instead, his hand drops onto hers, he
gives it a squeeze and then removes it.

"Wilma and I used to have this kind of discussion," he
says. "Did I mention she was soppy about animals too?"

Soppy. A horrible, childish word but she ignores it.

"When we were performing she was always picking up
pigeons with broken wings or legs – city streets are littered

with them, but you'd know that – and hiding them away in a corner of the dressing room until she could bring them back to our apartment and fatten them up with digestive biscuits. Pigeons, stray dogs. Once a baby mouse that she kept in a cigarette box and fed on grated apple."

Guy gets to his feet, stretches.

"Treated me like shit, but there you go."

He picks up his jacket, walks towards the front door.

"I'm taking Kevin to Barnstaple to look at a guitar someone's selling off cheap. The drums weren't his thing. He wants to play tunes, it seems."

Katie follows him.

"You can trust him," Guys says. "I know it doesn't make sense, not with that fox of yours being worth megabucks. And I realise you despise him for being involved with the hunt, and all that. But he won't let you down. It's not in his nature."

"If you say so."

Guy kisses her on the cheek, a small dry kiss, and steps outside. A distant honking sound grows louder and a skein of geese flaps slowly past overhead, dark shapes against a salmon pink sky. Soon it will be dark.

"Katie," Guy says. "Much as I'll miss you, it's time you went back to the city. This isn't the place for you. It's too real."


The phone yet again, her mobile.

In the early days Katie used to like to hear it going. It meant out of sight wasn't necessarily out of mind; that someone was still thinking of her. Lately she'd come to dread it.

She's resolved not to pick it up, to let the caller leave a message, but then, before she can stop herself, she's reaching for it. The silence this time is brief, only seconds, then an unfamiliar voice, a man's voice, with some kind of accent she doesn't recognise.

"Please, is this Mrs Tremain?"

Could be middle eastern.

"Yes."

"Good evening. I am contacting you on behalf of a client of mine, a man who appreciates beautiful things, and who has the money to spend on them. A very wealthy man, you understand? It is my information that you may be able to tell me the whereabouts of a certain animal."

For a moment Katie is too stunned to speak.

"It is a white fox, an albino, and my client is very keen to…"

"I'm sorry, I have no idea what you're talking about. Please don't call me again."

She sits down heavily. A private collector. But who'd have given him her mobile number? Not Kevin, certainly not Ben. Andrew? He wouldn't have done it on purpose, but he's talking to a lot of different people, she realises that and appreciates the effort he's making. Maybe he was careless, let something slip. He loves to talk, does Andrew. Or someone tricked him.

When the room is suddenly plunged into darkness her heart stalls, then thumps. She goes to swallow but her mouth is too dry. What the hell now? Is someone outside, cutting wires, waiting for complete darkness so he can force a door, or slide up one of the rickety windows and clamber inside to… what? Scared to move she sits like a statue, tries to steady her breathing. Why would someone want to break in? Surely if the fox is the lure then they'd go straight to the shed, haul her out and load her in a truck whilst Katie is trapped in the house?

From outside, nothing. The complete silence that goes with this impenetrable blackness.

"OK. Do something." She says it aloud, aware of the shake in her voice.

"A torch. Now where… in a drawer somewhere?"

She presses the palm of her hands against the wall, feels her way out of the room, heads towards the kitchen, her feet shuffling across tiles that feel cold through her socks. The first drawer she tries is full of bits of string. In the next one she finds a torch, presses the button. Sighs with relief as it comes on.

It has to be a fuse of course. It's happened before. Now she follows the ring of light across the hallway and back to a cupboard that's crammed with all sorts of things, brooms, mops, a ladder, and at the back, a fuse box. She can see at once that all the buttons are down, except for one. Squeezing an arm through she flicks the switch to line up with the others. And the lights are back on.

Briefly she closes her eyes. A simple fuse, and she's acting like she's being stalked by some evil kleptomaniac who'll stop at nothing to get her fox.

She's got to get a grip.

Even so, she can't resist the sudden need to check on the fox. Just in case. She looks around for her body warmer, can't find it, goes out without it, jogging across to the shed, cutting her finger on the cold, sharp bolt as she fumbles to slide it open.

> *That was the evening you let me touch you for the first time, wasn't it? I'd fed you and you'd settled down into the straw, actually pressed against the wire of the cage though you knew I was close to the other side of it, very close. I knelt down on the floor beside you, listened to your steady breathing mingling with my own. It was dusk. An owl hooted somewhere nearby and you opened your eyes and looked around, then at me.*
>
> *I knew then that you wouldn't mind.*

*I edged my fingers through the wire and gently, very gently, touched the top of your head, whispering something, I can't remember what. Some sentimental gibberish. You hesitated, yawned, then put your head back down on your paws and closed your eyes.*

*A couple more times, a couple more tentative touches was all I would have. But how many people have even had that?*

*Sleeping beside me you looked calm and contented. Yet once the moon was up I knew you'd revert back to being a wild animal, would start pacing and calling, scrabbling at the concrete floor as though convinced that you could do it, dig your way out. When you first came to me you needed a safe place to hide, to feed and grow strong again. You needed me. Now the cage that had protected you had become a trap, and your rescuer, your jailer. Soon you would begin to hate me, which was almost the very worst thing in the world that I could imagine.*

# TWENTY

There's something wrong.

Katie can't put her finger on it, but she knows. She's taken to standing outside the back door at night, when the blackness is thick and soft and the only light comes from a sliver of white moon, and thinking about things. Or thinking about nothing. But things are about to change. To end. She's sure of it. It's as though someone is whispering a warning in her ear: be calm, be careful. Watch out.

But watch out for what?

Ben arrives. He's come because he's worried about her. He wants to talk to her about the fox, about her going back to London, about a whole lot of things. He looks scruffier than usual: his hair needs cutting, his shirt is grubby around the collar. Ben, who she used to tease about being too fastidious. She thinks of a good friend they had years ago whose wife upped and left him for another woman. Everyone was amazed, but then delighted for her, said it was obviously the right thing to do, no point in living a lie, and that he'd get over once he'd accepted it. But he didn't. He was absolutely shattered. It was as though he was dissolving before their eyes, gradually shrinking into himself, getting thinner, shorter, even his hair starting to recede. He discovered drugs, lost his job. Lost contact with the gang, which they all agreed was awful.

Though Ben has put on weight there seems to be less of him too. Katie feels a prickling of guilt that this could be any of her doing.

"Come on. let's get some oxygen into those lungs of yours," she says. "I know where there's a whole bank of snowdrops out already."

Storms are forecast for the south west, more winds, gale force this time. There's a high probability of localised flooding. But at the moment the air is motionless and crisp, not a cloud in sight.

"Why not?" Ben says. "Give me half an hour."

He's brought his laptop with him, set it up in what she calls the spare bedroom – though there's no bed - and sits there tapping at the keyboard, leaning close to the screen. He has things he must go through, needs to find viable alternatives to at least some of the ludicrous suggestions made by the architect on the toy manufacturer's project. He's worried. The credit crunch is affecting the whole world. When Obama admits the US economy is sick and worsening, that's serious.  OK, it's encouraging that in the UK Gordon Brown has announced a loan to help smaller companies survive the downturn, but still.

He talks with his back to her. Katie stands in the doorway, unsure what to say.

"D'you think your company is in trouble? Really?"

"Everyone's in trouble."

"But you won't... I mean it's unlikely you'll close down.  Isn't it?"

He doesn't reply.

She looks at her watch, the heavy sky.

"Ben, if we don't go for this walk soon it'll be too dark."

"Five minutes. Ten at the most."

Half an hour later she goes out on her own. It's dusk and she can barely see the ground in front of her, but she's used to it. She marches on with her hands deep in her pockets, thinking that if she was to stay on in the country (now where did that idea come from?) she'd go to a rescue centre and get a dog, any kind, any age, she wasn't fussy. You never have to beg or bully dogs to go for a walk.

She gets back in time to see an unfamiliar car pulling away.

"You didn't wait for me," Ben says accusingly. He's in the kitchen buttering cream crackers.

"I did. Who was that?"

He pulls a face.

"Some reporter. Said he's been told we might know something about a white fox. I acted dumb but I'm not sure he wasn't snooping around the shed before I spotted him. Still, he wouldn't have seen her unless he'd somehow got inside."

He holds out a cracker which she ignores.

"But how would he have…?"

"Don't ask me," he says, munching, a few cracker flakes caught on his chin.

It has to be Andrew's fault, all of this. Who else? Katie snatches up her phone. He answers almost at once.

"Andrew?"

"Katie?"

From the babble in the background he must be in the pub again. With a new girlfriend probably. Even Ben can hear it. He shakes his head then wanders off.

"I'll be quick. It's just that I had a strange call on my mobile about the fox, a man wanting to buy her for some big shot tycoon client of his. Then today a reporter arrived on the doorstep. Someone knows, or at least suspects what we've got in the shed and…"

"And? You think it's down to me?"

"Could it be? Not on purpose, I know that, but could you have…?"

"Katie, listen carefully. I have not given your details to anyone. No-one. Not intentionally, not by accident. OK? Got that?"

"But how can you be so sure? You've been talking to all sorts of people, people you don't know, have never even met. You said so yourself."

"I'm sure."

She hears a sharp intake of breath, as though he's stopping himself saying more.

"You're angry with me."

"No I'm not."

But he is.

Ben comes into the room, drops a small white folder onto the table, taps the front.

"Came across this a few days ago."

On the label, clearly printed, her name, address, mobile number. She flips it open. Photos of old people in paper hats, a table littered with food and glasses, and on the bottom of the pile, a couple of hazy shots of what could be – if you narrow your eyes and use your imagination – two little white foxes.

Of course. How could she be so stupid? Of course.

"Katie? You still there?"

Andrew's voice is faint. She ignores it.

"Developed through the local newsagent, didn't you say?" Ben is looking pleased with himself. "Where some bored assistant might well have idly flicked through them, probably even forgotten about them? Until now, that is."

"Yes. That's it."

She pulls a face, holds the phone close again.

"Andrew, will you ever forgive me? I think Ben's found the answer."


They've eaten, shared a bottle of wine. They sit side by side on the fat sofa, not touching but almost, the room full of shadows cast by the one small sidelight they've left on.

She has so much she needs to talk to him about.

It's now or never.

"Help me, Ben. Please. I don't know what to do about the fox, and I have no-one else to ask."

Does he move away a fraction or does she imagine it?

"It has to be your decision."

"I know she'll be safe in a park or zoo, but I can't help it, I hate the thought. But if I release her she won't last a day."

Wind down the chimney is making the flames in the fire dance a jig.

"There is a third option."

He drains his wine glass, holds on to it, twirls it between his fingers.

"You'll hate it."

Katie waits.

"Have her put down."

She can't believe she heard him right.

"And why would I do that?"

"You say you don't want her to suffer. Have you seen the way she paces about in that cage, I mean, really watched her?"

"I know. I do know, Ben. But it's only temporary."

"Is it though? You said it, her options are pretty dire right now."

Katie is still reeling from his suggestion.

"Besides, imagine you've found someone - I don't know, a conservation group, a collector who's more interested in animal welfare than showing off his wealth. You'll never know if the conditions she's kept in really do match up to the promise. Or if for some unforeseen reason they have to pass her on. Or worse, are persuaded to sell her. You'll never know for sure."

He's right. But what he said has numbed her; she can't think straight.

"What d'you mean, kill her? Give her some kind of lethal drug? Drown her? Shoot her? I can't believe you said that."

Ben stands.

"Depends which you think is worse – a life of misery, or death?"

With that he heads back upstairs, back to his computer, his footsteps heavy on the newly polished wooden stairs. Though the room is warm Katie goes over to the fire and bends, holding the palms of her hands close to the flames.

The storm arrives shortly after midnight. First it's the banging that wakes Katie: a badly fitting window, loose tiles on the roof, a clay pot rolling around on the patio. Then the rain begins. It's torrential, noisier than the wind, and Katie imagines the rivers getting faster and higher, spilling over the banks, the roads turning into rivers. Sounds like the warnings of severe flooding weren't exaggerated.

Though he doesn't speak she's sure Ben is awake and she rolls over towards him and wraps an arm around his waist. Usually he'd turn to her but tonight he doesn't, he just leaves her arm lying there, and after a while she retrieves it and turns over onto her other side, hugging her knees instead.

Morning, and it's still raining.

Katie puts on wellies and holds an umbrella over her head as she splashes across the yard to the shed. Some water has seeped in under the door, but apart from that it's surprisingly dry inside. The fox looks subdued and though she eats the raw chop that Katie gives her, she's slower than usual, as though she's really not much interested. Or hungry? Without waiting to see if there's anything more, she turns and lopes to the back of the cage, spinning once before she settles. Her eyes remain open.

"What's wrong?" Katie asks softly. "Is it true, what everyone's saying?"

She walks to the door, changes her mind, comes back to crouch down beside the cage, and after a long moment the fox gets to her feet and approaches her, sniffing the outstretched fingers Katie has squeezed through the bars.

"Don't you dare give up on me," she says. "You hear? Don't even think of it."

Back indoors, shaking out the umbrella, Katie wishes Ben would forget about his work for just five minutes and talk to her. You'd think he could spare five minutes.

He's on the phone again, and she can hear from his voice that he's getting agitated. She takes him up a coffee and he lift a hand in thanks but carries on talking. She vacuums the downstairs rooms and then mops the kitchen floor, despite the fact that every time she steps outside she brings back with her more clumps of mud.

She'll find the answer, the right thing to do. It'll be something obvious that she's overlooking because she's too close to the problem. Too emotionally involved.

OK, she admits it. Too obsessed.

Midday. She takes Ben up a sandwich, avocado and mozzarella cheese, thanks to the supplies he brought with him. She makes one for herself too, eats it sitting on the carpet in front of the fire. By mid-afternoon the sky is already darkening and she goes around switching on lights. Through the window she looks across the yard to the shed, longing to go and check, to be sure that the fox is alright, yet putting it off a little longer. It's not the squally rain that stops her, nor the wind. It's that increasingly she can see that what everyone is saying is true. Of course the fox feels trapped. Of course she misses the outside world – the noises, the bird song, the smells, the rain and the morning dew. But what can Katie do? Early on she used to sometimes leave the shed door open so she could at least see out. Now she wouldn't dare.

Katie pours herself a glass of wine, goes upstairs and stands watching Ben who is still on the phone, still with his back squarely to the door, as though wanting to shut her out. She almost goes back downstairs, but doesn't.

He mutters something she can't catch, slides the phone down alongside his laptop, drops into the wicker chair letting his head fall back, gazes at the ceiling.

"You haven't eaten your sandwich."

No reply.

"Ben, I'm sorry, I know you're busy, I realise it bores you, but later could you just give me five minutes to run some ideas past you? Please?"

He turns and looks at her, puzzled.

"About the fox?"

He rests his hands on the sides of the chair, gripping them tightly. His knuckles are white.

"Know who that was on the phone?" His voice is low, the words clipped, precise. "Bill Taylor, our structural engineer. D'you know what he told me? She's walked out, Anita, our architect lady, complaining that both he and I are impossible to work with. And what has the polite, charming Chinese manager of Clever Clogs Europe got to say about that? That she's the one for them, that they want her on the job. And you realise what that means?"

He's on his feet now, pacing back and forth across the narrow room.

"What it means is that unless a miracle happens I'm off the job, I won't get paid, I might even have to pay them compensation."

He stops.

"And d'you know how many other jobs there are out there at the moment? None. Not a single one. The country's going into a recession and I'm not going to be able to pay for anything, our wine bill, running two cars, the mortgage. Nothing. And do you care? No way. All you go on and on about is that bloody freak you've got locked up in the shed!"

Katie reels, stunned by his outburst.

"Ben. I... listen, I'm sorry, I'd no idea things were so bad. How could I if you don't say anything?"

"Say anything? And how exactly do I get your attention?"

"That's not fair, Ben."

It's not like him to be cruel.

"And please stop calling her a freak," she adds, hearing how sulky she sounds.

He does have a point. But how the hell is she meant to know what he's going through if he doesn't tell her? How can she know what's happening in his life up there in the city when she's living in a different world tucked away amongst the trees down here? She's not a mind-reader.

"Come on, Ben. Be honest. Haven't I always been here for you?"

He doesn't reply.

"We agreed. We even wrote it down. That we'd always share things, everything, the good and the bad? That we were in this together. We made a point of always finding the time to talk, no matter how busy we were, no matter what else was going on in our lives."

He rubs a hand across his face, sighs.

"Remember?"

"Used to. You're right. But you've changed, Katie. Ever since you lost the job, and then coming down here. I feel we're…"

"Growing apart?"

She says it for him.

"Yes. No. Oh I don't know, Katie. Certainly not as close as we once were."

"And you're saying that's all my fault? I don't listen any more. I don't care." She hesitates. "Isn't that a bit unfair?"

She has his attention now. He's looking at her, waiting.

An especially fierce gust of wind squeezes through the window frame. The curtains ripple briefly. Katie thinks how back in their snug London house they're hardly aware of the weather, whatever it's doing. Back in her other life.

She's as caught out by what she says next as Ben is.

"Was that why you didn't tell me about Stefan? Was I too preoccupied then? Or did you just think it was none of my business?"

He blinks rapidly.

"Stefan?"

"Stefan. Your son. That Stefan."

It's as though time has stopped. Suspended animation; the words come into Katie's mind at the same time as she realises she's stopped breathing. It feels like it goes on forever. Then Ben speaks, his voice tight, uncomfortable.

"You know about Stefan?"

Katie bends her knees, slides down the wall until she's siting on the floor. There's no other chair and she needs to sit.

"I went to see Marta a few weeks ago. She told me everything."

Ben sits, leans forward, puts his face in his hands.

"Why, Ben?"

"Why what?"

He sounds genuinely confused.

"Why did you do it? Why didn't you tell me? Why do you still want to keep it secret? Keep him secret?"

He looks up, sighs.

"Oh Katie. Where do I start?"

If he's waiting for her to make things easier he'll wait a long time.

"OK. I suppose I felt sorry for her. She'd had a hard life, right from when she was a kid, the youngest of, I can't remember, six or seven. When her boyfriend let her down she was shattered. She wanted to have a child, to be a mother, the years were passing and she didn't…"

"She told me. But why you? And why couldn't she wait? She's attractive, intelligent, there was every chance she'd find someone else. She has. David Wheeler. He's forty-one years old, an accountant with a company that distributes American hot tubs and saunas."

She's said too much. He'll ask how she knows all that and she'll have to confess about the detective, and feel somehow sneaky, guilty even, which all things considered is ironic.

But he doesn't.

"She was convinced time had run out. She was desperate, Katie."

"Like you, you mean? Desperate to be a father."

"I'd have liked to have kids, yes. You know that."

"And the last thing your ambitious, heart-of-stone wife wanted was to have a baby so…"

"I never thought of you like that, Katie. Come on, you don't believe that? I loved you for being exactly who you were."

Loved? A slip of the tongue?

"Remember, I didn't have sex with her. it was a business arrangement. I've never been unfaithful to you, Katie. Never would be."

He pauses.

"Do you mind very much?"

Katie still isn't sure.

"Yes. I think I do," she says quietly. "It's strange to suddenly discover I'm sharing you with not one but two other people."

"But you're not. I never see her, or Stefan. I don't contact them."

"But you think of them, you must do. You helped give Stefan life, he's part of you, he shares your genes. He's your son. Whatever happens, you're linked to them forever."

Katie feels an unexpected stab of pure jealousy.

"You didn't tell me, when you could have. You should have. You made a decision to exclude me, to lie to me. That hurts, Ben."

"I didn't exactly lie. I just didn't tell you what you didn't need to know."

"Didn't need to know?"

"Guess I didn't want to risk hurting you."

"Thanks. Very thoughtful."

She's gone on long enough, but she can't stop.

"I still don't understand how you could have gone through all that with me having no idea, not an inkling."

She's pushing too hard. She should know by now there's only a certain amount of aggression Ben can take without switching into fighting mode.

The look he gives her is cutting.

"And you've never kept things secret from me, of course."

For a moment Katie can't think what he's talking about.

"You're not on again about that clinic appointment, all those years ago?"

Ben doesn't look away.

"Do you honestly still think I had a termination?"

"Who knows? How will I ever know for sure? When you thought you might be pregnant you seemed so annoyed. Not just annoyed. Horrified. Trapped."

Katie draws in a sharp breath. He's gone too far and he knows it.

"I didn't mean that."

"You know because I'd have talked to you before doing anything major like that. Don't you? I've never ever lied to you, Ben. If you don't believe me then…"

She was going to put it into words, and risk everything.

"… then maybe we should ask what sort of relationship we have? Do we even still have one, or have we grown so far apart that… that we might as well give up, cut our losses?"

A small sad smile. "That's a very good question."

So he's given up. And if he's given up on it then what chance do they have of sticking the broken bits of their marriage back together again?

"I'm going to the shed," she says, standing, knowing that if she doesn't get away from him she'll do or say something she'll regret.

"Stay," he says then. "Please. You can't keep running away from talking about us."

"Isn't it too late? We should have done it long ago."

She crosses the room.

"And besides, it's her feeding time."

Again she can feel his mood change. When did he become so edgy, so easy to irritate?

"Christ, Katie, she's a fox. An animal. Vermin. I'm your husband and still…"

This is not her Ben. She can't stand to be in the room with this stranger a minute more, but as she goes past he catches hold of her wrist.

"Tell you one thing, Katie. This obsession with the fox. It's good to know you do have a heart, that something at least can touch you. I was beginning to doubt it."

"Oh fuck off, Ben" she snaps, pulling free, stumbling down the stairs with no idea where she's going, needing only to be somewhere else, to not be there a minute longer.

"Just fuck off," muttered as she grabs her coat from the back of a chair, yanks open the door and lets in a blast of cold air.

## TWENTY-ONE

She'd intended to go to the shed, but changes her mind. Instead she grabs her keys and gets into the car. She has no idea where she's heading, just somewhere else, as far away as she can. She puts the car radio on, find some music – folk, on a local radio station which is one she can always tune in - and turns the volume up high. Though she longs to press her foot down hard on the accelerator, the windscreen wipers are struggling to cope with rain that's falling in sheets, and she's forced to slow down. The road is littered with twigs and even branches, some of them so big she has to steer the car around them, and it occurs to her that a tree could come down at any moment. People in cars are more vulnerable than they realise; she could be crushed to death in an instant.

She doesn't care. She doesn't have a choice.

Until the road in front of her turns into a pond, and she's forced to brake. Dare she drive through it? How deep is it? It could be alright, but then again, the water could come up to the doors, even seep inside. The engine might cut out. She could be stuck there all night.

Frustrated, she closes her eyes, tips back her head. It's like she's in a straightjacket. She can't move her arms, can't breathe, can't think.

There's no other option: she'll have to turn back.

Tugging at the gear stick – cursing that the car isn't an automatic which she keeps saying she'll get next time, and never does – she finally feels the gear slot into place. But as she starts to reverse she's aware the wheels aren't gripping, realises she's on a sheet of mud, and as the car slews to one side and the back wheels seem to drop down, she knows it for sure: she's about to slide into a ditch. As the car comes to a tentative halt she rests her forehead on the steering wheel and lets the tears flow warm and salty down her cheeks, into her mouth, even down her neck, whilst the rain continues to hammer on the roof.

She's stuck. Well and bloody truly.

She'll wait a few minutes and hope the rain eases. Then she'll have another go. And then she'll have to try to remember what lanes she took, and will go back to the house, get dry, make herself a hot drink, and do what she should have done instead of running away, which never solves anything. She'll talk to Ben.

The first thing she notices as she pulls back into the yard is that Ben's car has gone. Surely he wouldn't have tried to follow her? He'd have no idea which way she'd driven, it would be pointless. Would he have gone off back to London, defeated, exhausted, left without saying another word?

A sharp bang. She jumps. The shed door is open, being shoved back and forth by the wind. Her heart thumps. She'd left it locked, she knows she did, she always made sure of that. Locked with the padlock which then went under a terracotta pot round the side. She's across to it in seconds, sliding on the wet straw inside the door, holding onto the wall to steady herself. She wishes she had a torch. But as her eyes become accustomed to the dark, she can see that the cage door is also wide open, and the smaller container that the fox uses as her hideaway, her bolt hole, her bed, has gone too.

And so has the fox.

Katie starts to shake. She knows immediately what has happened. She turns and crosses the yard again, not caring that she's now so wet her sweater is sticking to her shoulders, her trainers squelching in the mud. The front door is open, all the lights still on. Slowly, reluctantly, she climbs the stairs. She reaches towards the grandfather clock, grasps the handle and turns it.

The gun too has gone.

Ben has taken them both.

She runs back downstairs, desperate to find her mobile, throwing cushions off the sofa, newspapers slithering onto the floor. If she can only talk to him, calm him down, make him see sense.

When eventually she finds it, there's no signal. Of course not. It's unreliable at the best of times. In a storm like this... what is she thinking of? She tries the landline which is crackly but goes though. She's invited to leave a message. She doesn't. She dials again. The same. She wants to scream but hasn't got the energy. Instead she slumps down onto the sofa and for a while – seconds, minutes, longer, she's no idea – it's as though she isn't there. But when, finally, she comes to again she knows she can't stay in the house alone, thinking, worrying, imaging all sorts of terrible things, the worst. She mustn't. She'll go mad.

At first she can see no lights at any of the windows, and it occurs to her that Guy could be in bed and asleep. But she can't go back. Not to the house, not after that terrifying drive during which she more than once thought her time was up. She stumbles across to the front door, searches frantically for a bell or knocker but can't find either, hammers on the door with her knuckles, then with the flat of her hands. She calls, not used to shouting but knowing she has to if she's going to be heard.

"Guy, are you there? It's Katie. Please, please don't be asleep."

When the door swings back she almost falls inside and he catches her arm to steady her. She's vaguely aware that he's wearing only his trousers so he must have been in bed. Is it late? She's completely lost track of time.

"Hey there, you're soaked through. What happened? Come in, sweetheart, come over to the fire, sit. I'll get a towel. Stay there a minute, OK?"

"Guy, I'm so sorry to wake you. Ben has taken her, we had a big row, and I think he's going to shoot her, he wants to punish me, and I didn't know who…"

"Shh, Katie. Stop talking. Here, drink this."

It could be brandy, whisky, she has no idea. As the warmth seeps through her veins Katie stops shaking, can feel her heart calming, the room around her coming back into focus. As it does she becomes aware of a figure at the top of the staircase up to Guy's sleeping area.

"Kevin?"

He too is wearing only his jeans. Without speaking he pads quietly down the stairs, and as he passes Guy reaches out and catches his arm, turns him towards him, gently holding his shoulders so Kevin has to face him.

"It's OK, Kevin. I promise you. Katie won't tell a soul."

He turns back to look at her.

"Will you?"

"Tell them what?" And then "Oh. God. No, of course not."

It's like a piece of a jigsaw, the final piece slotting effortlessly into place. The picture makes sense. Why hadn't she noticed before? So many clues she's overlooked. Her focus has been entirely on herself and her problems.

"About you two?" She manages a weak smile. "I won't say a word, I promise. Why would I? Whose business is it anyway?"

"It's difficult for Kevin. Let's just say rural communities are always a bit behind the times on these matters. His folk wouldn't understand, at least, he'd sooner not try them. Not yet anyway."

Guy drops his hands, grins.

"Of course, no-one gives a monkey's fart about what I do."

He turns Kevin around, pushes him towards the stairs. "Go back up. I'll be with you soon."

"Night, Katie," Kevin calls over his shoulder.

"Goodnight."

She wants to say more, to apologise for not understanding, to thank him for everything: his friendship, his support, his sad bags of chickens, everything. But she's running out of energy. She knows too that should go, leave them to their time together, but she can't move. And even as she feels her eyes closing Guy is back with blankets, a pillow, instructing her to shuffle over whilst he makes up the sofa.

As she gets to her feet he pulls her towards him and gives her an awkward hug.

"It'll be alright," he whispers in her ear. "Trust me. I don't know much but I do know Ben's one of the good guys. And that he's crazy about you, well, in that understated way you Brits have refined."

Almost tenderly he pulls a blanket up to her chin.

"Whatever he does it'll be alright. He's on your side. Trust me."


Still no car, and what a mess everything looks, Katie thinks when she arrives back late the next morning, parks by the far hedge. All the house lights are on and the front door is wide open, the hallway littered with twigs and leaves blown in during the night. Indoors the air is icy, the fire now a pile of white ash.

Katie takes a coat from the rail in the hall and goes back outside, looks up at a sky that's crowded with fat grey clouds, though at least the rain has stopped.

Though she doesn't want to, she knows she's got to get it over with. Got to face the empty cage. Right now..

Inside the shed the first thing that hits her is the smell, that familiar musky aroma still coming from the empty cage, from the small dark droppings on the floor, the frazzled straw, from the air itself. But even more powerful is the silence. She made next to no noise, the fox, and yet with her gone – with no tiny sounds of movement, or a yawn, or a snuffle as she pushed her nose into her thick white fur when grooming – the silence is like being inside a deep dark airless cave. Katie blinks hard, then reaches for the stiff broom she always keeps propped in a corner. She'll sweep it out and then go and get some hot soapy water, and wash everything down.

She remembers how she'd felt when she was getting it ready for the new arrival, having absolutely no idea what to expect. A mixture of determination, trepidation, and excitement. But most of all, excitement.

And all that for nothing. For the fox to end up dead.

When a car pulls up outside she doesn't hear it, or at least its arrival doesn't register. She's on her hands and knees brushing everything into a black polythene bag, the concrete floor hard and cold as ice, when she becomes aware of Ben standing in the doorway.

"Hi there."

She doesn't look up, brushes aside some straw.

"The things I said, Katie. I didn't mean any of them." Ben is finding it hard to speak. His voice is faint.

"I've been driving and thinking. Good time to think, when you're driving. How often have we said that?"

He grimaces.

"I've got no excuse. I've been so worried about the situation at work, and then worried about you too, and gradually realising I can't do anything about anything which is frustrating, frightening even. And it built up. But that's no excuse for lashing out at you. I'm sorry."

She sits back on her heels.

"Ben, I know."

"Wait. Please let me finish, Katie. I'm sorry for what happened too, with Marta, I mean. What was I thinking? At the time it didn't seem such a big deal. I didn't think it through and I should have. I do understand how betrayed you must feel."

Still she can't look at him..

"Ben, don't. Really. It's alright."

He moves into the dim shed, drops heavily onto the chair she's sat on so often, for hours, not noticing how hard it was. Now she lifts her head.. He's shattered, his eyes red, shoulders sagging.

"So, tell me. What have you done with her?"

"Who?" He lifts his head, his breath white in the chilled air.

She should get him indoors, make a hot drink for them both. She stays there kneeling at his feet.

"My fox, of course."

"The fox? What d'you think I've done with her?"

Must she put it into words?

"Shot her, I suppose."

He looks confused.

"Ben, you took the gun. Why else would you take the gun?"

"The gun?"

"For God's sake, Ben. The gun that you found in the attic?"

Still he hesitates, as though not sure what she's talking about, and Katie suddenly wonders if he's ill. Could he have had a breakdown of some kind? Could he genuinely not know what he did with the last twelve hours?

He shakes his head.

"No, no, no. D'you really think I could have killed her? Oh Katie, love. You don't know me at all, do you?"

"You… but so where is she?"

He shakes his head, as though he can't believe it himself.

"The Lake District."

"Where? Ben, I don't understand."

With difficulty he stands, walks to the door.

"I drove her to the Lake District. I got in touch with this guy who works with wild foxes. He's obsessed. You and he would get on well. He said the best place to release her was as far as possible from humans, where the climate's not too extreme and she'll be able to find food. Somewhere like the Lake District, he said. He'd even suggested a particular area."

He takes a deep, shuddering breath.

"I'd had it in the back of my mind for a few weeks now, but it seemed so far, and I thought you'd hate the idea anyway, and then with everything else happening…"

"Oh Ben. All that way."

He shrugs.

"But that's a crazy, ridiculous thing to do, driving, what, hundreds of miles in a storm."

"Yup. But it did ease off the further north I went. Up where I set her free it was very cold but dry. There was snow, a fine layer. It was another world. Quite magical really."

"So she's free?"

Ben nods. So it's all over; her snow fox has gone.

"Do you mind very much?"

"Mind?"

Does she? Katie feels a hotchpotch of emotions. Regret that she hadn't been with them, that she hadn't said goodbye. Joy. A fizzing of joy deep inside her that makes her feel lighter, as though a weight has been lifted. She could almost float.

"No. I don't. I don't mind at all. I love it. I love what you did. Really."

Again she's struggling for the right words.

"But how did she react? Was she frightened? Did she seem happy?"

Ben manages a smile.

"Both. But she'll be fine."

"Thank you," she says then. She thinks how small and feeble that sounds, how inadequate.

A vehicle goes past, a rare sound. Probably a cattle truck from the farm, taking another load of sheep off to be slaughtered. She hates the thought. But nothing is going to spoil today.

"Something I don't understand," he says. "Why did you never give her a name? All that time you spent together."

Kevin's words; she hasn't forgotten them.

"Because I'd promised her that one day I'd set her free. Well, that someone would. You would."

"On your behalf."

"On my behalf, yes."

She clambers to her feet, her knees sore, legs tingling now, brushes off the dust.

"And down here we don't name the animals we're not going to keep. OK, let's go inside, shall we?".

She takes his hand and together they crunch across the gravel.

In the kitchen she immediately puts the kettle on, takes down mugs. It's only then that she remembers.

"But if you didn't take the gun, where is it?"

"The gun? D'you really not know? OK. The day I shot the deer, remember? I hated doing it, Katie. It was the right thing, but I hated it."

He frowns.

"Anyway, I didn't even want the gun back in the house, I left it in the car. I thought you'd realised. I gave it to Rachael, it was hers anyway. She said she'd hand it in to the police. More likely she sold it, but that's her business."

And she hadn't even noticed the gun was gone. Yet another thing she'd missed. Katie takes teabags out of the packet. Through the window she can see the tree tops still swishing around though the wind is easing. Later in the week they say there could be snow.

"So what now?"

"Me, I'm going to bed for a few hours," Ben says. "Then I'll head off back to London to try to sort out this God-awful mess at work. And you?"

Katie has no idea.

"What d'you think I should do?"

Ben glances around. He downs his tea in two long slurps.

"See if you can get that fire going again? It's freezing in here."

"Ben, I…"

"Don't say anything now, Katie. Later. We'll talk later."

She watches him as he walks across to the stairs, winces slightly as his arm brushes the banister. Now she notices the gash on the back of his hand.

"Wait, Ben. Let me see."

She goes to him, peels back his sweater cuff to revel a red welt that's been bleeding sometime recently, the blood now drying to a crust.

"Did she…?"

"No. Not her fault. I had to change a tyre on the way back, I wasn't concentrating. Stupid of me."

"Honestly?"

"Honestly."

"Wait, let me at least clean it."

She gets a bowl, hot water, cotton wool, sits him alongside her on the stairs and dabs tenderly at the ragged gash. She pats it dry, then lifts his hand to her face, turns it over and kisses his palm. His fingers tighten around hers, he reaches, pulls her close, presses his lips to the top of her head. She closes her eyes.

And so they sit there, both of them reluctant to move apart.

*I found a tuft of your fur. It must have been torn free when it got trapped between two of the old wooden planks at the back of your cage, probably from your splendid fat tail. It wasn't very big but it was so white, and when I held it to my nose I knew instantly that it was yours. It was softer than I'd expected. Thought about making it into a tiny plait and keeping it in a locket, like people used to do with hair from a loved one who'd died. Then I could always have you with me. But it seemed a bit gruesome. So instead I went up to the place where I first saw you and the cubs and held it up, and let the wind take it. Free. Like you.*

*I'm over the moon that you have a second chance. It was absolutely, completely and utterly the right thing to do. Clever Ben. When I miss you I imagine you living your new life up there surrounded by all that nothingness, just empty space and vast skies. It worries me that we're going to cover this whole island with housing estates and factories and supermarkets and roads and soon there'll be nowhere left for wildlife. Except zoos and city rubbish tips.*

*No point in worrying though. What can I do?*

*I've decided to sell the photos, not for the money but because I want people to know about you, and your beautiful cubs and how they were so pointlessly murdered. Andrew is going to make some enquiries. I'll say that you died. Of course they won't believe me and they'll probably search the whole of Exmoor, but they won't find you, will they?*

*And so here I am, alone again.*

*Ben has gone back to London to sort things at work. He lost the Chinese contract of course. No surprise there. He's taken on another building project, something really mundane and not at all challenging. A youth club I think? He's happy enough. He enjoys helping kids, and of course with the economy in freefall he's grateful to have work. It'll pay a bill or two.*

*Me, I'm not ready to leave Exmoor yet. Which is just as well as Rachael suggested I might like to stay on for a bit, in fact, she asked me. Would I do her a favour? Keep the house feeling lived in, she said. Add more of your fancy Country Living Lifestyle touches. How could I say no?*

# TWENTY-TWO

Against all the odds, the fox is surviving.

It hasn't been easy. When she was first set free she was terrified. One moment she'd been in a cramped container, surrounded by unfamiliar noises, being thrown from one side to the other, joggled, bumped, unable to settle for hours. Then suddenly everything stopped. There was silence. The cage door was opened wide. And she'd hesitated, blinked, then shuffled herself back into a corner, turning her face away from the pale yellow light of dawn, the world outside that she instinctively knew was not her world.

But eventually she'd plucked up the courage to drop down out of the cage onto the frozen ground. She'd lifted her head, ears pricked, nose raised. High in an ice blue sky a single bird circled and trilled, its song unfamiliar to her. The distant rushing and tumbling of a wide white river sounded nothing like any river she'd heard before. Even the ground beneath her feet smelt different.

She'd glanced back at the car, the cage with its open door, the man who she could sense was standing motionless off to one side, watching, waiting. She could get back in the cage, of course. She could give up her freedom and be safe.

She looked around again, at the distant snow-capped hills, the trees stark as though drawn with a pencil, at a vast natural landscape empty of houses, shops, motorways, garages, farms, ye olde inns. Empty of her age-old enemy: man.

In a flash she was gone.

Somehow she'd managed to catch enough small creatures to eat, had discovered places to tuck herself away from the worst of the weather. She'd learnt quickly. Now the temperature is rising, the ground slowly turning green with lush new growth. Now – in some ways at least – her life will be easier. During the night there was a light rain, and as she stands there her dense white coat sparkles with droplets of water, just as it did when Katie took her photograph, one of the shots that has appeared in magazines around the world. Not that she knows of course. Not that she'd care. She shakes herself. Stretches, yawns. Then, for a moment, lulled by the warmth of the early morning sun sifting down through the trees, she sits. She's hungry, and soon she must go and find food, but not yet, not for a few minutes more.

The cracking of the twig is no louder than the clicking of fingers, but she hears it. Her eyes open wide, every fibre of her body suddenly alert. Startled, a flock of small brown birds is flung into the air like confetti. The fox is on her feet now. She's right: someone is coming.

And then she's running towards the newcomer making little whimpering sounds, her thick brush swishing from side to side. The young dog fox has in his mouth something that flops as he trots. It's a rabbit, still warm, and he drops it on the ground in front of her, stands proudly as she nuzzles him in welcome. Having sniffed the rabbit, then flipped it over with a delicate paw and examined it again, she settles down to eat, spots of blood a dazzling red against the white of her fur. The dog fox watches, knowing instinctively that his mate needs all the nourishment she can get before their cubs are born, and the cycle starts all over again.

Which will be soon now, very soon.

Overhead a pair of buzzards spiral upwards in the warming air currents, lifting effortlessly and silently as they soar, getting closer and closer to the cloudless blue sky.

> *The thing is, I've met this woman.*
> *Through Guy of course, who else? She's not*
> *young, short grey hair that I'd swear she*
> *cuts herself with nail scissors. Threadbare*

*trousers above the filthiest toes sticking out from orange plastic sandals. But she is so full of life. She sort of effervesces. And her laugh is one of those contagious types, you have to join in. you can't not.*

*Fiona, that's her name. She runs a wildlife rescue along the coast a bit and is desperate to find volunteers to help. I said I don't know anything about wildlife and she said no problem, you'll soon learn. She said anyway, you have a natural empathy for animals. Seems she has a nose for these things. So I'm going along for a look around tomorrow. Can't wait.*

*And there's the other thing. She used to have someone do the books, help keep track of money in, money out, donations, food and vet's bills and so on. She said he came up with some cracking ideas for raising funds too. Gone off to Zimbabwe to work with giraffes. Or was it Zambia? Anyway, I said I could do that. I mean, I could manage the business side of things for her. I'd like to. It would be a challenge, especially during the recession we're heading for.*

*Not sure if she's caring for any foxes right now. She said this is the time of year when she's inundated with cubs. Imagine. I can't wait. I'm sure none of them will be like you, but so what? They'll all be precious to me, every single one.*

THE END

# TAILPIECES*

## FROM THE TOP OF MY GARDEN

*Tailpieces: a piece forming an end; an appendage

## AUTHOR'S NOTE

This is a work of fiction. It never happened.

But it was inspired by a real-life event.

It's also based very closely on my own observations of life on Exmoor in the south west of England, and how I personally – born and bred in the big city – saw and reacted to this unique rural environment. There are many pluses to living here. There are some minuses. I hope I've done justice to both.

Thanks to everyone who gave me information, advice and encouragement as I worked.  You'll know who you are. And especially to G for being there - kind, patient, and always ready with the wine bottle opener.

Thank YOU for reading it.

And if you've any thoughts, comments or questions please do contact me via my website

www.janmazzoniwriter.com

Since The Snow Fox Diaries was first published readers have asked a variety of questions. Here are just a few of them, with my answers.

Q: WHERE AND WHEN DO YOU DO YOUR WRITING?

A: My new writing place – as you may have guessed - is a small summerhouse at the top of the garden. It's not that big a garden but it's ridiculously out of control and overgrown, and backs onto woodland, so that means it's full of wildlife, especially birds (who make it clear we're trespassing on their territory!) So this little wooden building – let's call it an upmarket shack – is more than an office. It also acts as a hide from which to watch the birds. As I occasionally take in nestlings or injured birds, it also serves as a secluded place where they can be attended to, and hopefully left quietly to recover. Then there's the comfy old Lloyd Loom chair that lures me and my other half to sit and meditate, dream, simply switch off. And as it's of course crammed with books, it's a library too.

I don't have a writing routine. The one thing I learnt from my many years as an advertising copywriter is that I work best to deadlines. A looming cut off point seems to do a brilliant job at sharpening my concentration, and (I hope) my ability with words. As a result I dither about doing other things for way too much time. Like walking my pack of elderly rescue dogs over the moors or on the beach, or trying – unsuccessfully of course - to teach them new tricks. Sometimes I'll cook, usually the same thing time after time until I get bored. Lately it's carrot muffins. Or I'll begin researching for a project that I haven't even yet started, but that seems so much more interesting than whatever I'm currently working on.

Then, when time is running out, I glue myself to my ergonomic chair and work from dawn to dusk, drinking way too much coffee (very strong with a splash of barista oat milk), feeling sorry for myself that I can't stop and dither, and vowing never again to leave things to the last minute.

Until the next time of course when I do exactly the same.

Q: HOW DID YOU GET THE IDEA FOR THE SNOW FOX DIARIES?

A: Ideas for novels usually tend to grow slowly, get added to and chopped and changed along the way. Not this one. This one came to me fully formed, and I remember the exact moment

It was years ago, a hazy summer's day, late afternoon. I was sitting having tea and biscuits in the garden of the naturalist and BBC wildlife filmmaker Eric Ashby and his delightful wife Eileen. In a paddock alongside us, a small herd of wild deer was grazing, completely relaxed even though it was obvious to the animals that they weren't alone. I guess they just felt safe hanging around with Eric. He had that effect on wildlife – as his vast output of films, photographs and books proved. If you shared his passion, you somehow got enveloped by that magical aura too.

As we'd just been playing with his rescued foxes it wasn't surprising that we got onto the subject of these very special animals. Suddenly Eileen got up, muttering about something she'd put aside to show me. When she returned it was with a tattered sheet of newspaper they'd come across amongst the hundreds of fox-related cuttings they kept in one of many files. file. She thought it might interest me. She was right.

It told of the sighting - somewhere in the north of the UK - of an albino vixen and two white cubs. The article explained that the rare genetic defect that made them so stunningly beautiful also made them especially interesting to both hunters and collectors. They were being monitored by conservationists who wanted desperately that this little family should survive. Needless to say, it didn't. The cubs were killed by youths. The vixen disappeared. And at this point my imagination took over. I wanted desperately to share her world, to help her, or at least to try. I wanted to make up for the cruel way she and her babies had been treated. I longed for her to have a second chance, and even, maybe - a happy ending.

That's the great thing about being a writer. You can work miracles. Well, in print at least.

## Q: WHY DO YOU THNK ALBINO ANIMALS ARE SO SPECIAL?

A: Ask a trophy hunter. They'll pay way over the odds to shoot an albino, whatever it is: kangaroo, deer, tiger, zebra, gorilla, moose, alligator, bear, penguin, koala. Killing things for fun – especially if it involves taking home an animal's body, or part of it, as proof of the hunter's bravery and skill – has now resulted in an international industry worth millions of pounds. Killing something rare, it seems, is even more satisfying.

Sadly, my research showed that there's a growing demand not just for hunting trips (professionally organised so that the hunter is guaranteed success), but for products, especially from rare animals. So for stay-at-home hunters there are poachers doing the job for them, then selling their illicit gains to taxidermists whose handiwork is then available online. Can't afford a lion? How about a cobra, or a hedgehog? Or some "quirky" collectables such as a two-headed duckling – or a giraffe's penis?

I do have another theory about why white animals have such a big oooh-factor. Beautiful though we may find them, their colouring makes their daily lives challenging, and they rarely survive for long. Wildlife relies heavily on camouflage. Albino predators struggle to catch their food. Albino prey animals have difficulty hiding from the predators. Worse still, if they live in a herd their colouring may make them a danger for the whole family, which can result in them being banished to cope alone. Often their sight and hearing is less than perfect. And even finding a mate can be a challenge.

So their look of innocence and vulnerability isn't just an illusion. That's exactly what they are. And doesn't that somehow make them even more precious?

Q. AND WHAT ABOUT THAT OTHER THREAT TO WILDLIFE, HUNTING WITH DOGS?

A: Foxes – as well as deer, hares and mink – are still being killed by the hunt, with literally thousands of deaths being reported each year. This is despite the fact that hunting with dogs was banned in England and Wales in 2004. Drag hunting was suggested as an alternative, and the law also allowed for dogs to be used to flush out any animal in hiding which could then be 'humanely' shot – that's if the frenzied dogs could be persuaded to release it.

Anti-hunt campaigners were over the moon when the ban came into force, but soon discovered that most of the hunts had no intention of being told what to do. And this still applies. The loopholes and grey areas in a badly thought-out law are being used by up to 300 hunts which are still active on the British mainland. These are frequently followed and filmed by passionate and determined hunt monitors who risk limb and (literally) life to get evidence of what's really happening in the countryside, away from the public. Videos confirm that not only is wildlife being killed, but the hunts are causing havoc on the roads, damaging private property, crossing railway lines. Still the courts and their judges seem to find it hard to be convinced of any wrong-doing. Strange, that.

Personally, I find it perplexing that in this day and age anyone can get pleasure out of chasing, terrifying and then watching as a small animal is all too often shredded by a pack of dogs. Exmoor is an absolutely stunning part of the UK. I think it's time it joined the 21st century and started to see its wildlife as something to be treasured and enjoyed by everyone, not a plaything for the hunt.

Q. YOU DESCRIBE THE SNOW FOX DIARIES AS BEING ECOFICTION. NOT HEARD OF THIS GENRE BEFORE. CAN YOU TELL ME MORE?

A: It sounds like something new, but it isn't. Ecofiction (also called ecolit) has in fact been around for decades, but it's only now becoming more widely known. You'll be lucky if you find anything under this genre on Amazon. But they'll catch on soon enough, with more publishers realising that this is exactly the kind of fiction people are looking for right now.

So what exactly is it? Ecofiction can be a love story, thriller, family saga, dystopian horror, children's book, but the one important thing is that there should be a strong environmental theme woven through it. This is fiction that raises important concerns – usually about the natural world, climate change, animal rights, and so on – yet without sacrificing a good story, written in a way that shows how these issues affect our daily lives. Which of course they do, and increasingly so.

Probably the earliest example of ecofiction (written before the genre was invented!) is Moby Dick. Look around and you'll likely find some you've already read, maybe by best-selling authors better known for other types of novel. What about Jodie Picoult's Leaving Time, with its passionate plea for elephants? Or Louise Beach's The Lion Tamer Who Lost? A weirdly wonderful read is Drive Your Plow Over the Bones of the Dead by Olga Tokarczuk. Wolves – those powerful symbols of the wilderness that are under growing threat – are a natural starting point for ecofiction. Try The Wolf Border by Sarah Hall, or the beautiful and very moving Winter of the Wolf by Martha Hunt Handler. I've recently read and loved The Tourist Trail by John Yunker who's written a number of novels that fit this genre (I'm delighted to say – more to add to my to-be-read pile).

You get the idea. If you're interested you'll find plenty of ecofiction book lists online. These are books with a difference. I'm hoping they'll inspire you not only to extend your reading choices, but to take more care of this amazing planet of ours which is more fragile than we ever dare admit. Time is running out.  Thank you.

BY JAN MAZZONI

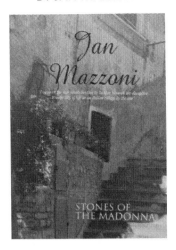

It's 1939 and the world teeters on the brink of war. But here, in this southern Italian fishing village, life goes on much as it always has.

Lily – newly arrived from London with her doctor husband James – thinks she has found paradise. Instead, she is about to discover things that will shatter her world, secrets she'd sooner not know...

## STONES OF THE MADONNA

Available from Amazon

BY JAN MAZZONI

Satisfy your literary wanderlust with this collection of evocative short stories set just before package tourism took off – and the Amalfi coast was about to be invaded, and changed forever.

Upbeat, sometimes ponderous and sad, always rich in descriptions that bring alive the smells, colours and sounds of this unique part of Italy, these are stories that will take you to a place that may look familiar, but is already – sadly – part of the past.

## DREAMLAND

Available from Amazon

Printed in Poland
by Amazon Fulfillment
Poland Sp. z o.o., Wrocław

61880942R00164